STEVEN SAYLOR

RUBICON

ST. MARTIN'S PRESS
NEW YORK

Production Editor: David Stanford Burr
Design: Anne Scatto / PIXEL PRESS

Library of Congress Cataloging-in-Publication Data
Saylor, Steven.
    Rubicon / by Steven Saylor.—1st ed.
        p.   cm.
    ISBN 0-312-20576-7
    1. Rome—History—Civil War, 49–45 B.C.—Fiction.   I. Title.
PS3569.A96R8   1999
813'.54—dc21   99-18090
                                                CIP

First Edition: May 1999

10   9   8   7   6   5   4   3   2   1

ALSO BY STEVEN SAYLOR

Roma Sub Rosa

CONSISTING OF:

Roman Blood
The House of the Vestals
Arms of Nemesis
Catilina's Riddle
The Venus Throw
A Murder on the Appian Way

RUBICON

For my brother, Ronny,
THIS BOOK

CONTENTS

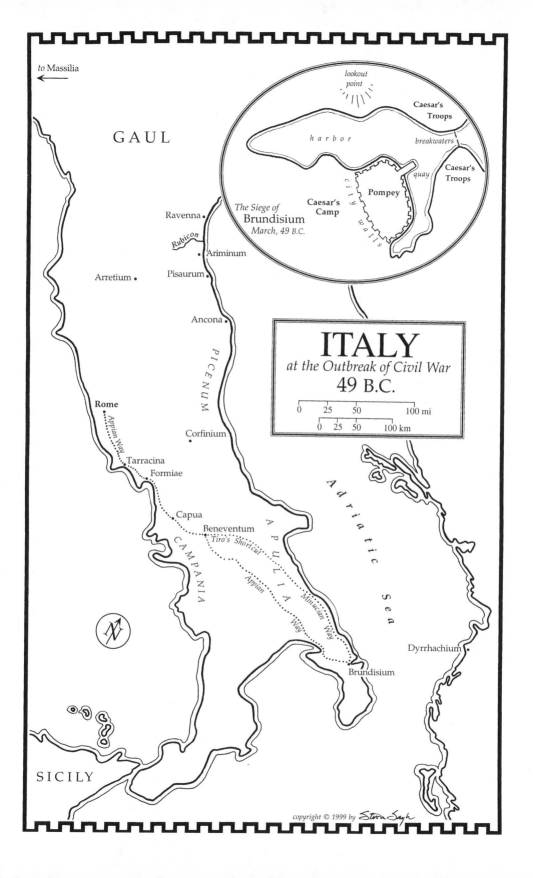

to Massilia

GAUL

Ravenna

Rubicon

Ariminum

Arretium

Pisaurum

Ancona

P I C E N U M

Rome

Appian Way

Corfinium

Tarracina

Formiae

Capua

Beneventum

Tiro's Shortcut

Appian Way

A P U L I A

Minucian Way

C A M P A N I A

Adriatic Sea

Dyrrhachium

Brundisium

SICILY

**The Siege of
Brundisium**
March, 49 B.C.

*lookout
point*

**Caesar's
Troops**

harbor

breakwaters

quay

city walls

Pompey

**Caesar's
Troops**

**Caesar's
Camp**

ITALY
at the Outbreak of Civil War
49 B.C.

| 0 | 25 | 50 | 100 mi |

| 0 | 25 | 50 | 100 km |

N

copyright © 1999 by *Steven Sagh*

PART ONE

MINERVA

I

"Pompey will be mightily pissed," said Davus.

"Son-in-law, you have a penchant for stating the obvious." I sighed and knelt and steeled myself to take a closer look. The lifeless body lay face-down in the middle of my garden directly before the bronze statue of Minerva, like a prostrate worshiper at the goddess's feet.

Davus turned in a circle, shielding his eyes from the morning sunlight and peering warily at the four corners of the peristyle roof surrounding us. "What I can't see is how the assassin got in and out without any of us in the house hearing." He wrinkled his brow, which made him look like a perplexed and much overgrown boy. *Built like a Greek statue, and just as thick;* that was Bethesda's joke. My wife had not taken kindly to the notion of our only daughter marrying a slave, especially a slave who had been brash enough, or stupid enough, to get her pregnant. But if Davus had a penchant for the obvious, Diana had a penchant for Davus. And there was no denying that they had produced a beautiful son, whom I could hear even now screaming at his mother and grandmother to be let out into the garden, crying as only a two-year-old can. But Aulus could not be let out to play on this bright, mild Januarius afternoon, for there was a corpse in the garden.

And not just any corpse. The dead man was Numerius Pompeius, who was somehow related to Pompey—one of the Great One's cousins, though a couple of generations younger. He had arrived at my house, alone, half an hour earlier. Now he lay dead at my feet.

"I can't understand it." Davus scratched his head. "Before I let Numerius in the door, I took a good look up and down the street, like I always do. I didn't notice anybody following him." When Davus had been a slave, it was Pompey who had owned him, and Davus had been a bodyguard—an obvious choice, given his hulking physique. He had been trained not just to fight but to keep a look-out for danger. As my son-in-law, Davus was the physical protector of the household, and in these perilous times it was his job to greet visitors at the door. Now that a murder had occurred within the house, practically under his nose, he took it as a personal failure. In Pompey's service, such a lapse would have called for a harsh interrogation, at the least. In the face of my silence, Davus seemed determined to interrogate himself. He paced back and forth, using his fingers to tick off each question.

"Why did I let him in? Well, because I knew him by sight, back from my days with Pompey. He was no stranger; he was Numerius, my former master's favorite young cousin, who always had a good word for everyone. And he came alone—not even a bodyguard to worry about—so I didn't see any need to make him wait outside. I let him into the foyer. Did I ask if he had any weapons? It's against the law to carry weapons inside the city walls, of course, but nobody pays attention to that these days, so yes, I did ask, and he didn't make any fuss at all and handed over his dagger right away. Did I search him for more weapons, as you've told me to do, even with citizens? Yes, I did, and he didn't even protest. Did I leave him alone, even for a moment? No, I did not. I stayed with him there in the foyer, sent little Mopsus to tell you there was a visitor, then waited until you sent back word that you'd see him. I escorted him through the house, back here to the garden. Diana and Aulus were out here with you, playing in the sunny spot at Minerva's feet . . . right where Numerius is lying now . . . but you sent them inside. Did I stay with you? No, because you sent me inside, too. But I knew better! I should have stayed."

"Numerius said he had a message for my ears alone," I said. "If a man can't safely have a private talk in his own home . . ." I looked about the garden, at the carefully pruned shrubbery and the brightly colored columns that lined the surrounding walkway. I gazed up at the bronze statue of Minerva; after all these years, the face that peered down from her great war helmet remained inscrutable to me. The garden was at the center of the house, its heart—the heart of my world—and if I was not safe here, then I was safe nowhere.

"Don't chastise yourself, Davus. You did your job. You knew that Numerius was whom he claimed to be, and you took his weapon."

"But Pompey would never be left unguarded, even for—"

"Have we reached a point where a common citizen needs to mimic Pompey or Caesar, and have a bodyguard standing over him every moment of every hour, even when he's wiping his ass?"

Davus frowned. I knew what he was thinking—that it was unlike me to talk so crudely, that I must be badly shaken and trying not to show it, that his father-in-law was getting too old to deal with ugly shocks like a corpse in the garden before the midday meal. He stared up at the rooftop again. "But Numerius wasn't the danger, was he? It was whoever followed him here. The fellow must be half lizard, to scurry up and down the walls without making a sound! Did you hear nothing, father-in-law?"

"I told you, Numerius and I talked for a while, then I left him for a moment and stepped into my study."

"But that's only a few feet away. Still, I suppose the statue of Minerva might have blocked the view. And your hearing—"

"My ears are as sharp as those of any man of sixty-one!"

Davus nodded respectfully. "However it happened, it's a good thing you weren't out here when the assassin came, or else . . ."

"Or else I might have been strangled, too?" I touched my fingers to the rope that still circled Numerius's neck, cutting into the livid flesh. He had been killed with a simple garrote, a short loop of rope attached to each end of a short, stout twisting stick.

Davus knelt beside me. "The killer must have come up behind him, dropped the garrote over his head, then used the stick to twist it tighter and tighter around his throat. A gruesome way to die."

I turned away, feeling queasy.

"But a quiet way," Davus went on. "Numerius couldn't even cry out! Maybe he managed a gurgle or a grunt at the start, but then, with his air cut off, the only way to make a sound would be to bang against something. See there, father-in-law, how Numerius gouged his heels into the gravel? But that wouldn't make much noise. If only he could have banged a fist against the bronze Minerva . . . but both hands are clutched to his throat. That's a man's instinct, to try to tear the rope from his neck. I wonder . . ." Davus peered up at the roof again. "The killer needn't have been a big fellow. It doesn't take a great deal of strength to garrote a man, even a big man, so long as you take him unaware."

"Do you speak from experience, son-in-law?"

"Oh, I learned lots of things like that, training to be Pompey's bodyguard." Davus smiled at me crookedly, then saw the look on my face. His smile vanished. "You don't think that I—"

"Of course not. But I wonder—might such an idea occur to Pompey? Is there any reason for you to bear a grudge against Pompey? Something I don't know about? When you were his slave, did he ever mistreat you?"

"No, father-in-law. Have I ever complained about him? He was a good master." Davus managed another crooked smile. "Besides, wasn't it Pompey who lent me to you, back during the Clodian riots, to guard the house—and wasn't that how I came to know Diana, and . . ." He flushed.

Pompey lent you to me, you became my daughter's secret lover, the two of you made a baby—and then it was up to me either to sue Pompey for damages and see you flogged to death, or else acquire you from Pompey, set you free, and make you my son-in-law. It's I who should bear a grudge against Pompey! I thought this, but did not say it.

"I only mean to say," Davus stumbled on, "that I harbor only good will toward Pompey, as he must know, if he ever gives me any thought at all."

"What about Numerius? You say he was Pompey's favorite young cousin. Did he take liberties with the slaves when he was in the Great One's house? Did Numerius ever mistreat you—make fun of you—abuse you in some other way?" Some men might have taken certain advantage of a slave who was thick as a Greek statue, and built like one.

"Never! I told you, Numerius had a good word for everyone. I liked him."

"Then there's no reason, no reason at all, why *you* might loom up as a suspect in Pompey's mind when he learns that Numerius was murdered under my roof?"

"None at all!"

"Because, son-in-law, if I thought Pompey might suspect you, I'd be tempted to drag Numerius into the street and pretend he never set foot in this house. These days it profits a man to go to whatever lengths he can to avoid trouble, especially trouble with the Great One." I studied Davus's face, which was incapable of deceit. I nodded. "Well, then, Pompey will have to be told. I suppose I must do it myself—make the trip outside the city walls to Pompey's villa, wait for an interview, give him the bad news, then let him deal with the matter as he chooses. Here, help me roll the body face-up."

From inside the house, I heard my little grandson shouting again to be let into the garden. I looked toward the doorway. Bethesda and Diana peered out anxiously. It was something of a miracle that they had so far obeyed me and stayed out of the garden. Bethesda started to speak, but I held up my hand and shook my head. I was rather surprised when she nodded and withdrew, taking Diana with her.

I forced myself to look at Numerius's strangled face. It was a sight to give anyone nightmares.

He had been young, in his twenties, probably a bit older than Davus. His broad, blandly handsome features were now discolored and distorted and almost unrecognizable in a rictus of agony. I swallowed hard. As I used two fingers to shut his lids, I saw my reflection in the black pool of his staring eyes. No wonder my wife and daughter had obeyed me without question. The look on my face was alarming even to me.

I stood, my knees crackling like the gravel beneath my feet. Davus sprang up beside me, as supple as a cat despite his size.

"Pompey will be mightily pissed," I said gravely.

"I said that already!"

"So you did, Davus. But bad news keeps, as the poet says. The day is young, and I see no need to rush across Rome to bring Pompey the news. What do you say we have a closer look, and see what Numerius may be carrying?"

"But I told you, I searched him when I took his dagger. There was only a small moneybag around his waist, with a clip for his scabbard. Nothing else."

"I wouldn't be sure of that. Help me take off his clothes. Be careful; we shall have to put everything back exactly as it was, before Pompey's men come to claim the body."

Beneath his well-cut woolen tunic, Numerius wore a linen loincloth. It was wet with urine, but he had not soiled himself. He wore no jewelry except for his citizen's ring. I took off the ring and examined it; it appeared to be solid iron, with no secret compartments or hidden devices. There were only a few coins inside his moneybag; considering the chaotic state of the city, it would not have been prudent for a man without bodyguards to carry more. I turned the bag inside out. There were no secret pockets.

"Perhaps you're right, Davus. Perhaps he was carrying nothing of interest, after all. Unless . . . Take off his shoes, would you? My back aches from bending over."

The uppers were made of finely tanned black leather stamped with an intricate design of interconnected triangles, closed and fastened by thongs that wound around the ankle and calf. The soles were quite thick, made of several layers of hardened leather attached to the uppers by hobnails. There was nothing inside them. They were warm and carried the scent of Numerius's feet; handling them was more intimate than handling his clothing or even his ring. I was about to hand them back to Davus when I noticed an irregularity in the layered sole, at the heel. The same irregularity appeared at the same spot in both shoes. There were two breaks in the middle layer of the sole, about a thumb's length apart. Near one of the breaks was a small hole.

"Do you have the dagger you took from Numerius?"

Davus wrinkled his brow. "Yes. Ah, I see! But if you mean to cut into his shoes, I can fetch a better knife from the kitchen."

"No, let me see Numerius's dagger."

Davus reached inside his tunic. I handed him the shoes and he handed me the dagger in its sheath.

I nodded. "What do you notice about this sheath, Davus?"

He frowned, suspecting a test of some sort. "It's made of leather."

"Yes, but what sort of leather?"

"Black." He saw that I was unimpressed and tried again. "It's decorated."

"How?"

"It's stamped—and the same pattern is carved on the wooden hilt of the dagger."

"Yes, a pattern of interlocking triangles."

Davus peered at the shoes in his hands. "The same pattern as on his shoes!"

"Exactly. Meaning?"

Davus was stumped.

"Meaning," I said, "that whatever shop made the shoes also made the dagger. They're a set. Rather unusual, don't you think, that the same shop should produce such dissimilar goods?"

Davus nodded, pretending to follow my thoughts. "So—are you going to pull out the dagger and cut open the shoes, or not?"

"No, Davus I am going to *unlock* the shoes." I left the blade in its sheath and studied the hilt, which was carved from the hard black wood of the Syrian terebinth, attached to the metal by bosses of ivory. The triangle design ingeniously concealed the hidden compartment in the hilt, but it slid open easily once I found the right place to press with my thumb. Inside the compartment was a tiny key, hardly more than a sliver of bronze with a little hook near one end.

"Son-in-law, hold up the shoes with the heels facing me." I started with the shoe on my left. The irregularity in the heel, the two breaks I had noticed in the center layer of leather, proved to be a narrow door, with a hinge at one side and a keyhole at the other. I inserted the tiny key into the tiny hole. After a bit of fiddling, the door gave a little snap and sprang open.

"Extraordinary!" I whispered. "What workmanship! So delicate—yet sturdy enough to be trod on." I took the shoe from Davus, held it under the sunlight and peered down into the narrow chamber. I saw nothing. I turned the shoe over and knocked it against my palm. Nothing came out.

"Empty!" I said.

"We could still cut into it," said Davus helpfully.

I gave him a withering look. "Son-in-law, did I not say that we must put back all of Numerius's things exactly as they were, so that Pompey's men will see no signs of our tampering when they come to fetch him?"

Davus nodded.

"That includes his shoes! Now hand me the other one." I inserted the key and fiddled until the lock sprang open.

There was something inside. I withdrew what appeared to be several pieces of thin parchment.

II

"What does it say, father-in-law?"

"I don't know yet."

"Is it Latin?"

"I don't know that yet, either."

"I see Greek letters and Latin letters both, all mixed together."

"Clever of you, Davus, to spot the difference." Davus had lately been taking instruction from Diana, who was determined to teach him how to read. His progress had been slow.

"But how can that be, Greek and Latin letters both?"

"It's in some sort of code, Davus. Until I figure out the code, I can't read it any better than you can."

We had stepped from the garden into my study, and now sat across from each other at the little tripod table by the window, peering down at the thin pieces of parchment I had extracted from Numerius's shoe. There were five pieces in all, each covered with writing so tiny that I had to squint to make out the letters. At first glance, the text appeared to be pure nonsense, a collection of random letters strung together. I suspected the use of a cipher, with the added complication of mixing Greek and Latin characters.

I tried to explain to Davus how a cipher worked. Thanks to Diana, he had mastered the basic idea that letters could represent sounds and collections of letters could represent words, but his hold on the alphabet was tenuous. As I explained how letters could be shuffled arbitrarily about, then unshuffled, his face registered mounting bewilderment.

"But I thought the whole point of letters was that they *didn't* change, that they always stood for the same thing."

"Yes. Well . . ." I tried to think of a metaphor. "Imagine the letters all taking on disguises. Take your name: The D might masquerade as an M, the A as a T, and so on, and altogether you'd have five letters that didn't look like any sort of word at all. But figure a way to see through those disguises, and you can unmask the whole word." I smiled, thinking this was rather clever, but the look on Davus's face was now of confusion verging on panic.

"If only Meto were here," I muttered. The younger of my two adopted sons had turned out to have a genius for letters. His natural gifts had served him well in Caesar's ranks. He had become the general's literary adjutant. To hear Meto tell it, he had done much of the actual writing of Caesar's account of the Gallic Wars, which everyone in Rome had been reading for the last year. No one was more brilliant than Meto at cracking codes, anagrams, and ciphers.

But Meto was not in Rome—not yet, anyway, though expectations of Caesar's imminent arrival continued to mount day by day, causing jubilation in some quarters, terror in others.

"There are rules about solving ciphers," I muttered aloud, trying to remember the simple tricks that Meto had taught me. "'A cipher is simply a puzzle, solving a puzzle is merely a game, and—"

"'And all games have rules, which any fool can follow.'"

I looked up and saw my daughter standing in the doorway.

"Diana! I told you to stay in the front of the house. What if little Aulus—"

"Mother is watching him. She'll keep him out of the garden. You know how superstitious she is about dead bodies." Diana clicked her tongue. "That poor fellow looks awful!"

"I wanted to spare you the sight."

"Papa, I've seen dead bodies before."

"But not . . ."

"Not strangled like that, no. Though I have seen a garrote before. It looks a lot like the one used to murder Titus Trebonius a few years ago, the fellow you proved was strangled by his wife. You kept the garrote as a souvenir, remember? Mother threatened to use it on Davus if he ever displeased me."

"She was joking, I think. Such weapons are as common as daggers these days," I said.

"Davus, are you doing a good job of helping Papa?" Diana moved to her husband's side and laid a slender arm over his brawny shoulders, then touched her lips to his forehead. Davus grinned. A strand of Diana's long black hair fell across his face, tickling his nose.

I cleared my throat. "The problem appears to be a cipher. Davus and I have practically solved it already. Run along, Diana, back to your mother."

"Isis and Osiris, Papa! How can you possibly read such fine writing?" She squinted at the parchment.

"Contrary to prevailing opinion in this household, I am neither deaf nor blind," I said. "And it is unseemly for girls to speak impiously in front of their fathers, even if the deities invoked are Egyptian." A passion for all things Egyptian was Diana's latest rage. She called it a homage to her mother's origins. I called it an affectation.

"I'm not a girl, Papa. I'm twenty years old, married, and a mother."

"Yes, I know." I looked sidelong at Davus, who was completely absorbed in blowing wisps of his wife's shimmering black hair away from his nose.

"If solving a cipher is the problem, Papa, then let me help you. Davus can go stand watch in the garden, to make sure no one else comes over the rooftop."

Davus brightened at this suggestion. I nodded. He strode off at once. "You, too, Diana," I said. "Off with you!" Instead, she took Davus's place in the chair across from me. I sighed.

"It needs to be done quickly," I said. "The dead fellow out there is a relative of Pompey's. For all I know, Pompey may have already sent someone looking for him."

"Where did these pieces of parchment come from?"

"They were hidden in a secret compartment in his shoe."

Diana raised an eyebrow. "This fellow was one of Pompey's spies?"

I hesitated. "Perhaps."

"Why did he come here? Why did he want to see you, Papa?"

I shrugged. "We hardly spoke before I left him alone for a moment."

"And then?"

"Davus came into the garden, found his body, and raised the alarm."

Diana eagerly reached for a sheet of parchment. "If we look for vowels, and common consonant combinations—"

"And common words, and case endings."

"Right."

"Or likely words," I added.

"Likely?"

"Words likely to occur in a document carried by Pompey's spy. Such as . . . such as 'Pompey,' for example. Or more likely, 'Magnus'—*Great One.*"

Diana nodded. "Or . . . 'Gordianus,' perhaps?" She looked at me askance.

"Perhaps," I said.

Diana fetched two styluses and two wax tablets for scribbling notes. We studied our separate pieces of parchment in silence. Out in the garden, Davus paced back and forth in the sunlight, whistling tunelessly and scanning the roof. He pulled Numerius's dagger from its scabbard and cleaned his fingernails. From the front of the house came more screams from Aulus, and then the sound of Bethesda crooning an Egyptian lullaby.

"I think . . ."

"Yes, Diana?"

"I think I may have found 'Magnus.' I see the same sequence of letters three times on this piece. Look, there it is on your piece, too."

"Where?"

"There: λVΨCΣQ."

"So it is. By Hercules, these letters are small! If you're right, that gives us λ for M, V for A . . ."

"Ψ for G . . ."

We scribbled on our wax tablets. Diana scanned her piece of parchment, put it down and scanned two others. "Papa, may I see your piece?"

I handed it to her. Her eyes moved down the page, then stopped. She sucked in a breath.

"What is it, daughter?"

"Look, there!" She pointed to a group of letters. They began with Ψ and ended with CΣQ—or, according to our cipher, began with a G and ended with NUS—and had five letters between.

"'Gordianus,'" she whispered.

My heart pounded in my chest. "Maybe. Forget the other pieces for now. Let's work together on this one."

We concentrated on the section of text immediately following my name. It was Diana who spotted the large numbers strewn throughout; rather than quantities, they appeared to be years, following Varro's fashionable new system of dating everything from the founding of Rome. The cipher letters for D and I (presumed already from GORDIANUS) turned out to stand as well for the numerals D (five hundred) and I (one). Deciphering the years also gave us the letters for C, L, X, and V.

Using our growing list of deciphered letters, we quickly spotted familiar names embedded in the text. There was METO, and CAE-SAR . . . ECO (my other son) . . . CICERO . . . even BETHESDA and DIANA, who seemed more amused than alarmed at seeing her name in a dead man's document. As we made further progress, the most devious feature of the text became obvious: not only did the ci-pher mix Greek and Latin letters, but the text alternated between phrases in both languages, with a patchwork of truncated and irregular grammar. My Greek had grown rusty in recent years. Fortunately, Diana's Egyptomania had included brushing up on the language of the Ptolemies.

With her sharper eyes and quicker stylus, Diana drew ahead of me. Eventually, despite some remaining gaps here and there, she managed to make a hasty translation of the entire passage into Latin, scribbling it out on a long piece of blank parchment. When she was done, I asked her to read it aloud.

"'Subject: Gordianus, called the Finder. Loyalty to the Great One: Questionable.'"

"A loyalty report!" I shook my head. "All these bits of parchment must constitute some sort of secret dossier on various men in Rome—someone's evaluation of where they each might stand in the event of a—"

"In the war that's coming between Pompey and Caesar?" How matter-of-factly Diana was able to say the words I choked on; she had no experience of civil war, no memories of Rome besieged and conquered, of enemy lists and seized property and heads on stakes in the Forum.

Diana read on. "'Plebeian. Family origins obscure. No known military service. Age about sixty.' Then there's a sort of résumé, a chronological list of highlights from your illustrious career."

"Let's hear it."

"'Little known of activities prior to Year of Rome 674, when he gathered information for Cicero for the parricide trial of Sextus Roscius. Earned gratitude of Cicero (his first major defense), enmity of the dictator Sulla. Numerous episodes of employment by Cicero and others in subsequent years, often related to murder trials. Travel to Spain and Sicily.

"'Year of Rome 681: Vestal Virgins Fabia and Licinia accused of intercourse with Catilina and Crassus, respectively. Gordianus thought to have some hand in the defense, but his role obscure.

"'Year of Rome 682: Employed by Crassus (on the eve of his command against Spartacus) to investigate the murder of a relative in Baiae. Again, his role obscure. His relations with Crassus strained thereafter.

"'Year of Rome 684: Birth of his brilliant and beautiful daughter, Diana . . .'"

"That's not in there!"

"No. Clearly, whoever compiled this little review doesn't know *everything*. Actually, the next entry reads: 'Year of Rome 690: Death of his patrician patron Lucius Claudius. Inherited Etruscan farm and moved out of Rome.

"'Year of Rome 691: Played murky role in conspiracy of Catilina. Spied on Catilina for Cicero, or vice versa, or both? Relations with Cicero strained thereafter. Traded Etruscan farm for his current residence on the Palatine Hill. Assumed pretense of respectability.'"

"Pretense? Don't read that part to your mother! Go on."

"'Year of Rome 698: Assisted Clodia in prosecution of Marcus Caelius for the murder of the philosopher Dio.'" There was a catch in her voice. "'Further estrangement from Cicero (defending Caelius).'"

I grunted. "The less said about that case . . ."

". . . the better," concluded Diana, who shared with me a secret about the untimely death of Dio. She cleared her throat. "'Year of Rome 702: Employed by the Great One to investigate murder of Clodius on the Appian Way. Service satisfactory.'"

"Satisfactory! Is that all, after what this family suffered to find the truth for Pompey?"

"I'm sure Pompey would say we were well rewarded." Diana cast a wistful glance toward the garden. Davus smiled back at her and waved.

"And the less said about *that* the better, as well," I muttered. "Are those all the entries?"

"There's one more, dated last month. 'December, Year of Rome 704: No known activity for either side in recent . . .'" She frowned and showed me her text. "It's a Greek word I couldn't translate."

I squinted. "That's a nautical term. It means 'maneuvering.'"

"Maneuvering?"

"In the sense of two ships getting into position so as to engage in battle."

"Oh. Well, then: 'No known activity for either side in recent *maneuvering* between Pompey and Caesar.'"

"Is that it? My whole career, reduced to a few arbitrary episodes? I don't think I care for this business of being epitomized by some stranger."

"There a bit more, about the family."

"Let's hear it."

"'Wife: A former slave, acquired in Alexandria, named Bethesda. Of no political significance.

"'One natural offspring, a daughter, Gordiana, addressed as Diana, age about twenty, married to a manumitted slave, one Davus, *formerly property of the Great One.*' That last part was underlined in the ciphered text."

I nodded. "That would make sense, if this document is what it appears to be, a confidential report intended for Pompey. Davus constitutes my only flesh-and-blood tie to Pompey. It's the sort of thing he'd want to see highlighted. Go on."

"'Two sons. Eco, adopted as a street urchin, age about forty, married to a daughter of the Menenius family. No military career. Resides in old family house on Esquiline Hill. Sometimes assists his father. Political connections resemble his father's—wide-ranging but fluid and uncertain. Loyalty to the Great One: Questionable.'"

She glanced up from her text. "The next part was also underlined: '*Of particular interest: second son, Meto, also adopted.* Originally a slave owned by Marcus Crassus. Age about thirty. Military career from early age. Rumored to have fought for Catilina at battle of Pistoria. Briefly served under Pompey in Year of Rome 692. Since 693, with Caesar. Numerous episodes of bravery in Gaul. Worked his way up through ranks to join inner circle. Notable for literary skills: handles correspondence, helped to edit Caesar's account of Gallic campaigns. Firmly in Caesar's camp—some say in Caesar's . . .'" Her voice trailed off.

"Yes? Go on."

"'Some say in Caesar's bed, as well.'"

"What?"

"That's what it says, Papa. More or less; the original was a bit more uncouth. That part was in Greek, but I knew all the words."

"Outrageous!"

"Is it?"

"Meto loves Caesar, of course; you'd have to love a man to risk your life for him on any given day. Hero worship—it's a cult among military men. I've never understood it, myself. But that's not the same as . . ."

Diana shrugged. "Meto's never said anything explicit to me about himself and Caesar, but even so, just from the way he talks about their relationship, I've always assumed there must be . . ."

"Assumed what?"

"Papa, there's no need to raise your voice."

"Well! It appears you're not the only one who's been making wild assumptions. In a confidential report intended for Pompey's eyes, no less! Caesar's enemies have been spreading this kind of tale about him for thirty years, ever since he befriended King Nicomedes. You can still hear him called the Queen of Bithynia in the Forum. But how dare they draw Meto into their rumormongering? Don't roll your eyes, Diana! You seem to think I'm making something out of nothing."

"I think there's no need to shout, Papa."

"Yes. Well . . ."

She laid her hand on mine. "We're all worried about Meto, Papa. About his being so close to Caesar . . . and what's going to happen next. Only the gods know how it will all turn out."

I nodded. The room seemed suddenly very quiet. The sunlight from the garden was already softening; days are short in Januarius. My temples began to throb. We had been working for hours. The only break had been to stoke the fire in the brazier, to ward off the growing chill. The brazier had been burning since first light. The room was smoky.

I glanced at Diana's text and saw that she had more left to read. "Go on," I said quietly. "What else?"

"'Few slaves in the household. Among them: two boys, brothers acquired from the widow of Clodius shortly after his death, originally stableboys at his villa on the Appian Way. Mopsus (older) and

Androcles (younger). Often act as messengers for Gordianus. Little jugs have big handles.'" Diana frowned. "I'm sure that's what it says."

"It's a quotation from a play by Ennius," I said. "It means that little boys have big ears—implying that Mopsus and Androcles might make useful informers. Go on."

"There's a bit more about Mopsus and Androcles: 'Given Gordianus's inclination to adopt orphans and slaves, will he end up with two more sons?'" She raised an eyebrow and waited for a comment.

"Go on," I finally said. "What else?"

"A summary: 'Subject possesses no political power and little wealth, yet is held in high regard by many who do. Once called by Cicero "the most honest man in Rome," but where does his reputation for integrity come from? By never firmly taking sides in any dangerous controversy, he manages to appear above the fray and so remains able to move freely back and forth between sides. Even when employed by one side, he maintains an appearance of independence and neutrality, committed to finding "truth" rather than achieving a partisan agenda. He combines the skills of the investigator with those of the diplomat. This could be his chief value in a crisis: as a go-between trusted by both sides.

"'On the other hand, some see him as a wily pragmatist, exploiting the trust of powerful men without giving them full allegiance. What sort of man hires out his integrity, case by case?

"'In the event of an unprecedented crisis, where will his true allegiance lie? He has a fine house on the Palatine and has managed to stay out of debt (another factor in his independence); it is hard to see how revolution or civil war could be to his interest. On the other hand, his unconventional family of adoptees and manumitted slaves indicates a man with little concern for traditional Roman values. Most troublesome is his connection to Caesar through his son Meto. This, more than anything else, may act to pull him into Caesar's orbit.

"'Conclusion: Gordianus may be of use to the Great One, but should be carefully watched.'"

Diana looked up. "That's all of it."

I wrinkled my nose. "'A wily pragmatist?'" That stung as sharply as the gossip about Meto.

"Actually, I think it's flattering, on the whole," said Diana. "It makes you out to be a rather subtle fellow."

"Subtle fellows lose their heads in times like these."

"Then Davus shall be safe, at least." She looked at me with a straight face, then laughed. I managed a smile. She was only trying to cheer me up, I knew; but she really had no idea of the enormity of the danger that was looming. I suddenly felt a great tenderness for her. I touched her hair.

There was some sort of commotion from the front of the house. Davus left the garden. A moment later he was back. He strode into my study. "Another visitor," he said. His face was pale.

"This late in the afternoon?"

"Yes, father-in-law. The Great One himself."

III

"Pompey? Impossible!"

"Even so, father-in-law, he's waiting in the foyer, with armed bodyguards."

"He's breaking the law, then! Pompey has a standing army. Never mind that his legions are off in Spain—proconsuls in command of armies are not allowed to enter the city walls."

Diana spoke up. "'Stop quoting laws to us. We carry swords.'" She quoted a phrase which Pompey had made famous when he was in Sicily and some locals objected that he was overstepping their treaties with Rome.

I took a deep breath. "How many men are with him, Davus?"

"Only two in the foyer. The rest of the bodyguards are waiting in the street."

I looked at the pieces of parchment on the tripod table. "Numerius! Where in Hades did his shoes end up? If Pompey finds him barefoot—"

"Calm yourself, father-in-law. His shoes are back on his feet. What do you think I've been doing in the garden all afternoon? I dressed Numerius, put the ring back on his finger, and replaced his moneybag. The body's just as we found it."

"What about his dagger?"

"I put the little key back inside and slipped the dagger back into his sheath."

"And the garrote around his throat?"

Davus nodded grimly. "Still there."

I lowered my gaze to the table. "Everything in place, then—except these pieces of parchment. I meant to put them back before anyone came for the body. If Pompey discovers they're missing—"

Davus frowned. "Perhaps, if we can keep Pompey from seeing Numerius . . ."

"Hide the body? I don't think so, Davus. Pompey must know that Numerius came here; that's why he's here himself. If we make some clumsy attempt to hide the body, and Pompey discovers it, how would that look?"

Diana touched my arm. "If you're worried about Pompey catching you with the documents, Papa, we could burn them. There's a fire in the brazier. It would take only a moment."

I stared at the pieces of parchment. "We could burn them, yes. Or stuff them back into Numerius's shoe, if there's time. Either way, we'll never know what else they contain. Perhaps there's more about your brothers, or someone else we care about . . ."

"Shall we hide them, then, so we can decipher them later?"

"And what if Pompey decides to search the house, and finds them? Gordianus, the 'wily pragmatist' of dubious allegiance, caught in possession of secret documents, with one of the Great One's kinsmen lying dead in his garden . . ."

Diana crossed her arms. "Pompey has no right to come barging in here. He has no right to search a citizen's house." The fire in her eyes reminded me of her mother.

"Are you sure of that, daughter? Ten days ago, the Senate passed the Ultimate Decree. The last time that happened was when Cicero was consul and accused Catilina of plotting insurrection. You were too young at the time to remember—"

"I know what the Ultimate Decree means, Papa. I read the notices in the Forum. The consuls and proconsuls are empowered to use any means necessary to safeguard the state."

"Any means necessary—and you think Pompey would hesitate to ransack this house? For all practical purposes, Rome is under martial law. The very fact that Pompey dares to come into the city with armed men means that ordinary laws no longer exist. Anything could happen. Anything!"

Diana's composure wavered. She crossed her arms more tightly. "Knowing all that, Papa, what do you want to do about these documents?"

I stared at them uncertainly, paralyzed with indecision. I had succeeded in frightening myself more than Diana.

I heard voices from the front of the house and looked up to see Pompey emerge through the doorway into the garden, accompanied by two bodyguards. All three wore expressions of grim determination. I had waited too long. The situation was out of my hands.

I watched through the window as they turned sharply right, then left, following the colonnaded walkway around the perimeter of the courtyard, heading for my study. Pompey glanced to his left. He halted so abruptly that one of his men bumped into him. From the look on his face I knew what he had seen. I followed his gaze, but the statue of Minerva blocked my view. All I could see of the body of Numerius was one of the feet, wearing the shoe from which we had taken the documents.

I looked at Pompey. In the blink of an eye, his face become contorted with anguish. He gave a cry and ran to the body. His two guards drew their swords in alarm.

Without a word from me, Diana scooped the documents from the tripod together with the parchment with her decipherings, walked to the brazier, and added them to the flames. The moment had passed when Davus or I could have done so; Pompey or one of his guards might have seen us, and remembered later. But who would take any notice of the daughter of the house tending to the brazier?

I drew a deep breath. So much for the documents; whatever other secrets they might have contained were beyond deciphering now.

From beyond the statue of Minerva, I heard Pompey let out another wail of anguish. His guards quickly circled the garden, poking their swords into the shrubbery and gazing up at the roof, as Davus had done. One of then tried to draw Pompey away from the body, back toward the foyer. Pompey waved the man off. A moment later more bodyguards flooded into the courtyard, drawn by Pompey's cry.

"Diana! Davus! Back against the wall!" I said. "Davus, take out your dagger and throw it on the ground. Quickly! If they see you draw it out, they're liable to swarm all over you."

Davus's dagger was on the floor and his hands were pressed flat to the wall even before I finished speaking. In the next instant, three of Pompey's men were in the room, eyes wide and swords drawn.

From the garden, Pompey bellowed my name. "Gordianus!"

I cleared my throat and straightened my shoulders. I turned to the brazier and pretended to warm my hands while I gazed into the flames to make sure that only ashes remained, then I turned back toward the door.

I looked the nearest guard in the eye. He was outfitted in full battle gear, including a helmet that hid most of his face. "Let me by," I said. "That's my name the Great One is calling."

The man stared back at me for a long moment, then grunted. The three guards drew apart just enough to let me pass through the doorway. One of them deliberately breathed in my face, making sure I caught the stench of garlic on his breath. Gladiators and bodyguards eat whole heads of garlic raw, claiming it gives them strength. Another made sure that my arm slid against the flat edge of his sword. I knew by such behavior that they were Pompey's private slaves, not regular legionaries; some slaves like to take liberties when circumstances put a citizen at a disadvantage. I didn't like the idea of leaving Diana and Davus alone in the room with three such creatures.

I took a breath and walked to the center of the garden. Pompey heard the sound of gravel crunching under my feet and looked up. His plump, round face was made for laughter or casting sardonic glances; expressing grief, his features seemed all askew. I would scarcely have recognized him.

He loosened his embrace of the body, gazed at his kinsman's face for a moment, then looked back at me. "What happened, Gordianus? Who did this?"

"I thought you might have an answer to that question, Great One."

"Don't answer me in riddles, Finder!" Pompey released the body and got to his feet.

"You can see for yourself, Great One. He was strangled here in my garden. You see the garrote still around his throat. I was about to set out for your villa, to bring you the news myself—"

"Who did it?"

"No one in the household saw or heard anything. I left Numerius alone for a moment, to go into my study. And then . . ."

Pompey clutched a fistful of air and shook his head. "He's the first, then. The first to die! How many more? Damn Caesar!" He glared at me. "Do you have no explanation for this, Finder? No explanation at all? How could it have happened, here in the middle of your house, without anyone knowing? Am I to believe Caesar can send down harpies from the sky to kill his enemies?"

I looked him straight in the eye. I swallowed hard. "Great One, you've brought armed men into my house."

"What?"

"Great One, I must ask you, first of all, to call off your bodyguards. There are no assassins lurking in my house—"

"How can you assure me of that, if you never saw the man who did this?"

"At least call your men out of my study. They have no reason to stand watch over my daughter and son-in-law. Please, Great One. A crime has occurred here, yes, but even so, I ask you to respect the sanctity of a citizen's house."

Pompey gave me such a look that for a long, dreadful moment I expected the worst. There were at least ten bodyguards in the garden. There might be more, elsewhere in the house. How long would it take them to ransack the place and kill everyone in it? Of course, they wouldn't destroy everything or kill everyone, only Davus and me. The things of value and the slaves would be confiscated. As for Bethesda and Diana . . . I couldn't bear to follow the thought to its conclusion.

I looked into Pompey's eyes. In his youth he had been extraordi-
narily handsome—a second Alexander, people called him, just as
brilliant and just as beautiful, a commander touched by the gods.
With age he had lost his beauty, as his bland features receded amid
the growing fleshiness of his face. Some said he had lost his brilliance
as well; his lack of foresight and unwillingness to compromise
had allowed the current crisis, with Caesar defying the Senate and
marching on Rome while Pompey responded with indecision and
uncertainty. Pompey was a man with his back against a wall, and at
that moment he was in my house, furious with grief, accompanied
by a large bodyguard of trained killers.

I looked at him steadily. I managed not to flinch. At last the moment passed. Pompey took a breath. So did I.

"You have nerve, Finder."

"I have rights, Great One. I'm a citizen. This is my home."

"And this is my kinsman." Pompey lowered his gaze, then stiffened his jaw and looked at the guard in the doorway to my study.
"You, there! Call your fellows out of there. All of you, back into the
garden."

"But Great One, there's a man in here with a dagger at his feet."

"And a very pretty girl in his arms," added a sniggering voice
from inside.

"You idiots! Numerius wasn't killed with a dagger. That much is
obvious. Come out of there and leave the Finder's family alone."
Pompey let out a sigh, and in that moment it seemed to me that the
worst possible outcome had been averted.

"Thank you, Great One."

He made a face, as if displeased at his own restraint. "You can
show your gratitude by offering me a drink."

"Of course. Diana, find Mopsus. Have him bring wine." She
looked at Davus, then at me, then went into the house. "You, too,
Davus," I said. "Into the house."

"But father-in-law, don't you want me to stay and explain—"

"No," I said, grinding my teeth, "I want you to go with Diana.
Look after Bethesda and Aulus."

"If he knows something, then he must stay!" snapped Pompey.

He looked Davus up and down. "You look familiar. Oh, yes, it comes back to me now. You're the one I lent to Gordianus a couple of years ago, to guard his house while he was off down the Appian Way doing some work for me. Only you guarded his daughter a bit too well, as I recall. I'd have taken your hide off, and then your head. But Gordianus wanted you, and so I let him have you, and here you are. What do you know about this?"

I watched the color drain from Davus's face. Pompey spoke to him in a tone suitable for addressing a slave, and Davus responded subserviently out of ancient habit. He lowered his eyes. "It's as my father-in-law says, Great One. There was no scream, no cry. No one heard footsteps, or anything else. The assassin came and went in silence. The first I knew of it was when my father-in-law gave a yell and I came running."

Pompey looked at me. "How did you come to find him?"

"As I said, I left him alone here in the garden while I stepped into my study for a moment—"

"Only a moment?"

I shrugged and gazed down at the dead man.

"What was he doing here? Why did he come to visit you?" asked Pompey.

I raised an eyebrow. "I thought *you* might be able to answer that question, Great One. Did you not send him to me?"

"I sent him into the city to deliver some messages, yes. But not to you."

"Then why did you come here, if not to find him?"

Pompey scowled. "Where is that wine?"

The slave boys appeared, Androcles bearing cups and Mopsus a copper flask. Casting furtive wide-eyed glances at the corpse, they made a mess of pouring the wine. I joined Pompey in his first cup, but he drained his second cup alone, downing it without relish as if it were medicine. He wiped his mouth, handed his cup back to Androcles and dismissed the boys with a curt wave of his hand. They ran back into the house.

"If you must know," he said, "I came here straight from Cicero's house up the road. I sent Numerius to Cicero with a message earlier today. According to Cicero, Numerius's next stop was your house. I didn't expect to still find him here. I only thought that you might know where he'd gone next. What business did he have with you, Finder?"

I shook my head. "Whatever it was, he's silenced forever now."

"And how in Hades did anyone get in and out of this garden? Do you think a man could have come down from the roof and then retreated the same way? I don't see how it's possible. The roof is above any man's reach, and the columns are too recessed to be of any use for climbing onto the roof. Not even an African ape could have done it!"

"But two men might have," noted Davus. "One to boost the other, and then to be hoisted up in turn."

"Davus is right," I said. "Or one man alone could have done it, with a sufficient length of rope."

Pompey's scowl intensified. "But who? And how did they know to find him here?"

"I'm sure, Great One, if you make inquiries—"

"I've no time for that. I'm leaving Rome tonight."

"Leaving?"

"I'm heading south before dawn. So will anyone else with a shred of sense, or an iota of loyalty to the Senate. Is it possible that you haven't heard the latest reports? Do you never come out of that study of yours?"

"As seldom as possible these days."

He flashed me an angry look that held a glimmer of envy. "You do know that six days ago Caesar crossed the Rubicon River into Italy with his troops, and occupied Ariminum. Since then he's taken Pisaurum and Ancona, and sent Marc Antony to take Arretium. He moves like a whirlwind! Now there's word that both Antony and Caesar are marching on Rome, closing on us like a vise. The city is defenseless. The closest loyal legion is down in Capua. If rumors are true, Caesar could be here in a matter of days, perhaps even hours."

"Rumors, you say. Perhaps they're only that."

Pompey looked at me suspiciously. "What do you know about it, holed up here in your garden? You have a son with Caesar, don't you?

That boy who used to be one of Crassus's slaves, and claims to have fought with Catilina. He sleeps in the same tent with Caesar, I'm told, and helps him write those pompous, self-serving memoirs. What sort of contact does he keep with you, Gordianus?"

"My son Meto is his own man, Great One."

"He's Caesar's man! And whose man are you, Finder?"

"It took many years and a great many Romans to conquer Gaul, Great One. Many a citizen has a relative who's served in Caesar's legions. That hardly makes us all partisans of Caesar. Look at Cicero—his brother Quintus is one of Caesar's officers, and his protégé Marcus Caelius has run off to join Caesar. Even so, no one would ever call Cicero a Caesarian." I refrained from pointing out that Pompey himself had been married to Caesar's daughter, and it was only after Julia's death that their differences became irreconcilable. "Great One, I served you loyally enough when you hired me to investigate the murder of Clodius, did I not?"

"Because I paid you, and because in that instance there was no choice to be made between Caesar and me. That's not loyalty! Loyalty comes from slaves and soldiers—from beatings, bloodshed, and battle. Those are the only ties that truly bind men together. 'The most honest man in Rome,' Cicero called you once. No wonder no one trusts you!"

Pompey turned from me in disgust and knelt beside his kinsman. He observed the body more closely than he had in his initial shock. "Here's his moneybag, with coins in it—the killer was no thief. And here's his dagger, still in its sheath. He didn't even have time to draw it. It must be as you said—the killer came silently and took him from behind. He never saw the face of the man who murdered him!"

In truth, Numerius had been without his dagger when he died; Davus had taken it from him, and replaced it after we searched the body. I could explain none of this to Pompey. He was right not to trust me.

Pompey touched the dead man's face with his fingertips. He gritted his teeth, fighting back his grief. "Someone must have followed him here when he left Cicero's house. Perhaps they followed him from the moment he left my villa this morning, waiting for the chance to strike. But who? Someone from Caesar's camp? Or one of my own men? If there's a traitor in my household . . ."

He lifted his angry gaze to the statue of Minerva looming over us. The goddess of wisdom was portrayed in battle gear, ready for war, an upright spear in one hand and a shield in the other, with a crested helmet on her head. An owl perched on her shoulder. A snake coiled at her feet. She had been toppled and broken in two during the Clodian riots. I had spent a small fortune to have the bronze repaired and freshly painted. The colors were so lifelike that the virgin goddess seemed almost to breathe. She looked directly at us, and yet her gaze remained aloof, oblivious of the tragedy at her feet.

"You!" Pompey rose to his feet and shook his fist. "How could you allow such a thing to happen, right before you? Caesar claims Venus for an ancestor, but you should be on my side!"

There was a rustle among the bodyguards, made uneasy by their master's impiety.

"And you!" Pompey turned to me. "I charge you with finding the man who did this. Bring me his name. I'll see to justice."

I shook my head, averting my eyes from Pompey's wild gaze. "No, Great One. I can't."

"What do you mean? You've done such work before."

"Very little since I last worked for you, Great One. I have no stomach for it anymore. I made a promise to myself to retire from public life if I managed to reach sixty years. That was a year ago."

"You don't seem to understand, Finder. I'm not *asking* you to find Numerius's killer. I'm not *hiring* you. I'm ordering you!"

"By what authority?"

"By the authority vested in me by the Senate's Ultimate Decree!"

"But the law—"

"Don't quote the law to *me,* Finder! The Ultimate Decree empowers me to do whatever is necessary to preserve the state. The murder of my kinsman, acting as my agent, is a crime against the state. Discovering his killer is necessary to protect the state. The Ultimate Decree empowers me to enlist your assistance, even against your will!"

"Great One, I assure you, if I had the strength, and if my wits were as sharp as they once were—"

"If you need a helper to guide you about like blind Tiresias, call on your other son. He's here in Rome, isn't he?"

"I can't draw Eco into this," I said. "He has his own family to look after."

"As you wish. Work alone, then."

"But, Great One—"

"Say no more, Finder." He stared at me coldly, then turned his gaze to Davus. "You there! You still look to be a healthy fellow."

"Never sick a day, Great One," said Davus warily.

"And not a coward."

"Certainly not!"

"Good. Because one of the powers granted to me by the Ultimate Decree is to muster fresh troops. You, Davus, shall be my first recruit. Get your things together. You're leaving Rome with me tonight."

Davus's jaw dropped. Diana, who had been watching from the doorway, ran to his side.

"This isn't right, Great One," I said, as calmly as I could. "Davus is a citizen now. You can't coerce him into—"

"A citizen, yes, but also a freedman, and a freedman has obligations to his former master. I've pledged to raise a certain number of troops from among my own dependents. Davus shall be among them."

"But he's no longer of your household. You gave him to me, as payment for my services. I manumitted him."

"Ah, but he still has certain obligations to his original master."

"Not legal obligations."

"Yes, legal obligations! If you don't think so, I suggest you examine the contract you signed when I handed him over to you, notably the clause regarding previous servitude and contingent future obligations in case of martial emergency. It's a standard clause in every contract when I sell or release a slave; otherwise I might see my former slaves being used to fight against me, instead of for me. This is a martial emergency, and Davus must submit to military service, when and where and how I choose. And *you* would presume to quote the law to *me!*"

"Papa, is he right?" Diana clutched her husband's arm.

I looked at the circle of armed men around us. Whether Pompey was right or not hardly seemed to matter. "Great One, the city may soon be in chaos. I need my son-in-law to protect the household."

"He seems to have done a poor enough job of that!" Pompey's voice broke as he gazed down at Numerius. He swallowed hard. "But I won't deprive you of protection for your women and slaves, while you're out finding the killer of my kinsman. I shall leave you a body-guard in Davus's place. You, there!" He called to one of the guards who had barged into my study, the one who had breathed garlic in my face. He was even bigger than Davus, and would have been ugly even without his broken nose and the hideous scar across one cheek. "You're called Cicatrix, aren't you?"

"Yes, Great One."

"You shall stay here and watch this house for me."

"Yes, Great One." Cicatrix gave me a surly look.

"Gnaeus Pompey, please, no!" I whispered.

"Yes, Gordianus. I insist."

I looked at the stunned faces of Davus and Diana. I felt as if a great stone was on my chest. "Great One, your kinsman is dead. That such a thing happened in my home fills me with shame. But as you yourself said, he's only the first. Thousands may die. What does one murder mean, when all the laws are suspended?"

"You ask questions, Finder. I want answers. Discover who murdered Numerius, and then we shall see about returning your son-in-law to you."

~

As the last of the sunlight retreated from the garden, so did Pompey's men, taking Davus with them and carrying the body of Numerius. Pompey left the device that had been used to strangle him with me, thinking it might be of some use in finding his killer. I could hardly stand to touch it.

Diana wept. Bethesda emerged from the house and gave me an accusing look. Mopsus and Androcles followed after her with my grandson between them, all holding hands. At the sight of the ugly giant Pompey had left to take Davus's place, little Aulus burst into tears, pulled free and toddled frantically back into the house.

IV

Cicero's house was only a short distance from my own, along the rim road of the Palatine Hill. Even on such a brief walk I would normally have taken Davus with me for protection, especially after dark. On this night, of all nights, I sorely missed him.

All around me I felt the uneasiness of the city, like a sleeper in the throes of a nightmare. The rustling of many footsteps rose up from the Forum in the valley below. Torches, like tiny fireflies at such a distance, darted to and fro across the open squares. What were so many people doing out after dark? They were lighting votives in the temples, I thought, praying for peace . . . making preparations for hasty departures . . . banging on their bankers' locked doors . . . buying up the last scraps of food and fuel in the market stalls. I rounded a corner, and the Capitoline Hill came into view. At its summit, great fires had been lit in the braziers before the Temple of Jupiter—watchfires to alert the people that an invading army was on the march.

Two guards were stationed outside Cicero's door. They appeared supremely unimpressed by the approach of a gray-haired visitor without even a bodyguard to accompany him.

My relations with Cicero were strained at best. I asked to see his private secretary, with whom I had always been on closer terms.

The younger of the guards scratched his head. "Tiro? Never heard of him. No, wait—isn't that the one who died while the Master was on his way home from Cilicia?"

The other guard, a fellow with a bristling beard, saw my alarm and laughed. "Pay no attention to this young idiot. He's been around only a few months, never even met Tiro, who isn't dead, just too sick to travel."

"I don't understand. Is Tiro here or isn't he?"

"He isn't."

"Where is he?"

The older guard looked thoughtful. "Now what is the name of that place? In Greece, close to the water . . ."

"What town in Greece isn't close to water?" I said.

"This one starts with a P . . ."

"Piraeus?"

"No . . ."

"Patrae?"

"That's it! I was with the Master during his stint as governor of Cilicia, you see, and so was Tiro, of course. Last summer, we all started back to Rome. Took a slow, easy route. Along about November, Tiro fell sick and had to stay behind with one of the Master's friends in Patrae. The Master pushed on, and we got back to Rome this month, just in time to celebrate his birthday."

"Cicero's birthday?"

"Three days before the Nones of Januarius. Fifty-seven—same age as Pompey, they say."

"What about Tiro?"

"He and the Master write each other back and forth, but it's always the same. Never seems to get much worse, but never gets much better, either. Still not well enough to travel."

"I see. I had no idea. This is bad news."

"For Tiro? I don't know about that. I figure he's in a good place about now. Lots of peace and quiet in Patrae, I should think. Nice place to convalesce. Wouldn't want to be in Rome these days if I didn't have two strong legs and felt up to running."

"I see your point."

"Was there somebody else in the household you wanted to see?"

"*Want* to see? No. Nonetheless, tell your master that Gordianus the Finder requests a visit."

Whatever recriminations had passed between us in former days seemed to have been forgotten by Cicero. I waited in the foyer for only a moment before he came to greet me. I received his embrace stiffly, startled by his warmth. I wondered if he had been drinking, but I smelled no wine on his breath. When he drew back I took a hard look at him.

I had braced myself to encounter Cicero in one of his less pleasant moods—the self-righteous, self-made man, smug friend of the powerful, peevish settler of old scores, priggish arbiter of virtue. I saw instead a man with jowls and receding hair and watery eyes, who looked as if he had just received the worst news of his life.

He gestured for me to follow him. The mood in his house matched the mood of the city—a panic barely contained by purposeful activity, as slaves hurried back and forth and spoke in hushed voices. Cicero led me first to his study, but the room was like a beehive, with slaves packing scrolls into boxes.

"This won't do," he said apologetically. "Come, there's a little room off the garden where we can talk quietly."

The little room was an exquisitely appointed chamber with a sumptuous Greek rug underfoot. A brazier on a tripod in the middle of the room illuminated walls painted with pastoral landscapes. Herdsmen dozed amid sheep, and satyrs peeked from behind little roadside temples.

"I've never seen this room before," I said.

"No? It was one of the first rooms Terentia decorated when we came back and rebuilt, after Clodius and his gang burned down the house and sent me into exile." He smiled ruefully. "Now Clodius is dust, but I'm still here—and so are you, Gordianus. But for what? To see it all come to this . . ."

Cicero paced nervously in a circle around the brazier, casting deep shadows across the walls. Abruptly he stopped his pacing and shot me a quizzical look. "Can it really have been thirty years since we first met, Gordianus?"

"Thirty-one, actually."

"The trial of Sextus Roscius." He shook his head. "We were all so young then! And brave, the way young men are, because they don't know any better. I, Marcus Tullius Cicero, took on the dictator Sulla in the courts—and bested him! I think back now and wonder how I could ever have been so mad. But it wasn't madness. It was bravery. I saw a terrible wrong and a way to redress it. I knew the danger and went ahead anyway, because I was young and thought I could change the world. Now . . . now I wonder if I can be that brave again. I fear I'm too old, Gordianus. I've seen too much . . . suffered too much . . ."

In my own recollections, Cicero's motives had never been quite as pure as he was painting them, colored as they were by shrewd ambition. Was he brave? Certainly he had taken risks—and been rewarded with fame, honor, and wealth. True, Fortune had not always smiled on him; he had suffered defeats and humiliations, especially in recent years. But he had caused others to suffer much worse. Men had been put to death without trial when he was consul, in the name of preserving the state.

Could any man advance as far in politics as Cicero had, and keep his hands entirely clean? Perhaps not. What rankled me was his insistence in presenting himself as the untarnished champion of virtue and reason. It was not a pose; it was the picture he had of himself. His unflagging self-justification had often exasperated, even infuriated, me. But now, in the darkness that had fallen on Rome, with the choice narrowed between one military leader and another, Cicero began to seem like not such a bad fellow after all.

He shook his head. "Can you believe it? That it's happening

again? That we must go through the same madness all over again? Our lives began with civil war, and now they shall end with it. A generation passes, and people forget. But do they really not remember how it was, in the war between Sulla and his enemies? Rome itself besieged and taken! And the horrors that followed, when Sulla set himself up as dictator! You remember, Gordianus. You were here. You saw the gaping heads mounted on bloody pikes in the Forum—decent, respectable men, hunted down and murdered by bounty hunters, their property seized and auctioned off to Sulla's favorites, their families impoverished and disgraced. Sulla got rid of his enemies—cleansing the state, he called it—made a few reforms, then stepped down and put the Senate back in charge. From that day until this, I have spent every hour of every day doing everything I could to fend off another such catastrophe. And yet—here we are. The Republic is about to come crashing down around us. Was this inevitable? Was there no way this could have been avoided?"

My mouth was dry. I wished that he would offer me some wine. "Pompey and Caesar may yet patch up their differences."

"No!" He shook his head and gestured wildly. "Caesar may send messages of peace and pretend that he's willing to parlay, but that's just for show, so that he can say later on, 'I did my best to keep the peace.' The moment he crossed the Rubicon, any hopes for a peaceful settlement vanished. On the far side of the river, he was a legally commissioned promagistrate in command of Roman legions. Once he crossed the bridge into Italy with armed men, he became an outlaw at the head of an invading army. There's no way to answer him now except with another army."

"Some people," I said, speaking slowly and carefully, "would say that the hope for peace vanished a few days before Caesar crossed the Rubicon, on the day the Senate passed the Ultimate Decree and drove Caesar's friend Marc Antony out of the city. That was as good as declaring Caesar an enemy of the state. You did the same to Catilina, when you were consul. We know how Catilina ended. Can you blame Caesar for mustering his troops and making the first move?"

Cicero looked at me darkly. The old antagonism between us began to stir. "Spoken like a true Caesarian, Gordianus. Is that the side you've chosen?"

I walked to the brazier and warmed my hands. It was time to speak of something else. "I was sorry to learn of Tiro's illness. I understand he's still in Greece. Have you heard from him lately? Is he better?"

Cicero seemed disconcerted by the change of subject. "Tiro? Why—? But of course, you and Tiro have always remained friends, even when you and I have not. Yes, I think he may be somewhat better."

"What is his malady?"

"Recurring fever, poor digestion, weakness. He can't leave his bed, much less travel."

"I'm sorry to hear it. You must miss him terribly, under these circumstances."

"There's no man in the world I trust more than Tiro." A silence ensued, finally broken by Cicero. "Is that why you came tonight, Gordianus? To ask after Tiro?"

"No."

"Why, then? Surely it wasn't concern for your old friend and patron Cicero that drew you out alone on such a night, without even that hulking son-in-law of yours to look after you."

"Yes, without even my son-in-law," I said quietly, seeing in my mind the look on Diana's face, and Davus looking over his shoulder as Pompey's men dragged him off. "I understand that Pompey came to visit you earlier today. And before that, Pompey's kinsman, Numerius."

Cicero scowled. "Those damned guards at the door! Their jaws are always flapping."

"It wasn't the guards who told me. It was Pompey himself. After he left you, he came to my house. So did Numerius, earlier in the day. Numerius came to see you, and then to see me."

"What of it?"

"Numerius never left my house alive. He was murdered in my garden."

Cicero looked aghast. His reaction seemed almost too extreme. I reminded myself that he was an orator used to performing to the farthest person in a crowd, and was prone to overact by force of habit. "But this is terrible! Murdered, you say. But how?"

"Strangled."

"By whom?"

"That's what Pompey would like to know."

Cicero tilted his head back and raised his eyebrows. "I see. The old hound has been put to the scent again."

"The first place the scent leads is back to this house."

"If you think there's any connection between Numerius's visit here and . . . what happened to him later, that's preposterous."

"Still, you were one of the last people he spoke to. One of the last . . . besides myself . . . to see him alive. Did you know him well?"

"Numerius? Well enough."

"From the tone of your voice, I take it you didn't care for him."

Cicero shrugged. Once again, the gesture seemed too broad. What was Cicero really thinking? "He was likable enough. A charming young fellow, most people would say. The apple of Pompey's eye."

"Why did he come to visit you this morning?"

"He brought news from Pompey. 'The Great One is vacating Rome, heading south. The Great One says that any true friend of the Republic will do the same at once.' That was his message for me."

"It sounds almost like a threat," I said. "An ultimatum."

Cicero looked at me warily but said nothing.

"And then Numerius left?"

"Not immediately. We . . . talked a bit, about the state of the city and such. Pompey hasn't called on all his allies to leave immediately. The consuls and some of the magistrates will stay on, a sort of skeleton government, enough to keep the city from falling entirely into chaos. Even so, the treasury will be closed, the bankers will flee, everything will come to a standstill . . ." He shook his head. "We talked a bit . . . and then Numerius left."

"Was anyone with him?"

"He came alone and he left alone."

"Odd, that he should go abroad in the city on Pompey's business without even a bodyguard."

"You've just done the same, Gordianus, and after dark. I suppose Numerius wished to moved as quickly and freely as he could. There must have been plenty of other senators he had to call on, all over the city."

I nodded. "There were no harsh words between you, then?"

Cicero glared at me. "I may have raised my voice. Those damned guards! Did they tell you they heard me shouting?"

"No. Did you shout at Numerius that loudly? What was the altercation about?"

He swallowed hard. The knob in his throat bobbed up and down. "How do you think I felt, when Numerius told me to leave the city by daybreak? I've been away from Rome for a year and a half governing a miserable province, and now that I'm back I hardly catch a breath before I'm told to pack up and flee like a refugee. If I raised my voice, if I shouted a bit, what of it?"

"You're raising your voice now, Cicero."

He pressed a hand against his chest and took several deep breaths. I had never seen him so overwrought; it unnerved me. Whatever their flaws, Pompey and Cicero represented models of Roman self-assurance and self-discipline, the military giant and the political genius. Both had known setbacks, but always triumphed in the long run. Now something was different, and both seemed to sense it. Born the same year, they were a few years younger than I, yet I felt like the child who sees his parents in a panic: if *they* have lost control, then all must be chaos.

He went on at a lower pitch. "It's a mistake for Pompey to flee. If Caesar is allowed to enter the city without opposition, he'll break into the treasury and squander the wealth of our ancestors to bribe the street gangs. He'll call together whatever's left of the Senate—debtors, discontents, rabble-rousers—and claim it's the legitimate government. Then it will be Pompey and those who fled who are outlaws."

"Have you said as much to Pompey?"

"Yes. Do you know what he replied? 'Sulla could do it, why not I?' It always comes back to Sulla!"

"I don't understand."

"Sulla abandoned the city to his enemies and then retook it, with Pompey as one of his generals. Thirty years later, Pompey thinks he can do the same if the need arises. Can you imagine the city under siege? Disease, hunger, fires spreading out of control—and then the horror of the conquest . . ."

He stared into the flames of the brazier and again tried to calm himself. "For a long time now, Pompey's mind has been set on playing Sulla. Once Caesar is defeated, Pompey will do what Sulla did. He'll make himself dictator and purge the Senate. He'll draw up a list of enemies. Confiscations, heads on stakes in the Forum . . ."

"But surely not *your* head, Cicero." I tried to make light of his fear, but the look he shot back at me was ghastly.

"Why not? If I'm still in Rome tomorrow, Pompey will call me his enemy."

"Follow him, then."

"And make myself Caesar's enemy? What if Caesar wins? I shall never be able to return. I was exiled from Rome once. Never again!" He circled the brazier until he stood opposite me. His eyes flashed, catching the light. The flickering flames and shadows transformed his face into a grim mask. "We must all choose sides, Gordianus. No more argument, no more procrastination. This side, or that. But toward what end? No matter who wins, we shall end up with a tyrant. What a choice—beheaded if I pick the wrong side, a slave if I pick the right one!"

I stared back at him across the flames. "You sound as if you have yet to make up your mind between Caesar and Pompey."

He lowered his eyes. "In the next hour . . . I keep telling myself, before another hour passes, I shall cast the dice, and let Fortune choose for me!"

He stared at the floor with his hands tightly clasped before him, his brow rigid, his mouth turned down. He raised his eyes at a sound from the doorway. A female slave stole into the room and whispered in his ear.

"My wife calls me, Gordianus. Poor Terentia! Shall I leave her here, in charge of the household, or take her with me? And what of my daughter? While I was off in Cilicia, behind my back Tullia married that wastrel Dolabella! The young fool has both feet firmly in Caesar's camp. He'll do his best to drag her along with him. And now she's expecting his baby! What a world for my grandchild to be born into. And my son! Marcus turns sixteen this year. When the day comes for him to put on his toga of manhood, will we be in Rome for the ceremony? By Hercules, will we even be in Italy?"

On that abrupt note, Cicero left the room and the slave hurried after him.

I was left alone.

I took a deep breath. I warmed myself at the fire. I studied the images on the walls. The face of one shepherd in particular fascinated me; he reminded me of my old bodyguard, Belbo. I looked up at the ceiling, where firelight and shadow flickered across the black spot made by the smoke. I turned my eyes down and traced my toe over the geometric pattern of the carpet.

Alone and forgotten in another man's house, surrounded by silence, I felt overcome by a curious paralysis, unable to depart. It was the only moment of peace I had experienced all day. I was reluctant to give it up. To be abandoned and forgotten by the world, to be left alone, truly alone, without fears or obligations—for a few brief moments in that quiet room I indulged in a fantasy of what that would be like, and savored it, sank into it like a man into dark, deep, soothing water.

I pondered Cicero's dilemma. Pompey and Caesar were not only tearing apart the state; they were tearing apart families. Rome was not easily split into two factions. Rome was a hopelessly tangled skein of blood ties overlaid and interlinked with ties of politics, marriage, honor, and debt. How could such a complex web of mutual obligations be severed down the middle without being destroyed altogether? How many households in Rome that night mirrored Cicero's house, with the occupants rushing about in an agony of indecision? Without eyes to see the future, how could any man be sure of his choice?

In the end it came down to this: that a man might have a willful daughter who chose her own husband against her father's better judgment, and that fellow, intruding from the outside, might have a link—Dolabella to Caesar, Davus to Pompey—that might in the end prove the whole household's undoing. Cicero's Tullia and my Diana: we created them, and now they were out of our control, showing what vanity it was that any man should think to plot his destiny.

At last I forced myself to leave the peaceful room. I passed a few scurrying slaves as I made my way through the house, but none took notice of me. In the vestibule, the slave on duty lifted the bar and opened the door for me.

There was more activity in the street than there had been when I arrived. Handcarts and litters, messengers and torchbearers hurried back and forth. The Palatine Hill was home to many of Rome's richest and most powerful men, those who had the most to lose, or gain, in the event of civil war. Pompey's decision to abandon the city had stirred up the neighborhood like a stick poked into an anthill.

The same two guards were stationed in front of Cicero's house. They had moved to one side, where the trunk of a great yew tree shielded them from the hubbub of the street. I considered asking one of them to walk me home—a common courtesy Cicero would surely have approved—but I decided against it. However unwittingly, I had got them into enough trouble already, arousing their master's suspicion against them.

But if they were as loose with their tongues as Cicero seemed to think, it seemed foolish not to ask them a few questions.

"A wild night," I commented.

"Inside and out," noted the older one.

"Inside? In the house, you mean?"

"It's crazy in there. Has been all day. Glad I'm out here, never mind the cold."

"I understand there was shouting earlier."

"Well . . ."

"Your master himself told me so."

This freed the man's tongue. "It was him who did most of the shouting."

"This was when that fellow Numerius was here, Pompey's kinsman?"

"Yes."

"Did Numerius come often to see your master?"

The guard shrugged. "A few times since the Master got back to Rome."

"So they had quite a shouting match, did they? For you to hear them all the way out here, I mean."

He ducked his head a bit and lowered his voice. "Funny thing, how the sound from the courtyard in the middle of the house seems to carry over the roof and land right here in front of the door. Acoustics, they call that. This spot by the yew tree is like the last row of seats in Pompey's theater. You may be too far away to see the stage, but you can hear every word!"

"Every word?"

"Well, maybe not quite. Every other word."

"Words like . . . ?"

The older guard frowned and drew back a bit, realizing that I was fishing, but the younger one now seemed eager to speak up. "Words like 'traitor,'" he said. "And 'secret' . . . and 'liar' . . . and 'the money you owe to Caesar' . . . and 'what if I tell Pompey?'"

"Was this Cicero speaking, or Numerius?"

"Hard to tell, the way they were talking on top of each other. Though I'd say the Master's voice carried better, probably on account of his training."

Poor Cicero, betrayed by his oratorical expertise. "But which of them said what? Who said the word 'traitor'? Who owes a debt to—?"

The older guard stepped forward, brusquely elbowing his companion aside. "That's enough questions."

I smiled. "But I was only curious to know—"

"If you've got more to ask, you can ask the Master. Do you want to be announced again?"

"I've already taken up enough of Cicero's time."

"Well, then." He crossed his arms. His bristling beard grazed my chin as he backed me into the street.

"Just one more question," I said. "Numerius came to this house alone and left alone—so your master told me. But *did* he come alone? Was there no one loitering in the street while he visited Cicero? And when he left, did you notice anyone who joined up with him—or who might have been following him?"

The guard said nothing. His companion now joined him in backing me farther into the street, almost into the path of a careening handcart pushed by two reckless slaves. The handcart swerved and almost struck a team of litter-bearers. The litter lurched and almost ejected its passenger, a fat, bald merchant who appeared to be wearing every jewel and bauble he possessed, fleeing the city and loath to leave behind anything of value.

The string of near collisions momentarily distracted the guards. They backed away, then moved toward me again. I stood my ground and looked from one to the other. The situation suddenly seemed comic, like a pantomime in the theater. The menace the guards projected was all for show. They were overgrown boys compared to the brute Pompey had stationed in my house.

I took a deep breath and smiled, which seemed to confound them. As I turned to walk away, I saw the older guard cuff the younger against the back of the neck. "Loudmouth!" he muttered. His companion cringed and accepted the rebuke in silence.

The rim road around the crest of the Palatine Hill is wider than most roads in Rome. Two litters can pass one another and still leave room for a pedestrian to walk on either side without brushing against a sweaty litter-bearer. Such congestion would be rare; the rim road is less traveled than most in Rome, lined by large houses and situated high above the turbulence of the Forum and the marketplaces. But on that night, the road was crowded with vehicles and people and lit up as bright as day with what seemed to be an army of torchbearers. Illuminated by those torches I saw a succession of unhappy faces—dazed citizens fleeing the city, weary slaves toting loads, determined messengers shoving past the rest.

Several times I imagined I was being followed. Whenever I turned around to look, the confusion in the street made it impossible to tell. My sight and my hearing were not what they once had been, I told myself. I was mad to be out without protection on such a night.

I arrived at the door of my house and took one last look behind me. Something caught my eye. It was the man's carriage and his overall bearing that attracted my notice. I felt that I recognized him at once, in the way that one often knows a familiar person at a distance or from the corner of one's eye. The man turned about before I could get a clear look at his face and headed back in the direction I had come from, walking very fast. He vanished into the crowd.

I could have sworn by Minerva that the man I had just seen was Cicero's secretary, Tiro, who was supposed to be in Greece, too sick to leave his bed.

V

I passed a cold, fitful, sleepless night. It would have been warmer if Bethesda had been beside me. She slept in Diana's room. I suspected that her abandonment of our bed was as much to punish me as to comfort our daughter; if Diana had to sleep without her spouse, then so should I. I rose several times to pass water and pace the house. From Diana's room I heard the two of them talking in low voices, sometimes weeping, long into the night.

The next morning, before I had dressed or eaten, even before my first disparaging glance of the day from Bethesda, who remained shut away with Diana, a slave arrived at the front door with a message. Mopsus ran into my room without knocking and handed me a wax tablet. I wiped the sleep from my eyes and read:

> If you are still in Rome and this message finds you, I beg you
> to come to me at once. My messenger will show you the way.
> We do not know one another. I am Maecia, the mother of Nu-
> merius Pompeius. Please come as soon as you can.

While the messenger waited in the street, I withdrew to the garden, still wearing my nightclothes. I paced back and forth before the statue of Minerva, looking furtively up at her. On some days her eyes gazed back, but not that morning. What could the virgin goddess know of a mother's grief?

My stomach was empty but I had no appetite. I shivered in my woolen gown and hugged myself. After a certain age, a man's blood grows thinner year by year, until it becomes like tepid water.

At last I returned to my bedchamber. To show respect for the dead, and for a dead man's mother, I would put on my best toga. Wearing it would also serve to demonstrate to anyone who saw me that Gordianus, at least, was going about his business as calmly as on any other day. I opened the trunk and smelled the chips of cedar scattered inside to ward off moths; nothing looks sadder than a moth-eaten toga. The garment was just as it had come from its last washing at the fullers, lamb-white, neatly folded, and loosely bound with twine.

I summoned Mopsus and Androcles to help me dress. Usually Bethesda assisted me in donning my toga; she had grown so skilled that the procedure was effortless. Mopsus and Androcles had helped a few times before, but still had only a vague idea of what to do. Following my instructions they laid the irregular oblong of wool over my shoulders, wrapped it across my chest, and attempted to arrange the folds. There seemed to be four of us in the room: myself, two slave boys, and a very unruly toga intent on thwarting the rest of us. As soon as one fold was tucked, another came untucked. The boys became flustered and sniped at one another. I rolled my eyes, admonished myself to be patient, and kept my voice low.

At last I was ready. On my way out I encountered Bethesda emerging from Diana's room. She coolly looked me up and down, as if I had no right to wear such finery when my daughter's life was ruined. Her unpinned hair hung in tangles and she could scarcely have had more sleep than I; even so, she looked remarkably beautiful to me at that moment. Time had never yet diminished the luster of her dark eyes. Perhaps she read my thoughts. She paused to give me a fleeting kiss and whispered in my ear, "Be careful, husband!"

In the foyer I encountered Cicatrix. The hulking monster was leaning with his back against the front door, arms crossed, idly scratching the ugly scar across his face. He gave me an impertinent look, then stepped away from the door to let me pass.

I cleared my throat. "Let no one in while I'm gone," I told him. "Take orders from no one except my wife or my daughter. Do you understand?"

He nodded slowly. "I understand that I'm to keep an eye on this house for my Master, the Great One." He gave me an unsettling smile.

As I stepped out the door to join the waiting messenger, I whispered a prayer to Minerva to watch over my household.

⁓

"Where are we going?" I asked the slave.

"Yonder." The big fellow pointed beyond the Forum, toward the Esquiline Hill. I suspected he was a bit simple. The powerful often prefer to use illiterate slaves to carry messages, and only a slave too simpleminded to learn to read can be trusted not to.

The rim road was as busy in the early morning as it had been the night before. We crossed to the other side, threading between litters and carts, and onto the Ramp, which would take us down to the Forum. The pathway was so crowded that people were pressed shoulder to shoulder and no vehicles could possibly have passed. The descent was slow and tedious. We found ourselves pressed against the sheer rock face of the Palatine, the view of the Forum to our right blocked by the crowd. People jostled, stepped on each other's feet, squealed in pain and spat insults. At one point a fist fight broke out nearby.

As we descended farther, any glimpse of the Forum was blocked by the massive rear wall of the House of the Vestals. At last we reached the bottom of the incline, packed as tightly as sheep in a run.

Here the Ramp narrowed even more as it made a sharp right turn into the gap between the House of the Vestals and the Temple of Castor and Pollux. The crush became dangerous. Behind me I heard a woman scream.

Panic spread through the crowd like a wave of prickling heat. A stampede began.

I clutched the messenger's arm. He looked over his shoulder and gave me a simpleminded grin, then gripped my arm and pulled me forward, practically lifting me off my feet. Around me swirled a sea of faces. Some grimaced in pain. Some shouted. Some screamed. Some were wild-eyed with fear, while others stared blankly, dumbfounded. I was punched and prodded from all directions by elbows and flailing arms. I felt as helpless as a pebble in an avalanche.

Then, all at once, the narrow path emptied into the open space of the Forum. The messenger pulled me around a corner. We staggered onto the steps of the Temple of Castor and Pollux. I sat down, gasping for breath.

"We could have been trampled to death!" said the big fellow. His penchant for stating the obvious reminded me of Davus. As we watched, people spilled out of the narrow passageway into the Forum, looking dazed and shaken, many of them weeping. At last the torrent thinned, and the trickle of stragglers emerging from the Ramp seemed utterly unaware of the panic that had preceded them.

As soon as I caught my breath, we set out again. The Forum had an air of unreality, a continuation of the nightmare that had begun on the Ramp. I felt as if we were walking through a succession of theatrical scenes staged by some maniacal director. People ran in and out of temples, waving votive tapers and shouting prayers to the gods. Huddled family members took leave of one another, holding hands and weeping, kneeling together to kiss the ground of the Forum, while street urchins perched on nearby walls threw pebbles at them and made rude remarks. Angry crowds outside the banks and exchanges threw stones against doors that were locked up tight. Despondent women wandered through empty market stalls picked clean by hoarders and profiteers. The oddest thing was how little notice strangers seemed to take of one another. Everyone appeared to be boxed inside his own little tragedy, to which the rushing panic of others was merely a backdrop.

Not everyone was leaving Rome. Hordes of people were coming into the city from the countryside to seek refuge. Caesar, according to one rumor, was on the outskirts of Rome no more than an hour away, leading an army of savage Gauls to whom he had promised full citizenship—one Gaul to be enrolled for every Roman killed, until the entire male population of the city was replaced by barbarians loyal to Caesar.

Amid so much chaotic movement, my gaze was suddenly arrested by the sight of a formal cordon of magistrates wearing their senatorial togas with purple stripes—the only togas besides my own I had seen in the Forum that day. The entourage strode through the Forum at an unusually quick pace, preceded by twelve lictors in single file, each bearing on his shoulder the ceremonial bundle of rods called the fasces. A dozen lictors meant a consular procession, and sure enough, within the cordon of senators I recognized the two newly installed consuls, Lentulus and Marcellus. They looked grim-jawed but rabbit-eyed, as if a sudden loud noise could send them scurrying for the nearest cubbyhole.

"I wonder what that's about," I said aloud.

"They're leaving the Temple of the Public Lares," said Maecia's messenger. "I saw them going in on my way to your house. They were performing a special ceremony. What's it called? A 'rite of safe-keeping'—asking the hearth-gods to watch over the city while the two consuls are away."

"Only one consul at a time ever leaves Rome," I explained, remembering he was simple. "One may go off to lead an army, but the other stays to run the city."

"Maybe so, but this time they're *both* leaving town."

I took a last, fleeting look at Lentulus and Marcellus, and knew the fellow was right. They had been consuls for less than a month, but this might well be their last formal walk across the Forum. Hence the grim jaws; hence the rabbit eyes and the unseemly pace of the procession. The consuls were abandoning Rome. The state was deserting the people. In a matter of hours—however long it took

Lentulus and Marcellus to return to their homes and join in the mad rush to get out of Rome—there would be no government remaining in the city.

~

Maecia's house was in the Carinae district on the lower slopes of the Esquiline Hill, where a great deal of real estate had been in the hands of the Pompeius family for generations. Pompey's private compound was not far away. Maecia's house was not as grand as that. It faced onto a quiet street and was freshly painted in bright shades of blue and yellow. The black wreath on the yellow door struck a discordant note.

The slave knocked with his foot. Someone inside peered at us through a peephole, then the door swung open. As I stepped across the threshold, I hardened myself for the sight that awaited me.

Just beyond the foyer, the body of Numerius Pompeius lay upon a bier in the atrium, beneath the skylight. His feet pointed toward the door. The smell of the evergreen branches surrounding him mingled with the heady odor from a pan of incense set in a brazier nearby. The overcast morning light surrounded his white toga and waxen flesh with a pale ivory nimbus.

I forced myself to step closer and look at his face. Someone had done a good job of removing the horrible grimace. Embalmers sometimes break a jaw or stuff the cheeks to achieve the proper effect. Numerius seemed almost to be smiling, as if enjoying a pleasant dream. His toga had been arranged to hide the ugly marks around his throat. I saw him in memory nonetheless, and clenched my jaw.

"Is it so hard to look at him?"

I looked up to see a Roman matron dressed in black. Her hair was undressed and her face without makeup, but the ivory glow from the skylight was kind to her. I thought for a moment that she might be Numerius's sister, then looked again and decided she must be his mother.

"I think he looks rather peaceful," I said.

She nodded. "But the look on your face—I think you must have been remembering how he looked when you found him. I didn't see him until later, of course, and not . . . not until Pompey made sure he was presentable. That was kind of Pompey, to think of a mother's feelings, with so much else on his mind. Was Numerius so terrible to look at, when he found him?"

I tried to think of an answer. "Your son . . ." I shook my head. "The older I become, the more of death I see, yet the harder it is to look at."

She nodded. "And we shall be seeing so much more of it, in days to come. But you haven't answered me. I think you know what I'm asking. Did he look as if . . . as if he suffered a great deal? As if his final thoughts were of the horror of what was happening to him?"

The skin prickled across the back of my neck. How could I possibly answer such a question? To avoid her gaze I looked down at Numerius. Why could she not be content to remember him as he looked now, with his eyes closed and a serene expression on his face?

"I've seen the marks on his throat," she said quietly. "And his hands—they couldn't quite unclench them. I imagine him with that thing around his neck, reaching up to claw at it. I imagine what he must have felt . . . what thoughts went through his mind. I try not to think of those things, but I can't stop myself." She looked at me steadily. Her eyes were red from weeping, but there were no tears in them now. Her voice was calm. She stood erect, with her hands clasped before her.

"You needn't worry that I'll collapse to the floor sobbing," she said. "I don't believe in hair-tearing, especially in front of an outsider. I have no more tears. None I intend for a stranger to see, anyway." She smiled bitterly. "The men of this house have all run off, except for the slaves. They've left me to bury Numerius by myself."

"Your husband?"

"He died two years ago. The men of this house are Numerius's two younger brothers and his uncle Maecius; my brother moved in to head the household when I became a widow. Now they've all run off with Pompey, and left me to handle this. They know I can do it, you see. They saw how strong I was when my husband died, how strong I've been every day since then. I never flinch, never shirk. I'm famous for it. I'm the model of a Roman matron. So you see, when I ask you to tell me what it was like for my son at the end—and I ask you because it happened in your house, because you were there, and who else could tell me?—you mustn't avoid answering out of fear that you'll reduce me to tears and have a sobbing, hysterical woman on your hands. You must answer as if I were a man."

She had gradually moved closer to me, so that now she stood very near, her face turned up to mine. Her son's beauty came from her. Her undressed hair fell back from her face in dark, shining tresses. Her black gown emphasized the creamy flesh of her throat and the gentle flush of her cheeks. Her green eyes gazed up at me with disconcerting intensity. It was impossible to think of her as a man.

"Surely the Great One told you all you need to know. It would be his duty to you, as the boy's cousin and your kinsman—"

"Pompey told me what he thought I needed to know, that Numerius was . . . strangled. That he must have been taken by surprise from behind, off his guard, with no chance to respond. Pompey said that meant it must have been quick. Quick and . . . not so terribly painful."

Not necessarily, I thought. Did Maecia really want me to confirm her worst fears? To tell her that a man strangled by a garrote, with no chance to escape, might nonetheless struggle against the inevitable for quite some time—an eternity for him, no doubt—before succumbing? Did she truly wish to dwell on what Numerius might have thought and felt in those final panic-stricken moments of life?

"Pompey . . . told you the truth."

"But not the exact details," she said. "When I pressed him . . . you must know how he is. When the Great One has no more to say, no more will be said. But you were there. You found my son. You saw . . ."

"I saw a young man lying in my garden, before my statue of Minerva."

"And the instrument used to kill him . . ."

I shook my head. "Don't do this."

"Tell me, please."

I sighed. "A garrote. A simple device that serves no other purpose than to kill."

"Pompey says he left it with you, because you might need it for your inquiries. I can't even imagine what such a thing must look like."

"A piece of wood as long as my forearm, but not so thick, with a hole bored near each end; a slightly longer piece of stout rope, pulled through the holes and tied into knots."

"How does it work?"

"Please—"

"Tell me!"

"You slip the rope over a man's head, then twist the piece of wood."

"Pompey said it was still around his throat."

"There are ways to catch the rope over the wood so that it stays twisted tight and can't be removed by the victim."

She touched the creamy flesh of his throat. "I saw the marks. Now I understand." Her eyes glistened. "When you found him, with that thing still around his neck, what did his face look like?"

I lowered my eyes. "Just as he looks now."

"Yet you won't look at me as you say that. Can you look at him?"

I tried to turn my gaze to Numerius, but couldn't.

"He must have looked quite horrible, to have such an effect on a man of your experience."

"He was hard to look at, yes."

She shut her eyes. Tears glistened in her lashes. She blinked until they vanished. "Thank you. I had to know how he died. Now I can turn to asking why, and by whose hand. Pompey says you make your livelihood following such inquiries."

"I used to."

"Pompey says you'll help us now."

"He gave me no choice." Her eyebrows lifted. She had demanded unflinching answers, after all. "Did the Great One not explain that he coerced me into accepting this duty?"

"No. I never ask after his methods. But you will help?"

I thought of Davus and Diana, and Cicatrix in my home. "I'll do what I must to satisfy Pompey."

Maecia nodded. "There's something . . . something I couldn't tell Pompey."

"A secret? Anything you tell me may end up in the Great One's ear. I can't promise you otherwise."

She shrugged uncertainly. "If there's anything to be found out, Numerius has already suffered the consequences. I'm not even sure there's anything to it. A mother's suspicions . . ."

"What do you mean?

"Between Numerius and Pompey, everything may not have been as it seemed."

"Numerius was the Great One's favorite, wasn't he?"

"Yes, Pompey doted on him. And Numerius had always been loyal to Pompey. But in recent months . . ." She had broached the subject herself, but seemed reluctant to pursue it. "In recent months . . . as the situation with Caesar grew more tense, and the debates in the Senate became more acrimonious . . . as it became evident that war might come, and soon—I began to think that Numerius might not be quite so loyal to Pompey as we all thought."

"What made you doubt him?"

"He was mixed up in something. Something he kept secret. There was money . . ."

"Money and secrets. Are you saying he was a spy?"

"A spy . . . or something worse." Now it was Maecia who could neither look me in the eye nor stand to look at her son.

"What do you mean?" I said quietly.

"I discovered a box in his room. It was full of gold coins—so heavy with gold I couldn't lift the box. We're not a rich family and never have been, in spite of our connections to Pompey. I couldn't imagine where Numerius had come by so much money."

"When was this?"

"About a month ago. I remember, it was the day one of the tribunes—Caesar's attack dog, Marc Antony—made that horrible speech against Pompey in the Senate, ridiculing his whole career, demanding amnesty for all the political criminals expelled from the city by Pompey's reforms. 'Every virtuous Roman in exile must be returned and given back his property, even if it takes a war to do it!' You see, a woman can follow politics."

"More closely than many men, I'm sure. But the gold?"

"That night, I asked Numerius where it had come from. I caught him by surprise. He was flustered. He wouldn't tell me. I pressed him. He refused. He spoke . . . harshly to me. That was when I knew something was very wrong. Numerius and I never argued. We were always very close, from the day he was born. And after my husband died . . . it was Numerius who reminded me most of his father, more than his younger brothers. It upset me very much that he had kept something secret from me. It worried me. The city in such a state, and Numerius somehow piling up money and refusing to explain, acting guilty when I questioned him . . ."

"Guilty?"

"He said that I mustn't tell Pompey about the money. So you see, the money couldn't have come from Pompey. From whom, then? And why must it be a secret from Pompey? I told him I didn't like it. I said to him, 'You're doing something dangerous, aren't you?'"

"What did he say?"

"He told me not to worry. He said he knew what he was doing. Blind certainty! Every man on his father's side of the family is just the same. I've yet to meet a Pompeius who doesn't think he's indestructible."

"Did you have any idea of what he was up to?"

"Nothing specific. I knew Pompey had made him a confidential courier. Pompey trusted him. Why not? Pompey was in and out of this house all the time while Numerius was growing up; Pompey watched him grow from child to man. Numerius was always his favorite of the younger generation. But these days, everything is twisted and turned upside down. The young have no sense of what it means to be a Roman. Every man looks out for himself, not even putting family first. So much money pours in from the provinces, corrupting everything. Young men become confused . . ."

She took refuge in abstractions; it was easier to talk about Rome's problems than about her own suspicions. I nodded. "When you say that Numerius was a confidential courier for Pompey, you mean that he carried secret information."

"Yes." She bit her lip. Her eyes glistened. "Secret information has value, doesn't it? Men will pay gold to get it."

"Perhaps," I said carefully. "You say you found a box full of gold. Did you find any other boxes with surprises inside?"

"What do you mean?"

"If Numerius possessed valuable information—documents—he must have kept them somewhere."

She shook her head. "No. Only the box with the gold."

"Have you looked again? I mean, since . . ." I glanced at the body.

"I stayed up all last night searching the house, pretending to help my brother and sons pack. If there were any more surprises to be found, I wanted them to be found by me—not by my brother, or by Pompey . . . or by the assassin who killed my son. I found nothing." She exhaled wearily. "You take it for granted, don't you—that Numerius was a spy? It doesn't even shock you."

"It's as you say, we live in a world turned upside down. Men become capable of . . . anything. Even good men."

"My son was a spy. There, I've said it, for the first time aloud. It wasn't as hard as I thought it would be. But to say the rest . . . to call him a . . ."

"A traitor? Perhaps he wasn't. Perhaps he spied *for* Pompey, not against him."

"Then why did he insist the gold be kept secret from Pompey? No, he was doing something behind Pompey's back. I'm sure of it."

"And you think this was the reason he was killed?"

"Why else? He had no personal enemies."

"Unless there were other secrets he kept from you."

She gave me such a fierce look that a shiver ran up my spine. The atrium suddenly seemed very cold. The light from the overcast sky grew even weaker, dwindling to a soft, uncertain radiance that cast no shadows. Numerius on his bier, bloodless and dressed in white, glowed like a statue carved from solid ivory.

VI

As I made my way homeward from Maecia's house, the scene in the Forum was even more hectic than before, the people more frantic, the rumors wilder.

Before the Temple of Vesta an old man gripped my arm. "Have you heard? Caesar is at the Colline Gate!"

"Odd," I said. "Just moments ago a fishmonger told me Caesar was on the opposite side of town, coming in the Capena Gate at the head of an army of Gauls, carrying Pompey's head on a stake."

The old man reeled back in horror. "He and his barbarians have surrounded us, then! Jupiter help us!" He ran off before I could say a word. I had thought to comfort the poor man by mocking his rumor with another that contradicted it; instead he believed both rumors and now was off to tell people the city was doomed.

I continued to make my way across the Forum, alone. Maecia had offered to send her messenger back with me for protection. I had declined. It was one thing to have him lead me to her house, another to take advantage of her generosity. She was without her brother or sons and had only her male slaves to protect her. Who knew how lawless the city might become in the next few hours, especially if rumors of Caesar's approach were true?

From the Temple of Vesta I could see that the Ramp was crowded, but not jammed. Foot traffic was passing in both directions. Still, my heart beat faster as I entered the confined passage between the House of the Vestals and the Temple of Castor and Pollux. I saw no sign of that morning's panicked stampede until I took the sharp leftward turn onto the Ramp. I sucked in a breath when I saw blood on the flagstones, smeared by the passage of hundreds of feet. I remembered the screaming woman. Someone had been trampled by the crowd, after all. I quickened my pace and began the ascent.

Parts of the Ramp are like a tunnel, densely shaded by overhanging yew trees. It was in one of these patches, looking up ahead, that for the second time in two days I thought I saw Tiro.

I couldn't see the man's face, only the back of his head. The climb had apparently warmed him, for he was in the process, never breaking his stride, of pulling a dark cloak from his shoulders, revealing a green tunic beneath. It was something about the way he moved that seemed to stir my memory, keying that unsettling, powerful yet fleeting sensation that one sometimes has of reliving a moment already experienced. Had I once walked up the Ramp behind Tiro, perhaps thirty years ago, and seen him shrug off a cloak in that exact same way? Or was my mind playing tricks? You're an old man, I told myself, slightly out of breath with spots before your eyes, looking at the back of someone under the shade of a dense tree on an overcast day. The idea that I was seeing an old friend who was supposed to be hundreds of miles away across the sea was hardly worth a second thought. Still, if only I could see the man's face, I could at least be satisfied of my mistake.

I quickened my stride. The path grew steeper and my breath shorter. More spots danced before my eyes. Other pedestrians blocked my view. I lost sight of the man ahead of me, until I thought I had lost him entirely. Then I caught a glimpse of the green tunic, farther ahead of me than before.

"Tiro!" I called out.

Did the man pause for a moment, cock his head, then hurry on? Or did I imagine it?

"Tiro!" I shouted, gasping for breath.

This time, the man in the green tunic didn't pause. If anything, he walked faster. He reached the top of the Ramp well ahead of me. Before he vanished, it seemed to me that he turned to the right, in the direction of Cicero's house.

I reached the top of the Ramp and sat heavily on a yew stump. The stately tree had stood in that spot for years, since long before I came to live on the Palatine; I had been able to see the top of it from my garden courtyard. Early that winter, a particularly violent storm had blown the tree over. The limbs had been cut up for firewood, but the stump had been left as a convenient spot to sit and rest after the climb from the Forum. Poor old yew, I thought, not good for much but still good for something. I would have laughed, had I breath to spare. Pompey expected me to track down a killer for him. I couldn't even follow a man up the Ramp.

❧

Begrudgingly, a glowering Cicatrix admitted me to my own house. "You've got a visitor," he said in a surly voice, breathing garlic at me.

In the garden, I found Bethesda, Diana, and little Aulus waiting for me. They had been joined by Eco.

"Papa!" He gave me a forlorn look and a bruising hug. "I've heard the news about Davus. Damn Pompey to Hades!"

"Not so loud. Pompey's man is only a few steps away."

"Yes, I saw him on the way in. Mother and Diana explained about that, too. Pompey is such a bully."

"Lower your voice."

Instead Eco spoke louder, as if intentionally pitching his voice for Cicatrix to hear. "Absurd, that a citizen in his own home should have to whisper every time he makes reference to the so-called Great One!"

I couldn't remember the last time I had seen my even-tempered son in such a belligerent mood. The crisis was provoking reactions in all of us. "Did you bring Menenia and the twins with you?" I asked.

"Through that mob in the Forum? No, they're safe at home."

"How are they taking things?"

"Titus and Titania are old enough to know that something's very wrong—you can't hide much from two eleven-year-olds. But they don't really understand what's happening, or likely to happen."

"I'm not sure anyone does, not even Caesar or Pompey. And their mother?"

"Serene as the face of Lake Alba, even though the Menenii are as divided as any family in Rome—some for Pompey, some for Caesar, the rest trying to find a hole to hide in till it's all over. But don't worry about us, Papa. After the Clodian riots, I put a lot of effort and expense into making the old family house secure. It's practically a fortress now, there are so many bars on the doors and spikes around the roof. It sounds as if you could have used something to keep climbers off the roof here." He turned his eyes up to the roof surrounding the courtyard. "Too bad about Pompey's unfortunate kinsman. And the outrage of it, that Pompey should use such a tragedy to force you into his service, and practically kidnap Davus—"

"What's done is done," I said.

He nodded. "Just another problem to be solved, eh? You always told me there was no such thing as a big problem, just lots of smaller problems intertwined, like knots in a rope. Start at one end and work your way to the other. A good attitude to have when the whole world is falling apart. Where shall we start?"

"*You* should start by going home to Menenia and the twins. We may be in for a dangerous night."

"But what about our problem with—"

"Satisfying Pompey and getting Davus back is not *our* problem, Eco. It's *my* problem. I'm responsible for what happened. I'll find a way out of it."

Diana spoke up. "Papa, don't be silly. You'll need Eco to—"

"No. I won't have him involved in this. So far, neither Pompey nor Caesar has any particular claim on Eco. Let's keep it that way."

Eco shook his head and started to speak, but I raised my hand. "No, Eco. You have your own family, your own problems. Who knows what may happen in the coming days and months? It's best that you remain as independent as you can, for as long as you can. In the long run, that may help to save us all."

I could see they were not satisfied, but even in a family as unconventional as mine, as unmindful of "traditional Roman values," as the report in Numerius's shoe had put it, there is a point beyond which the will of the paterfamilias cannot be disputed. I had a hard time seeing myself as a stern Roman father in the mold of the elder Cato, but if pressed I can perform a convincing enough imitation. Eco and Diana fell silent.

Two others in the garden were unawed, however. Little Aulus, paying no attention to me at all, tripped over one of his feet and burst into screams. Bethesda crossed her arms and peered at me. "What about tonight?" she said. "If the city is as dangerous as you say, what shall we do? Without Davus there's not a bodyguard in the house, unless you count that monster Pompey left at the front door."

"I doubt if anyone is likely to slip by Cicatrix, wife."

"Unless they come over the roof, husband," she said wryly.

"I suppose Mopsus and Androcles could at least keep watch," I said dubiously.

"I can spare a man to come over and help protect the house," offered Eco. "You could post him here in the courtyard, or up on the roof."

"For that I'd be grateful," I said, laying aside my mantle as paterfamilias with the relief one feels at taking off an uncomfortable pair of shoes.

"And if things grow even worse?" asked Bethesda.

"Perhaps we'll all take refuge in Eco's house on the Esquiline, since it's more defensible. But it may not come to that. These rumors about Caesar may be only rumors. He may have withdrawn beyond the Rubicon, for all we know."

"But with so many abandoned houses, isn't there likely to be looting?" observed Diana, between making faces at Aulus to distract him.

"Perhaps not. The rich have left factotums and gladiators to guard their property. A few would-be looters hung in the streets may be enough to keep things quiet."

Bethesda looked down her nose. "Rome is as bad now as Alexandria was when I was a girl. Worse! Riots and assassinations and insurrections, one after another, and no end in sight."

"I suppose it will end only when either Pompey or Caesar is dead," said Eco. He lowered his voice without being asked.

"I'm afraid that might be only the beginning," I said. "If Cicero is right, it's inevitable that one or the other will make himself dictator, and not for a year or two as Sulla did, but for life. Romans may have forgotten how to run a republic, but they certainly can't remember how to live under a king. The end of this crisis may mark the start of another, far worse."

"What a time for Aulus to grow up in," said Diana. Cicero had expressed the same anxiety for his expected grandchild. She turned her face away, hiding sudden tears from Aulus, but the boy was not to be fooled. Confusion crossed his face, then he opened his mouth to join her quiet weeping with a pitiful wail of his own. Bethesda hurried over and spread her arms to embrace them both, shooting a sharp glance at me over her shoulder.

Eco and I, with Androcles and Mopsus surreptitiously peering from the doorway, looked on helplessly. What good was the much vaunted power of the paterfamilias, if it could not stop a woman from weeping?

VII

As it turned out, Caesar did not lay siege to Rome that day, nor the next, nor the day after. The remaining days of Januarius slipped past. Every dawn spawned new rumors and fresh panic. Every sunset faded without the arrival of Caesar before the gates.

From south of the city came news that Pompey had joined the loyalist legions in Capua, had appointed Cicero to organize resistance along the Campanian seacoast, and was daily consulting the consuls and the coterie of senators who had fled with him.

The talk of Rome for several days had to do with the famous training school for gladiators in Capua owned by Caesar and notorious for the ferocity of its pupils. First I heard that five thousand gladiators, promised freedom by their master, had broken out, massacred Pompey's troops, and were marching on Rome to rendezvous with Caesar. Then word spread that Pompey had anticipated Caesar's gambit, freed the gladiators himself and enlisted them in his army—over the furious objections of his advisors, who argued that wholesale manumission of slaves in a time of crisis set a dangerous precedent. The last rumor to trickle in—least spectacular and most likely—

claimed that the school had been shut down and the gladiators dispersed to various new masters throughout the region, purely as a precautionary measure.

Daily, Bethesda asked what progress I had made in getting Davus back from Pompey. I explained to her that staging a serious inquiry into the death of Numerius was virtually impossible. Both Caesar's and Pompey's partisans had left Rome to join their respective leaders. Anyone with reason enough to kill Numerius, or to know who did, was probably in one camp or the other, and miles from Rome.

Bethesda was not impressed. "Pompey won't give back Davus until you find his kinsman's killer. If you lack the energy, husband, why don't you ask Eco to do it?"

"It occurs to me, wife, that your job is to see that this household is kept warm and fed—which so far you have done brilliantly, in spite of the shortages and outrageous prices at the markets. Are those duties not enough to keep you busy, and out of my affairs?"

A chill settled between us in those first days of Februarius, making the house as cold inside as out. Around us the crisis wore on.

Despite my protests to Bethesda, I was not entirely idle. If Rome was a foundering ship from which captains, crew, and paying passengers had fled, the rats remained aboard—and rats have keen eyes and ears. I called upon old contacts and put out feelers among the lower orders of the city—petty thieves, poison-dealers, pimps, and tavernkeepers—seeking knowledge of Numerius's shady dealings.

The few scraps of information I was able to find—or more precisely, purchase, at prices as outrageously inflated as everything else for sale in the city—were piecemeal and second-hand, largely unreliable and mostly useless. Repeatedly, I was told what I already knew, that Numerius had spent most of his time running errands for Pompey, which meant that he had frequently been seen all over the Forum and on the doorsteps of senators and wealthy merchants. His contacts among the powerful ranged far and wide. But at least occasionally the Great One's favorite cousin had patronized far more humble surroundings; more than one of my contacts claimed to have seen Numerius entering or leaving a particularly notorious establishment in the seedy warehouse district between the Forum and the river. I knew the place from previous investigations: the Salacious Tavern.

I had not been to the tavern for a long time; it had been over two years since I last spent an afternoon there, with Tiro of all people, drowning our sorrows after the trial of Milo. On the chilly afternoon I decided to pay a visit I almost got lost in the maze of narrow streets surrounding it. Once I found the right alley, it was impossible to miss the familiar sign, an upright post surmounted by an erect marble phallus. A phallus-shaped lamp hung over the door, sputtering fitfully beneath the overcast sky. I knocked.

A peephole slid open, then shut. The door swung open to reveal a fleshy eunuch in a capacious white tunic, ostentatiously bedecked with glass jewelry. Rings glittered like little rainbows across his fingers. Baubles of faux topaz, amethyst, and emerald were strung around his neck and dangled from his elongated earlobes. The long, dimly lit room behind him exhaled the warm smell of moldering wood, oily smoke, and sour wine. To my eyes, unadapted to the dark, the place looked as black as a cave.

"Citizen!" The eunuch smiled. "Do I know you?"

"I think not. I don't know you. I take it the tavern is under new management?"

"Yes! Did you know it before?"

"I came here once or twice."

"Then you'll find it much improved. Come in!" He shut the door behind us.

"Funny, it smells the same." I wrinkled my nose. "Same rancid lamp oil, smoking up the place. Same foul wine, stinking up the floors."

The eunuch's smile wavered.

My eyes adjusted a bit to the dimness. Leaning against a wall a few feet behind the eunuch, I made out a bored-looking redhead. She, too, was familiar. Ipsithilla was already a fixture in the tavern the first time I stepped foot in the place, six years before, with the drunken poet Catullus. By the orange glow of a nearby lamp she still looked relatively young and fresh, testament to just how dim the lighting was. "Even the girls are the same!" I said.

The eunuch shrugged. "There are only so many pleasures to be had in this world, citizen. But you'll find them all here, I promise—for a price."

"What I really crave is a bit of information. Might I find that here, for a price?"

The eunuch raised an eyebrow.

I left the Salacious Tavern that day without having indulged a single vice, but with a few intriguing bits of information. Numerius Pompeius had indeed been a frequent patron; the eunuch knew him by sight, and had heard the news of his death. Numerius, the eunuch told me, always arrived at the tavern alone and left alone. He always sat in the same corner. Sometimes he met with others, but what they discussed, and who those others were, the eunuch couldn't say; it was his practice never to eavesdrop, and the men Numerius met with were strangers to the Salacious Tavern who never came again—except for one.

"Ah, yes," the eunuch told me, "I remember, one day Numerius shared his corner bench with that fellow Soscarides."

"Soscarides?"

"Odd name, isn't it? Greek, I suppose. From Alexandria. Swarthy little fellow with a beard. Been coming in for a couple of months now. A philosopher—rather famous, to hear him tell it. Perhaps you know him, citizen?"

"I'm sure I don't."

"Well, Numerius Pompeius did. They sat in the corner for a long time that day, he and Soscarides, talking and drinking, drinking and talking."

"Talking about what?"

"Alas, citizen, I never eavesdrop, and neither do my girls. A man's secrets are safe in the Salacious Tavern, even from the gods."

"When was this?"

"Oh, let me think—why, just before Pompey fled the city, so I suppose it must have been only a day or two before Numerius was murdered."

I nodded and mouthed the name Soscarides. I was sure I had never heard of him. A philosopher; a dark, swarthy little fellow with a beard . . .

The eunuch, fingering his already-swollen coin purse, was eager to be helpful. "As I said, Soscarides comes in here every so often. When I see him next, shall I tell him you're looking for him, citizen?"

I shook my head. "I was never here." I gave him another coin, to be sure he understood.

Several days of stormy weather followed my visit to the Salacious Tavern. The weather was so foul that no one went abroad in the city; even the Forum was deserted. I spent those days holed up in my study, reading philosophy. In rare moments when the rain broke I paced in the garden, gazing up to contemplate Minverva's inscrutable features. She was the only witness to everything that happened the day Numerius Pompeius died. She had heard his final words, had seen the face of his killer. "What shall I do next?" I asked her. She gave no indication of hearing.

The storm passed. Two days after the Ides of Februarius I made my way down to the Forum to catch the latest flock of rumors. At Bethesda's insistence, I took Mopsus and Androcles along with me, to give the boys a chance to use up some of their pent-up energy from being housebound by the storm. Going down the Ramp, they ran ahead of me and then back up to me over and over, making a game of it. Just watching them exhausted me.

The daily panic over an immediate occupation by Caesar receded.

Reliable reports now placed him to the northeast, along the Adriatic coast. All of Picenum had surrendered to him. It was said that the people of the towns he passed through had welcomed him jubilantly, offering prayers as if he were a god. He had garrisoned strategic cities with troops, and now was heading south, where Pompey and the loyalist forces had occupied the region of Apulia, but were split in two. Lucius Domitius Ahenobarbus—who by the Senate's decree was supposed to have replaced Caesar as governor of Gaul at the first of the year—had occupied the central city of Corfinium, only seventy-five miles east of Rome, with thirty cohorts, eighteen thousand men. Pompey, in the meantime, had moved farther south. There seemed to be a tug of war between the two loyalist generals, Domitius wanting Pompey to reinforce him in Corfinium, Pompey demanding that Domitius abandon the city and join him.

If Domitius had his way, would the deciding battle take place at Corfinium, with Caesar's legions confronting the combined loyalist forces? Or would Corfinium be abandoned in a loyalist retreat? If that happened, it was easy, looking at a map, to imagine Caesar's troops forcing Pompey relentlessly southward into the heel of the Italian boot, toward the seaport of Brundisium. Some rumors claimed that Pompey was already assembling a navy at Brundisium, and had all along intended to flee across the Adriatic Sea to Dyrrhachium rather than engage Caesar.

Hearing such tactical questions discussed by citizens standing in line for pots of rancid olives and loaves of stale bread was a strange experience. It was common enough to hear men in the Forum speculate about battles and troop movements in faraway provinces—but never on Italian soil, and with the fate of Rome in the balance.

The sky began to drizzle. I had had enough of the Forum.

I made my way back to the Ramp, with Mopsus and Androcles running circles around me. Halfway up, beneath the branches of a towering yew that blocked the drizzle, I happened to look ahead. My heart skipped a beat.

Had I lost my sense? Or was the same uncanny experience happening again? Up ahead, I thought I saw a familiar figure, except that this time the man in the green tunic was pulling on his cloak, not shrugging it off.

"Boys!" I said, calling them in from their orbit. "Do you see that fellow up ahead, walking alone?"

Mopsus and Androcles nodded in unison.

"I want you to follow him. Not too close! I don't want him to know. Do you think you can do that?"

"*I* can, Master," said Mopsus, hooking his thumb to his chest.

"And so can I," insisted Androcles.

"Good. When he arrives at his destination, one of you find a hiding place to keep watch while the other runs back to tell me. Now go!"

Off they went. When they drew close to the man in the dark cloak, one broke to the left, the other to the right, like jackals hunting in tandem. One by one, all three reached the upper end of the Ramp and disappeared. I resisted the urge to quicken my stride. I whistled a comic Egyptian tune, one that Bethesda used to sing to herself back in the days when she was my slave instead of my wife and had no slaves of her own to do the household chores. Happy days, I thought. Those were the days when I first met Tiro.

I came to the top of the Ramp. The stump of the fallen yew was out of the drizzle, so I sat there to wait. If I was correct, the man in the dark cloak would not be going far, and it would not be long before one of the boys came running back with news.

I waited. And waited some more. At last I began to wonder if I had been wrong after all, and had sent the boys on a fool's errand. The drizzle stopped. I got up from the stump and walked in the direction of Cicero's house. It occurred to me that if the man was not who I thought he was, I might have put the boys in danger. The crisis had frayed everyone's nerves. Even a respectable citizen might react unpredictably if he discovered he was being followed by two unknown slave boys.

I followed the rim road to Cicero's house and stopped in the deserted street. There was no one to be seen. I had been wrong, after all, I thought—and then heard a hissing from the opposite side of the street, where the cedars and cypress trees had been thinned to allow a view of the Capitoline Hill.

"Master! Over here!"

I peered into the underbrush of shaggy bushes dotted with tiny red berries. "I can't see you."

"Of course not. You said to hide." It was Mopsus.

"He said for *me* to hide." That was Androcles.

"No, *I* was to hide, and *you* were to run back and tell him."

"No, *you* were to run back, while *I* stayed to watch."

"Boys," I interrupted, "you can both come out now."

One head emerged, then another. Both had bits of twigs and red berries stuck in their unruly hair. "Isn't that right, Master?" said Mopsus. "I was to stay and watch, and Androcles was to run back and tell you."

I sighed. "Meto says that one mark of a great general is that he never gives an unambiguous order. Clearly, I'm no Caesar. And you two are as bad as Domitius Ahenobarbus and Pompey Magnus, squabbling like that instead of doing what needs doing."

"Did you hear that?" said Mopsus to Androcles, emerging into the street and swaggering a bit. "He compared you to Redbeard, and me to the Great One!"

"He did not. I'm Pompey and you're Domitius!"

"Boys, enough! Tell me where the fellow went and what you saw."

"We followed him here, to Cicero's house," said Androcles, eager to deliver the news ahead of his older brother.

"And he went in the door?"

"Not exactly . . ."

"They let down a ladder from the roof. He climbed up. Then they drew back the ladder," explained Mopsus.

I nodded. "Thank you, boys. You both did a good job. Better than Pompey and Domitius seem to be doing, anyway. Now you can both run along home."

"And leave you alone, Master?" said Mopsus, alarmed. "But isn't the fellow terribly dangerous? A thief or a murderer?"

"I don't think so." I smiled at the thought of mild, bookish Tiro as an assassin.

Once the boys were off, I banged on the door. There was no answer. I stepped back and surveyed the roof, but saw no signs of life. I banged on the door again. At last, the peephole opened and a brown eye peered out.

"No one's home," said a gruff male voice.

"You are," I said.

"I don't count. The Master's gone. The house is closed."

"Even so, I have business with someone inside."

The eye disappeared, then reappeared some moments later. "Who—?"

"My name is Gordianus. Cicero knows me. I saw him the night before he left Rome."

"We know who you are. Who is it you want to see?"

"The man who arrived ahead of me. The one you let up by ladder."

"No such person."

"He wasn't a phantom."

"Maybe he was."

"No more games! Tell Tiro I need to see him."

"Tiro? The Master's secretary is away in Greece. Too sick to travel—"

"Nonsense. I know he's here. Tell him that Gordianus needs to see him."

The eye disappeared and was gone for a long time. I stood on tiptoes and tried to peer inside through the peephole, but could see only shadows. Something moved among the shadows. I drew back. The eye reappeared.

"No, there's no Tiro here. No one by that name."

I banged on the door. The brown eye gave a startled blink and drew back. "Tiro!" I shouted. "Let me see you! Or shall I stand here in the street, shouting your name until every wretched soul left in Rome knows that you're back? Tiro! *Tiro!*"

A hissing issued from the peephole. "All right, all right! Stop shouting."

"Very well, then, open the door."

"Can't."

"What? *Tiro!*"

"Shhhh! Can't open the door."

"Why not?"

"It's barricaded shut."

"Barricaded?"

"Boards nailed across the door, and sandbags piled behind the boards. I have to crawl through a tunnel just to get to this peephole! Step back into the street."

I backed up to the middle of the street and looked up. A few moments later two men appeared on the roof. I recognized them as the two guards who had been posted at Cicero's door the night I last saw him. Together they lowered a long wooden ladder to the street.

"Don't tell me Cicero's wife and his pregnant daughter go up and down this thing every time they leave the house!" I eyed the spindly steps and felt the brittleness in my bones.

"Of course not," said the older one. It was he who had been addressing me from behind the door. "The Mistress and Tullia left days ago. Stayed with Cicero's friend Atticus here in the city for a while, then went to join the Master down at the villa in Formiae, on the coast. There's nobody at all in the house now, except some of us slaves left behind to guard the valuables."

"Nobody else?" I said.

"Nobody except me." The speaker stepped into view between the two men on the roof, put his hands on his hips and looked down at me. He wore a green tunic and a dark cloak. I suddenly realized that I must have been mistaken all along, or else they were playing another game with me. The man was Tiro's height and bore a rough resemblance to him, but had to be younger. His skin was as dark as an Egyptian's, his hair had a reddish tinge without a hint of gray, he was slender as a youth and he wore a neat little beard of the sort that Tiro had despised ever since Catilina made it popular.

"I'm not sure what you're playing at," I said, "but I mean to find out." I stepped onto the ladder.

"No, don't come up," said the stranger. "I'll come down."

I backed away as he descended. His movements on the spindly steps gave him away; he wasn't nearly as young as he looked at a distance. By the time he reached the bottom rung and turned to face me, the stranger had been transformed back into Tiro—Tiro with skin stained and hair dyed with henna, with a thinner face and sporting a very unlikely beard, but Tiro nonetheless.

"You seem to have made a miraculous recovery," I said. "How did you get here from Greece so swiftly—riding Pegasus?"

He silenced me with a finger to his lips. Behind us the ladder withdrew. The two guards vanished.

"We can't talk here," he said. "But I know of a quiet place, where the host never eavesdrops . . ."

VIII

Directly across the road from Cicero's house, amid the shrubbery where Mopsus and Androcles had hidden themselves, Tiro pulled back a branch covered with little red berries and appeared to step into empty space.

"Mind that the branch doesn't fly back and hit you," he cautioned. "And watch your step on the trail. It's steeper than it looks."

That hardly seemed possible. The trail was hardly a trail at all, just a descending series of little cleared spots large enough for a man to place his foot amid the gnarled trees and thorny bushes sprouting out of the western face of the Palatine Hill. Directly below us was the congested warehouse district.

"Tiro, where are you taking me? If we're heading down, why not take the Ramp?"

"Too much risk of being recognized."

"But you don't avoid the Ramp. I've seen you on it twice myself."

"Oh, *I'm* not worried about being recognized. But you would be. And then someone would start to wonder, 'Who *was* that swarthy bearded fellow I saw with Gordianus the Finder today?' "

"Then why not talk privately inside Cicero's house?"

"The guards, for one thing. They tend to hear things they shouldn't. Then they talk."

That was true enough.

"And also . . ." Tiro hesitated, deliberating where next to put his foot. "To be candid, Cicero doesn't want people coming and going in the house while he's not there."

"You think I might snoop?"

"I didn't say that, Gordianus. But it's Cicero's house. While he's away, I'll obey his wishes."

A loose stone slipped from under my foot and skittered down the hillside. I gripped the branch of a cypress tree for balance, caught my breath, and cautiously sought the next foothold.

At last we reached the lower slopes of the Palatine, where the path gradually flattened and meandered amid trash heaps piled behind the warehouses. Tiro led me this way and that, undaunted by the maze of narrow alleys stinking of urine. At length we turned a corner and I saw ahead of us a familiar sign—an upright post surmounted by an erect marble phallus.

"Not the Salacious Tavern!"

"We ran into each other here after Milo's trial," said Tiro. "Remember? That was the last time I saw you—over two years ago."

"I remember the hangover," I said, but I was thinking of my last visit to the tavern, and the host's account of a swarthy, bearded foreigner . . .

Tiro laughed. "You were getting over a hangover the very first time we met. Do you remember that?"

"A bright-eyed young slave came to my house on the Esquiline Hill and asked if I'd help his ambitious young master defend an accused parricide."

"Yes, but before I could speak, you demonstrated a cure for your hangover."

"Did I? What was it?"

"Concentrated thought, so as to flush the brain with fresh blood. It was quite remarkable."

"You were hardly more than a boy, Tiro. You were easily impressed."

"But it was amazing! You deduced who'd sent me and why, without my saying a word."

"Did I? A pity I can no longer concentrate my mind so keenly. I can't begin to imagine, for instance, why Cicero's right-hand freedman is wandering about Rome incognito."

Tiro looked at me shrewdly. "You haven't grown less keen, Gordianus, just craftier. You could work it out, if you cared to, but you'd rather draw it out of me."

Over the door of the tavern, the hanging phallus-shaped lamp cast a faint glow to brighten the chilly, overcast afternoon. "A waste of oil," I remarked to Tiro, "considering the shortages in the city."

"Words like 'shortage' have no meaning at the Salacious Tavern," said Tiro, knocking on the door. "Have you been here in the last year or so?"

I shrugged. "Once, I think."

"The place is under new management," he went on. "But nothing's changed. Same girls, same smells, same foul wine—but the taste improves after the second cup."

The peephole opened, then the door. "Soscarides!" the eunuch practically shrieked, gripping Tiro's hands. He failed, as yet, to notice me. "My favorite customer, who also happens to be my favorite philosopher!"

"You've never read a word I've written, you dog. You told me so the first day I came here, two months ago," said Tiro.

"But I keep meaning to," insisted the eunuch. "I placed an order with a book dealer down in the Forum. Really, I did! Or I tried to. The fellow claimed he'd never heard of Soscarides the Alexandrian. Practically laughed at me. The idiot! Now all the book dealers have closed their shops and left town. I shall have to remain ignorant of your wisdom."

"Sometimes ignorance is the truest wisdom," quipped Tiro.

"Oh! Is that one of your famous sayings, Soscarides? I like having philosophers in the tavern. Cleaner than poets, quieter than politicians. Is your friend a famous philosopher, too?" The eunuch finally looked at me. His face fell.

"As much a philosopher as I am," said Tiro, "and even more famous. That's why we're here, to seek some peace and quiet."

The eunuch was nonplused for a moment, then recovered. He acted as if he had never seen me before. "Will a corner in the public room do? The private rooms upstairs are all taken by gambling parties."

"We'll take that corner bench over there," said Tiro, indicating a region so dark I could only conjecture the existence of a corner, let alone a bench. "And two cups of wine. Your best."

Tiro set out for the corner. I followed close behind him. "I didn't realize there was more than one quality of wine offered in this establishment," I said.

"Of course there is. For the best, you pay a bit more."

"And what do you get?"

"The same wine, but poured through a strainer. No nasty surprises floating in the cup."

I grunted as I bumped into something that grunted back. I apologized to a murky, growling shape and moved on, glad when we at last reached the far side of the room. The corner bench was built into the wall. I leaned back and waited for my eyes to adjust to the dimness. Our wine arrived. It was as foul as I remembered. The Salacious Tavern seemed unusually crowded, considering that the sun was still up. With all normal activities in the city at a standstill, what better way to pass the time on a cloudy afternoon than to indulge in a bit of vice? Amid the murmur I heard laughter and cursing and the rattle of dice.

"*The die is cast!*" shouted one of the players. A round of drunken laughter followed. It took me a moment to catch the joke. Caesar had uttered the same words to his men when he crossed the Rubicon.

"They've immortalized him with a throw, as well," remarked Tiro.

"A throw?"

"Of the dice. The Venus Throw is the highest combination and beats all else. The gamblers are all calling it the Caesar Throw nowadays, and shouting 'Gaius Julius' when they cast the dice. I don't think it means they've taken Caesar's side, necessarily. They're just superstitious. Caesar claims to be partly divine, descended from Venus. So the Venus Throw becomes the Caesar Throw."

"Which beats all else. Is there such a thing as the Pompey Throw?"

Tiro snorted. "I think that must be when the dice skip off the table."

"Is Pompey's position as bad as that?"

"Do you know what Cicero says? 'When he was in the wrong, Pompey always got his way. Now that he's in the right, he fails completely.' Caesar took them all by surprise. Not even his supporters believed that he'd dare to cross into Italy with his troops. You saw the panic that resulted. Pompey led the stampede! Ever since, he's been struggling to get a grip on the situation, day by day. In the morning he's elated and full of bluster. Come afternoon, he falls into a funk and orders his troops to retreat farther south."

I looked at him wryly. "You seem to be awfully well informed for a man who's been lying in a sickbed in Greece since November."

He smiled. "Tiro is still in that sickbed, and will be for some time yet. I'm Soscarides, an Alexandrian philosopher thrown out of work and cast adrift by the crisis."

"What's the point of this elaborate deception?"

"Cicero and I concocted the scheme together, on the trip back from Cilicia. At every stage of the journey, the news from Rome was more and more disturbing—Caesar mocking the constitution, refusing to give up his troops in Gaul, demanding to be allowed to stand for the consulship without coming back to Rome. Pompey likewise digging in his heels, refusing more concessions to Caesar, brooding outside the city gates and clinging to his own legions in Spain. And the Senate—our pathetic, confused, cowardly, grasping, greedy collection of the so-called best men in Rome—breaking down into acrimonious debates on the verge of open violence. You didn't have to be Cassandra to see that the situation was drawing to a crisis. Cicero decided it would be prudent if I were to arrive in Rome ahead of him; there was no one else he could trust to send back accurate reports."

"But why incognito?"

"So as to gather information without drawing attention to Cicero. The disguise is simple. A beard, a change of coloring; that's all."

"But you're slender again, as thin as when I first met you. It changes the shape of your face."

"As it happened, I did fall ill on the way back from Cilicia, early on, and lost quite a bit of weight. I decided to keep myself slim as part of the charade. No more sesame and honey cakes for me, I'm afraid! Altogether, the changes hardly constitute a disguise, but the combined effect suffices. No one seems to recognize me at a distance, or if they do, they decide they must be mistaken, because Cicero made a point of letting everyone know that his beloved Tiro is suffering a prolonged illness back in Greece. People put more faith in what they 'know' than in what they see. Except for you, Gordianus. I should have known you'd be the one to find me out."

"Since you got back, have you spent the whole time here in the city?"

"By Hercules, no! I've been all over Italy, visiting Caesar's garrisons, scouting Antony's movements, checking on Domitius's situation in Corfinium, relaying messages between Cicero and Pompey . . ."

"You've become Cicero's secret agent."

Tiro shrugged. "I rehearsed for the role during his term as governor of Cilicia. No one would talk to Tiro, the governor's secretary. Soscarides the Alexandrian, on the other hand, was everyone's friend."

I gazed at him over my wine cup. "Why are you telling me this?"

"Having made up your mind you'd seen me back in Rome, you'd have figured it out for yourself, sooner or later. And you might have jumped to some wrong conclusions."

"You could have refused to see me today."

"While you shouted my name in the street, and set those two little boys to dog my every step? No, Gordianus, I know how tenacious you can be, like a hound who can't remember where he buried a bone. Better to point you straight to it than have you digging holes all over the place. Holes are dangerous. They can hurt innocent people. So can jumping to wrong conclusions."

Our host brought more wine. The second cup *was* better than the first, but only by a little. My eyes had adjusted to the darkness. In the orange haze of the smoky lamps I could make out faces, but only vaguely. The noise would keep anyone from overhearing us.

I thought of something. "The guards told me that Cicero writes letters to you all the time, back in Greece."

"So he does. Our host in Patrae, who supposedly is nursing me back to health, is in on the scheme. As soon as he receives the letters, he posts back false ones, bearing my name."

"So Cicero's letters to you are blank?"

"Hardly! They're full of gossip, quotations from plays, exhortations to get better. You see, he always has the letters done in duplicate. Nothing unusual about that, except that he posts both copies. One goes by regular messenger all the way back to Patrae, to keep up the deception. The other is sent by secret messenger to me, wherever I actually happen to be."

"But if the messages are identical, Cicero is merely sending you gossip and get-well wishes."

"On the surface, yes. Safer that way." He smiled, seemed to mull something over, then produced a pouch from his tunic. From the pouch he pulled out a folded piece of parchment. He called for one of the serving girls to unhook a hanging lamp and bring it to our table. By its sputtering glow, I read the letter. It was dated the first day of the month, some fifteen days previous.

At Formiae, on the Kalends of Februarius.

Marcus Tullius Cicero, to Marcus Tullius Tiro at Patrae:

I remain very anxious about your health. The news that your complaint is not dangerous consoles me, but its lingering nature worries me. The absence of my skillful secretary vexes me, but more vexing is the absence of one dear to me. Yet though

I long to see you, I urge you not to stir until you are fully recovered, especially as long as harsh weather prevails. Even in snug houses it is difficult to escape the cold, to say nothing of enduring wet, windy weather at sea. As Euripides says, "Cold to tender skin is deadliest foe."

Caesar continues to make pretense of negotiating with Pompey even as he plays invader. Like Hannibal sending diplomats ahead of his elephants! He says now that he will give up Gaul to Domitius and come to Rome to stand for the consulship in person, as the law requires—but only if Pompey will disband all the loyalist forces recently levied in Italy and depart at once to Spain. Caesar says nothing of giving up the garrisons seized since he crossed the Rubicon.

Our hope is that the Gauls among Caesar's troops may desert him, for they certainly have reason to hate him after all the pain he inflicted in conquering Gaul. To the north he would have a rebellious Gaul; to the west, Pompey's six legions in Spain; and to the east, the provinces which Pompey pacified long ago and where the Great One is still held in high esteem. If only the center can hold long enough to keep Caesar from sacking Rome!

Terentia asks, are you wearing the yellow scarf she gave you when we left for Cilicia? Do all you can to ward off the chill!

I looked up from the letter. "His hope that the Gauls will desert Caesar seems far-fetched to me. My son Meto tells me they cling to Caesar with the fervor of religious converts. Otherwise, the letter seems straightforward enough."

"Yes, doesn't it?"

"What do you mean."

"Words can carry more than one meaning."

I frowned and scrutinized the text under the flickering light. "Are you saying that the letter is in some sort of code?" It was Tiro, during Cicero's consulship, who had invented and introduced the use of an abbreviated writing system for recording debates in the Senate. But this was not Tironian shorthand; nor was it ciphered.

Tiro smiled. "We all know what the word 'blue' means, for instance. But if I say to you ahead of time, 'Use blue to mean a legion and red to mean a cohort,' and later you write to me about a blue scarf, then only the two us know what you truly mean."

"I see. And if Cicero quotes a line from Euripides . . ."

"It might mean something very different than if he had cited Ennius. The actual content of the quotation is irrelevant. If he mentions sea travel, it might mean that Pompey has a head cold. 'Snug houses' might refer to a particular senator who bears watching. Even the mention of elephants might have a secret meaning."

I shook my head. "You and Cicero make quite a team. What need for swords, when you have words for weapons?"

"We've been together a long time, Gordianus. I helped Cicero write every speech he's ever given. I've transcribed his treatises, edited all his commentaries. I often know what he'll say next even before he knows. It wasn't hard for the two of us to concoct an invisible language to use between ourselves. Everyone can see the words. No one but us can see the meaning."

I gazed into the dim corners of the room. "I wonder if Meto and Caesar were ever that close?"

He seemed not to notice the rueful tone in my voice. He tapped his forehead. "Perhaps. Great men like Cicero—even Caesar, I suppose—need more than one head to store their intellects."

"Freedom hasn't changed you, Tiro. You still underestimate yourself and overestimate your former master."

"We shall see."

As he refolded the letter and slipped it back into his pouch, I had a sudden realization. "It was Cicero, wasn't it?"

"What do you mean, Gordianus?"

"It was Cicero who wrote that confidential report for Pompey, about me and my family."

Tiro hesitated. "What report?"

"You know what I'm talking about."

"Do I?"

"Tiro, you can hide behind words, but you can't hide behind your face, not with me. You *do* know what I'm talking about."

"Perhaps."

"It all makes sense. If Pompey wanted an intelligence report on various men in Rome, and needed it on short notice, and from someone he trusts—who better than Cicero, who's been seeing phantoms under beds ever since he sniffed out the so-called conspiracy of Catilina. Cicero's probably kept a dossier on me for years! That remark about my lack of 'Roman values,' the dig at me about adopting slaves out of habit—oh, yes, that's Cicero, looking down his nose at me, as usual. And who better to help Cicero transcribe his confidential report into ciphered code than you, Tiro—his trusted secretary, the inventor of shorthand, the other half of his brain? You were in town that day, weren't you—the day Numerius died? I caught a glimpse of you in the street,.after I left Cicero's house. Was that Numerius's last errand for the Great One, to pick up Cicero's secret loyalty report?"

Tiro looked at me shrewdly. "If there ever was such a report . . . the copy Cicero gave Numerius went missing. Pompey was never able to find it, even though he turned Numerius's clothing inside out and tore open the stitches. He assumed that whoever murdered Numerius must have absconded with it. How did you come to know about it, Gordianus?"

"I read it. The part about myself, anyway. I found it on Numerius's body, inside a hidden compartment in the heel of his shoe."

"His shoe!" Tiro laughed. "That's something new. But what did you do with the report? Do you still have it?"

"I burned it."

"But you said you read only the part about yourself. You burned it without having read it all? The cipher wasn't that complicated."

"Pompey arrived at the house unexpectedly. I had no time to replace it in Numerius's shoe. If Pompey found it in my study . . ."

"I see. Well, there's a riddle solved. Cicero and I have been wondering where that report ended up."

"When you write to him about this meeting—as I presume you will—I suppose you'll have to mention the 'rosy-colored dawn,' or whatever passed between the two of you for 'secret report went up in flames.'"

"That would be a particular quotation from Sophocles, actually. Do you think Numerius was murdered because someone knew he was carrying Cicero's 'loyalty list,' as you call it?"

I hesitated. "There may have been other reasons that someone wanted him dead."

"Such as?"

"His mother seems to think he had a secret livelihood. Working as a paid spy, perhaps."

Tiro frowned. "For someone other than Pompey?"

"Yes. She's ashamed of the possibility, but she told me her suspicions nonetheless. The poor woman is desperate to know the truth about her son's death."

Tiro nodded. "I met Maecia once. An extraordinary woman. Did she hire you to look into Numerius's murder?"

"No, Pompey did. Or rather, the Great One ordered me to investigate."

"Ordered you? He's not our dictator, yet."

"Nonetheless, he was very persuasive. He forced my son-in-law into his service, against Davus's will but following the letter of the law. Pompey was explicit: he won't return Davus to us unless and until I'm able to name his kinsman's killer. My daughter is distraught. Davus could end up in Greece, or Spain, or even Egypt. And if Pompey loses patience with me . . ." I shook my head. "Generals assign dangerous duties to men they don't like. Davus is at his mercy."

Tiro looked pensively into his wine cup, which was made of cheap yellow earthenware. He ran his finger over the chipped rim. "You've been very candid with me, Gordianus."

"And you've been candid with me, Tiro."

"The two of us have never been enemies."

"We never shall be, I hope."

"I'm going to tell you a secret, Gordianus. Something I probably shouldn't." He lowered his voice. I had to strain my ears to hear him above the bursts of laughter and the clatter of thrown dice. "Only a few days before his death, I met with Numerius Pompeius. We had messages to exchange, between Pompey and Cicero. We met here in the Salacious Tavern—in this very corner, as a matter of fact. *His* corner, he called it. I got the impression he transacted quite a bit of business from the very spot where you're sitting."

I shivered at the thought of the dead man's lemur sitting beside me. "What sort of business?"

Tiro hesitated. "So far as I know, Numerius was loyal to Pompey. I never had reason to believe otherwise. But the last time I met with him, he claimed to know some interesting things. Dangerous things."

"Go on, Tiro. You have my attention."

"Numerius drank more than he should have. That loosened his tongue. And he was very excited."

"About what?"

"About some documents he'd acquired. 'I'm sitting on something enormous,' he told me, smiling like a fox. 'Something so big it could get me killed if you breathe a word of this to anyone.'"

"What was it, Tiro?"

"Something to do with a plot to kill Caesar."

I managed a grim laugh. "Concocted by Pompey?"

"No! A conspiracy inside Caesar's own camp, involving men close to him. How Numerius could know of such a plot, and what sort of documents he had obtained, I don't know. But that's what he told me."

"When was this assassination supposed to take place?"

"It was supposed to have happened when Caesar crossed the Rubicon, the moment he invaded the motherland and showed his true intentions. For some reason it didn't come off. But this was the thing: Numerius seemed to think it still had a chance of happening."

"Wishful thinking!" I scoffed.

"Maybe. But he claimed to have proof of the plot in the form of documents." Tiro leaned closer to me. "*You* wouldn't know about that, would you, Gordianus?"

"What do you mean?"

"You say you found Cicero's report to Pompey in Numerius's shoe. What else did you find there? Be honest with me, Gordianus. I've been honest with you."

I took a deep breath. "I found exactly five pieces of parchment, all of the same color and quality, all written in the same hand and the same sort of cipher."

Tiro nodded. "That would have been Cicero's entire report; there were five pages in all. And you found nothing else?"

"That was all I found in Numerius's shoe."

Tiro sat back. After a moment he raised his cup and called for more wine. "And a decent cup as well, with a smooth lip!" he added, in a tone harsh enough to cause the eunuch's grin to vanish. I suddenly realized why he had been so generous with his information. He had hoped I would give him information in return, about the conspiracy documents. I had disappointed him.

We waited for our wine, then drank in silence. Across the room someone shouted, "Gaius Julius!" Dice clattered, and the gambler jumped from his seat. "The Caesar Throw! The Caesar Throw beats all!" The man did a victory dance and scooped up his winnings.

"Not a gracious winner," I muttered.

"I wonder if Caesar will be," Tiro muttered back.

"This talk you had with Numerius here in the tavern, about a plot to kill Caesar—that was a few days before he died."

"Yes."

"But on the day he died, it was the documents from Cicero he was carrying. And wasn't there . . ." I had to tread carefully. "Wasn't there some sort of altercation that day, between Cicero and Numerius, just before he left Cicero's house and came to mine?"

"Altercation?"

"Shouting, loud enough to be heard in the street."

"Those damned guards! Did they tell you that?"

"I hate to get them in trouble . . ."

Tiro shrugged. "Cicero may have raised his voice to Numerius that day."

"Raised his voice? He was practically screaming, according to the guards. Something about a debt owed to Caesar. Was it Numerius who owed money to Caesar . . . or was it Cicero?"

Tiro's face told me I had touched on something sensitive. "Lots of people owe money to Caesar. That hardly compromises their loyalty to Pompey or the Senate."

I nodded. "It's only . . . I got the impression from his mother that Numerius might have been blackmailing someone."

Tiro shifted in his seat. "I think I've had enough of this wretched wine. After a certain point it gets worse, not better. And this damned cup has more chips than the last!"

"You were in Rome that day, Tiro, the day Numerius died. Did you happen to . . . *follow* him . . . after he left Cicero's house?"

"I don't think I like the tone of your voice, Gordianus."

Did he think I suspected him of the murder? "I only wondered, if you did happen to follow Numerius, whether you might have seen anything significant. Someone besides yourself following him, for instance. Or someone to whom he might have passed documents before he entered my house . . .."

Tiro looked at me squarely. "Yes, I followed Numerius. Cicero was curious to know where he was headed next. So I followed him along the rim road to your house. I waited so long for him to leave that I finally assumed he'd given me the slip. How was I to know that he was dead inside? And no, I didn't see him pass anything to anyone, nor did I notice anyone else following him. And before you ask, no, I didn't see anyone climb over the roof into your garden, either—though I could hardly have seen all four sides of your house at once, could I?"

I smiled.

"And don't even think of asking if *I* climbed over the roof and into your garden!" He tried to inject some levity into his voice. "You saw how carefully I had to climb down that rickety ladder at Cicero's house!"

"Yes. Still, you do manage to climb up and down that ladder, don't you?" I likewise tried to keep my tone light.

I excused myself to go to the privy, which was out the back door and across an alley in a little lean-to. There were several holes in the paved floor, but the drunken patrons of the Salacious Tavern were poor marksmen and the place stank of standing urine. It occurred to me that the Cloaca Maxima, the central sewer line into the Tiber, was probably located just beneath my feet.

When I returned to the corner bench, Tiro had vanished. I stayed and drank another cup of wine, in no hurry to go home. The interview had yielded more than I expected. Where were the documents of which Numerius had boasted to Tiro only days before his death? Who else knew about them? Like poor Numerius, I felt I was sitting on something enormous, if only I could lay my hands on it.

IX

The remaining days of Februarius brought despair for Pompey's supporters, joy for Caesar's.

Flush with an unbroken chain of victories, Caesar continued his southward advance and surrounded Corfinium. Domitius Ahenobarbus, trapped in the city, sent desperate messages to Pompey begging for reinforcements. Pompey curtly replied that he had no intention of relieving Corfinium because Domitius had no business making a stand there in the first place.

Domitius concealed the contents of the letter from his officers and claimed that Pompey was on his way, but his agitated demeanor fooled no one. Behind his back, his officers decided to hand the city over to Caesar without a fight.

Domitius's longstanding grudge against Caesar was personal. Domitius's grandfather and father had begun the settlement of southern Gaul, conquering the Allobroges and the Arverni, building roads, establishing Roman colonies on the coast, and along the way amassing an enormous family fortune. The family had come to think of the region as their personal domain, to which Domitius should be heir. Caesar they considered an upstart who had built on their achievements to launch his own conquests. When Domitius made his first bid to acquire governorship of southern Gaul, six years ago, Caesar successfully thwarted him and held on to command of the region. Now Caesar's tenure had at last expired. Legally he was obliged to relinquish Gaul and let Domitius succeed him. Caesar's answer had been to cross the Rubicon with his army. Domitius had good reason to hate him, and better reason to fear him.

Finding himself betrayed and despairing of an ignoble death at the hands of Caesar or, even more ignobly, at the hands of his own rebellious men, Domitius asked his physician to give him poison. No sooner had Domitius swallowed the dose than word arrived that Caesar was treating all captives, even his bitterest enemies, with mercy and respect. Domitius wailed and tore his hair and cursed himself for acting too soon—until the physician, who knew his master better than his master knew himself, revealed that the dose was not poison, but a harmless narcotic. Domitius surrendered to Caesar and was allowed to keep his head.

In Rome, copies of Caesar's public pronouncement on entering Corfinium were posted in the Forum by his supporters:

> I did not leave my province with intent to harm anybody. I merely want to protect myself against the slanders of my enemies, to restore to their rightful positions the tribunes of the people, who have been expelled because of their involvement in my cause, and to reclaim for myself and for the Roman people independence from the domination of a small clique.

Fence-sitters among the rich and powerful were heartened by the news of Caesar's clemency. Some who had fled now began to return to the city.

His army swelled by the troops of Domitius Ahenobarbus and by fresh reinforcements from Gaul, Caesar continued his southward advance. Pompey fell back and ordered all loyalist troops to rendezvous at Brundisium, in the heel of Italy.

"Davus will die there," Diana said. "He'll die in Brundisium, trapped with the rest of Pompey's men. Caesar will put his foot into the boot of Italy and grind them all beneath his heel."

"Caesar has shown mercy, so far," I said cautiously. "He took Corfinium without spilling a drop of blood."

"But this is different. This is Pompey. He'll never surrender to Caesar."

"Perhaps Pompey will flee, rather than fight."

"Across the sea? But Davus can't swim!"

I tried not to smile. "I imagine they'll take ships, Diana."

"I know that! I'm thinking of the weather. No one sails at this time of year if they can help it. It's too dangerous, especially crossing the Adriatic. Storms and shipwrecks—I keep seeing Davus clinging to a scrap of flotsam, waves crashing over his head, lightning all around . . ."

The curse of an overactive imagination was something she inherited from her mother. "Davus is cleverer than you think," I said. "He can take care of himself."

"That's not true! He's sweet as honey on a cold morning and just as slow, and you know it. And what if Pompey *doesn't* flee, and there *is* a battle, Caesar's men against Pompey's? Davus would never do the sensible thing and run away. He'll feel obliged to stay and fight, for the sake of the other soldiers. It's like that for men in battle, isn't it? Comrades and loyalty, to the last drop of blood?"

I had no answer to that. I had been in one battle in my life, fighting with Catilina at Pistoria; what she said was true.

Diana grimaced. "Meto says you don't even feel the wounds when they happen. You just keep fighting until you can't fight anymore." She looked at me with sudden horror in her eyes. "Davus and Meto could be in the same battle, on different sides. They could kill each other!"

Now her imagination was definitely getting the better of her. I rose from my chair and crossed my study. I laid my hands on her shoulders. She leaned back against me and I circled her with my arms.

"Davus was trained to be a bodyguard, not a soldier. You know that, Diana. That's how Pompey will use him—to guard his person. He'll keep Davus close to him, day and night. Now I ask you, where could Davus be safer? Pompey is no fool. Look how cautious he's been so far, retreating two steps every time Caesar advances one. Davus is probably safer with Pompey than he would be in Rome."

"But what if there is a battle, and Pompey is at the head of the charge, leading his men? Caesar does that; Meto says so. Davus would be doomed then. It's as you say, he was trained to be a bodyguard. He'll sacrifice himself rather than let Pompey be harmed. He won't even stop and think. If there's a sword aimed for Pompey's heart, he'll throw himself on it!"

"Diana, Diana! You must stop imagining such things!" I sighed. "Listen, I want you to close your eyes. Now picture Davus. What's he doing this very instant? I'll tell you. He's standing at attention outside Pompey's tent, bored out of his mind, struggling not to yawn. There, can you see him? I can. I can even see the fly buzzing about his head. If he yawns, it may fly into his mouth!"

"Oh, Papa!" Diana sniffled and laughed in spite of herself. I held her close.

"What do you suppose Davus is thinking about right now?" I said quietly.

She laughed. "His next meal, probably!"

"No. He's thinking about you, Diana. About you and little Aulus."

Diana sighed and snuggled against me. I congratulated myself on having successfully comforted her—prematurely, as it happened, for the next moment she trembled and burst into tears and pulled herself from my embrace.

"Diana, what now?"

"Oh, Papa, I can't stand to think of Davus like that, so far from home, so lonely for us! He must be utterly miserable, and there's nothing he can do about it. Papa, you must promise me that you'll get him back. You must do whatever it takes to bring him back to us!"

"But Diana—"

"You must find whoever killed Pompey's kinsman, and tell Pompey, and make him give back Davus!"

I shook my head. "You don't know what you're asking, daughter."

She gave me a puzzled, dissatisfied, desperate look. In her eyes I saw something I had never seen before. For the first time, it occurred to her that her beloved father, upon whom she had always relied as upon a rock, might simply be too old now, too far past his prime to keep his family safe. I wanted to assure her that nothing could be further from the truth, but my tongue was like lead in my mouth.

That particular day, the first day of Martius, seemed to be my day to deal with distraught young women.

Diana had hardly left my study when Mopsus ran in. In my irritable state of mind, it occurred to me that he and his brother never seemed to walk anywhere, indoors or out. They had only two states of being: at rest, or scampering like hounds.

"Master, there's a visitor for you."

"Does he have a name?"

"It's not a he. It's a she."

I leaned back. "Still, I imagine she has a name."

He frowned, and I saw that between the foyer and my study he had forgotten the visitor's name. Humans are like Aesop's animals, I thought; they never change their essential nature. Davus would always be a bodyguard. My son Meto would always be a scholar and a soldier. And Mopsus, raised in a stable to look after beasts, would never make a decent door slave.

"What sort of woman is she?" I asked. "High or low?"

He thought. "She has bodyguards. Otherwise, it's hard to tell, from how she's dressed. All in black."

Could it be Maecia, come to inquire after my progress, or lack of progress, into her son's murder? I didn't relish the idea of seeing her again . . . unless she had found in her house new evidence of Numerius's activities—perhaps even the documents which gave details of the plot on Caesar's life . . .

"Old or young?"

Mopsus thought. "Young. Maybe Diana's age."

Not Maecia, then, but dressed in black, nonetheless. I frowned. Numerius had not been married. Nor had there been a sister. But perhaps . . .

"Show her in," I said.

"And her bodyguards?"

"They must remain outside, of course."

Mopsus grinned. "There's three of them, but I bet even three couldn't get past Scarface!" Of late, Mopsus and his brother had grown rather fond of Cicatrix. Curiously, the ugly monster seemed to return the sentiment; I often heard the three of them laughing in the foyer or outside the front door, Cicatrix's harsh bark making odd counterpoint to the boys' giggles. I remained suspicious of the fellow and would gladly have been rid of him, but I was not as afraid of him as I had been at first. He did an excellent job of guarding the front door. His demeanor to Bethesda and Diana was sullen but not threatening. He clearly preferred guarding the Great One and considered service in the household of a nonentity such as myself to be beneath him, but the two of us had worked out a begrudging means of communicating. I gave curt orders. Cicatrix scowled and grunted, but did as he was told.

Mopsus ran from my study. I stepped into the garden, thinking it a more suitable place to greet a young woman. The weather was mild for the Kalends of Martius, with little wind and only a few high, fleecy bands of clouds streaking the cold blue sky.

A few moments later, the visitor entered. She wore not a married woman's stola but a maiden's long tunic, all in black and covered by a heavy cloak as black as her hair, which was done up with pins and combs atop her head in a fashion too mature for her face. Her perfume seemed too mature for her, as well; I caught a whiff of jasmine and spikenard. Mopsus had estimated her to be Diana's age. She looked younger to me, no more than seventeen or eighteen. Her hands and face were as white as a dove's breast.

She looked at me warily from beneath her dark brows. "Are you Gordianus?"

"I am. Who are you?"

"My name is Aemilia, the daughter of Titus Aemilius."

I looked expectantly at the door through which she had come. "Where is your chaperone?"

Aemilia looked uncomfortable and lowered her eyes. "I came alone."

"A girl of your age and station, walking about Rome without a companion?"

"I brought bodyguards."

"Even so . . . Does your father know you're out?"

"My father is away. With Pompey."

"Of course. Your mother?"

"We returned to Rome only a few days ago. We were at our villa on the coast, but Mother says it's probably safer here in Rome now. She's busy today visiting the shops and markets. I was supposed to go with her. I told her I felt unwell and needed to stay at home."

"But instead you came here."

"Yes."

"*Are* you unwell? You look pale."

She didn't answer, but looked nervously about the garden until her eyes fixed on the Minerva behind me. The sight of the goddess seemed to give her strength. It was Minerva's face she looked at while she spoke, not mine. She probably had little experience addressing a grown man directly.

"I just came from Maecia's house. She told me about you."

"What did Maecia say?"

"That you were looking into . . ." Her nerve seemed to falter. She lowered her eyes to the ground. "Is this where it happened?"

I took a deep breath. "If you mean the death of Numerius Pompeius, yes, it happened in this garden."

She shuddered and clutched the black cloak to her throat.

"Were you kin to him?" I said.

"No."

"Yet you're dressed in mourning."

She bit her lips, which looked blood red against her pale cheeks. "He was . . . he and I . . . we were to marry."

I shook my head. "I didn't know."

"No one did."

"I don't understand."

"No one knew. Pompey had plans for him to marry someone else. But I was the one he chose. Numerius chose me."

From the way she touched herself, one hand unconsciously coming to rest above her belly, I suddenly understood. "I see."

"Do you?" Her face registered a confusion of pride and alarm. "Maecia could tell, too. Is it that obvious?"

I shook my head. "It doesn't show yet, if that's what you mean."

"Not here." She looked down and touched her belly. "But it must show on my face. And why not? I should have been his widow. The baby should have been born with his name. But now . . ."

"Why did you come here, Aemilia? To see the place where he died?"

She grimaced. "No. I don't like to think about that."

"Then why are you here? What do you want from me?" Her eyes met mine for an instant, then she looked beyond me, to Minerva, as she struggled to put her thoughts into words. I raised my hand. "Never mind. I know already. You want from me what everyone else wants—Pompey, Maecia, even Diana . . ." I shook my head. "Why was I able to tell at once with you, and yet with my own daughter, I practically had to be struck by lightning before I saw the obvious? And people think Gordianus is so clever, able to see what others don't!"

Aemilia looked at me, mystified. I sighed. "How long have you known?"

"About the baby? I knew before Mother and I left Rome. I wasn't certain, but I knew. Since then, the moon waxed and waned, and waxes again, and now there's no doubt. I can feel it inside me! I know it's too early for that, but I swear I feel it sometimes."

"His child . . ." I said. Like Aemilia imagining she felt the new life inside her, I seemed to sense another, very different kind of presence in the garden. What stronger lure than his unborn child might serve to call back the lemur of a murdered man to the spot where he was killed? I turned about and gave a start, almost certain I saw a shadow move behind the statue of Minerva. It was only a trick of the light.

"Did he know? Did you tell Numerius?"

She nodded. "The last time I saw him . . . the day before he died. We had a secret place to meet." She lowered her eyes. "We . . . afterward . . . I told him. I was afraid he'd be angry. But he wasn't. He was happy. I'd never seen him so happy. He said, 'Now Pompey will have to give up his plans for me and let us marry. I'll tell him tonight.' The next day Numerius was supposed to meet me again, to tell me what Pompey said, but he never came." She bit her lip. "That was the day everyone thought Caesar was coming, and Pompey decided to leave Rome, and my father decided to send Mother and me to the villa, and we spent the whole night madly packing our things and I didn't sleep at all . . ."

She took a breath, lifted her eyes, and stared hard at the face of Minerva. "The next morning we were in our wagon, lined up with all the other wagons to leave through the Capena Gate. A friend of Mother's came over. They talked about whether Caesar was really coming, and who was taking sides, and then—it was just another bit of gossip to her—the woman said, 'Did you hear? Numerius Pompeius was murdered yesterday! Strangled . . .' She said it so quickly, then moved on to something else so fast, I thought I must have imagined it. But I knew I hadn't. I knew it was true. I felt something sharp in my chest, like a jagged stone. I think I must have fainted. The next thing I knew we were out on the Appian Way. For an instant I thought I'd dreamed it, but I knew better. The stone was still in my chest. It hurt to breathe."

"Who else knows about the baby?"

"I kept it from my mother as long as I could. She knew something was wrong, but she thought I was only worried for Father, and upset by all that was going on. But once we started back to Rome, I couldn't keep it from her. She wasn't as angry as I thought she'd be."

"Then your father doesn't know?"

She lowered her face. "Mother says he must never know."

"But how can that be? Even if Pompey leaves Italy and takes your father with him, they may return before you come to term. And when you have the child, someone will talk; someone always does. You can hardly expect—" Then I fell silent, because I understood what she had told me.

"This morning, when I went to see her, I told Maecia everything—about Numerius and me, about the baby. We wept together. She says I mustn't get rid of it. She says it's all that's left of her little boy, her son. But it's not her choice to make. It's not my choice, either. Mother says I must get rid of it."

My mouth was dry. "It's not your mother but your father who has legal power over you and the baby inside you."

"If Father knew, he could put me to death! That would be legal and proper, wouldn't it?"

"Surely he'd never do that! What if he's gone for a year and comes back to find you and the child—"

"He might still get rid of the baby—expose it on a hill outside the city to let it starve or be eaten by jackals. Then he'd put me away somewhere, the way you hide a cracked vessel at the back of a cabinet." She swallowed hard. "No, Mother is right. If Father were here, he'd demand that I get rid of the baby while I can. They may yet be able to find a husband for me, don't you see? Mother says it wouldn't be right, anyway, to bring a child without a father into such a world . . ."

She began to weep.

I resisted the urge to comfort her. I stiffened my arms and clenched my fists. I glanced over my shoulder, and it seemed to me that Minerva regarded me with a mocking smile. "Aemilia, why have you come to me?"

"I don't know . . . except that Maecia said you were the last to see him . . . and that everything depends on you now."

"But Aemilia, there's nothing I can do to help you."

"You can at least find out who killed him—who killed . . . my baby." She saw the confusion on my face. "Don't you see? If Numerius hadn't been murdered, he would have found a way to marry me. I'm certain of it. I could have had our child! Then, even if Numerius was taken from me, killed in battle or lost at sea, I would have had the baby, and the baby would have had his name. But now . . . now there'll be no baby. Don't you see? Whoever murdered Numerius might as well have stuck a knife in my womb!"

Her grief erupted in a long, keening wail that carried all the way to the front of the house. I heard banging noises and a scuffle, and a few heartbeats later her three bodyguards rushed into the garden one by one, their swords drawn. Cicatrix followed after them, bellowing furiously, brandishing his own sword. The scar across his face was livid, like a fresh brand. He circled the bodyguards and ran to my side, where he assumed a defensive crouch, his arms extended and his knees bent to spring. The three armed men approached us with wild looks in their eyes.

Aemilia spun about, dazed, and realized what was happening. She stifled her sobs and held up her arms, calling her bodyguards to heel. They drew back and surrounded her. One of them exchanged whispers with her, then with his companions. The threat of bloodshed lingered in the air, like a raw, pungent smell.

Aemilia stepped toward me, her face lowered. Her bodyguards advanced with her, swords drawn, eying me warily.

"Forgive me," she whispered. "I never meant . . ."

I nodded.

"I'll go now. I don't know why I came. I only thought . . . I hoped you might . . . I don't know." She turned away. Her bodyguards withdrew with her, the hindmost walking backward and keeping his eyes on Cicatrix and me.

"Wait!" I said.

She stopped and looked over her shoulder. I stepped toward her, getting as close as I dared. It was too close for Cicatrix, who gripped my arm to hold me back.

"Aemilia, you said something about a secret meeting place."

Her face, already flushed, grew even redder. "Yes."

"Did this place belong to Numerius?"

"It belonged to his family. They own a lot of property in the Carinae district."

"And this place—where is it?"

She stepped toward me and motioned for her bodyguards to stand back. I gestured for Cicatrix to move away.

"It was a tenement building," said Aemilia, keeping her voice low. "An awful, smelly place. But there was a vacant apartment on the uppermost floor. From the window you could see a bit of the Capitoline Hill . . ." She gazed into space, her eyes glittering with tears.

"And only you and Numerius knew about this meeting place?"

"I don't know. I think he inherited the building from his father, but his uncle Maecius had a say in running it."

"But the room—it was Numerius's secret place?"

"Yes. He kept a few things there. A lamp, some clothing . . . some poems I gave him."

"Poems?"

"Greek love poems I copied out for him. We used to read them to one another . . ."

I nodded. "So this was a place where he might have kept . . . other secret things?"

"I don't know. Why do you ask?"

"Some documents may be there."

She shook her head. "I don't think so. There was no scroll cabinet. Not even a chest for keeping papers. He had to keep my poems beneath the bed."

"Even so, I need to see this place."

She bit her lip, then shook her head.

"Please, Aemilia. It may be very important. I may find the documents that were responsible for Numerius's death."

She looked at Minerva, then at me. Her gaze was steady. "The building is at the corner of the Street of the Basketmakers and a little alley that runs off it to the north. It's covered in a red wash, but the red is starting to wear off to show a yellow wash beneath. The room is on the fourth floor, in the southwest corner. The door has a lock, but the key is under a loose floorboard with a deep scratch across it, three paces up the hall."

I nodded. "I'll find it."

She touched my arm. "If you go there, you'll find the love poems. I'd be grateful if you could—"

"Of course. I'll find some way to return them to you."

She shook her head. "No, I could never have them in the house. But I can't bear to think of anyone else reading them. Burn them." She turned and rejoined her bodyguards.

I followed them through the house. Just before we reached the foyer, little Aulus appeared from nowhere and went stamping across the atrium, laughing and clapping his hands, directly in front of Aemilia. Mopsus and Androcles came running after him, but not before Aemilia gave a shudder and fled weeping through the foyer and out of the house, her guards trailing after her.

❧

That night I tossed and turned. At last Bethesda rolled toward me. "Can't you sleep, husband?"

The moonlight picked out glints of silver in her undone hair but left her eyes in shadow. "I'm thinking about the girl who came to visit me today." I had told her Aemilia's story over dinner.

"Very sad," said Bethesda.

"Yes. I was wondering . . . I don't know much about how it's done."

"What?"

"How a baby is gotten rid of."

Bethesda sighed in the darkness. "It's one of those things most men don't care to know much about. There are several ways. Sometimes a willow wand . . ."

"Willow?"

"With the bark stripped off. It needs to be thin and flexible to reach into the uterus."

I nodded.

"Or the girl may take poison."

"Poison?"

"Something strong enough to kill the child and expel it from her body. You brew a strong tea, using roots and herbs and fungi. Rue, nightshade, ergot . . ."

"But isn't that likely to kill the mother as well?"

"Sometimes that happens. I saw the girl on her way out. She looked rather frail to me." Bethesda sighed wearily and rolled away.

I stared at the ceiling. Aemilia believed that the killer of Numerius was equally responsible for the destruction of her unborn child. If Aemilia died, aborting the baby, would Numerius's killer then be responsible for three deaths?

I wondered, did men like Caesar in the cold, dark hours of the night ever ponder such chains of responsibility? To kill a man on the battlefield Caesar would consider an honorable act. But what of the man's widow and child left to starve, or the parents who die of grief, or the lover who kills himself in despair, or the whole villages that perish to famine and disease in the wake of war? How many such chains of suffering and death radiated from every battlefield in Gaul? How many such casualties would there be in Italy now that Caesar had crossed the Rubicon?

I tossed and turned, unable to sleep.

X

The next day, taking Mopsus and Androcles with me, I made my
way to the Carinae district. I had forgotten exactly where the Street
of the Basketmakers was located. Mopsus thought he knew. So did
Androcles. To the right, said Mopsus. To the left, said Androcles.
While they squabbled, I asked directions of a slave who passed by
carrying an armload of baskets. He pointed straight ahead. I followed and was nearly around a bend when the boys noticed and came
running after me.

The narrow, curving street was lined with shops, all with doors
flung open and wares on display. Baskets spilled out onto little tripod tables. More baskets hung suspended from ropes that criss-
crossed overhead. Many were local products, but the best and most
expensive came from Egypt, made of Nile reeds, with dyed strands
woven into the fabric to make intricate patterns and repeating pic-
tures. I made the mistake of pausing to look at a curious specimen
decorated with a circular band of Nile river-horses. The shop owner
descended on me at once.

"Those are called hippopotami," he said.

"Yes, I know. I lived in Egypt for a while when I was young."

"Then you'll want the basket as a souvenir. It was made for you!"

I smiled, shook my head and hurried on. The man followed me down the street, badgering me and waving the basket. When I refused to bargain, he threw down the basket with a curse. Times were hard on the Street of the Basketmakers.

It was not hard to locate the mottled red and yellow tenement Aemilia had described. It had a seedy, run-down appearance, with chipped plaster and broken shutters hanging from the windows. Someone was stewing cabbage inside. A baby was crying. The sound made me think of Aemilia.

Some tenement landlords post a slave at the front door to keep out thieves and troublemakers, but there was no slave at the entrance, and when I tested the door I found it had no lock, either. It was hard to imagine anything inside such a building to tempt a burglar.

"Mopsus," I said, "I want you to stand across the street while Androcles and I go inside. Try not to look like a runaway slave up to no good."

"I'll stand watch!" said Mopsus eagerly. "If anybody dangerous-looking goes in after you, I'll run up and tell you."

I shook my head. "No, Mopsus. I imagine any number of dangerous-looking men, and women for that matter, are likely to live in this building; this is a dangerous neighborhood. But tenement dwellers must come and go. How could you possibly know who has legitimate business in this building and who does not?"

Mopsus scratched his head.

"And if some assassin *were* to enter this building, intending to do me harm, how could you get past him to warn me?"

Mopsus frowned. Androcles covered his mouth, laughing at his older brother's consternation. I put my hands on their shoulders and walked them both across the street.

"Mopsus, I want you to stand precisely here. Now, do you see that corner window up on the fourth floor? The one with the shutters intact? I want you to watch that window. In a moment, if all goes well, I'll open those shutters and give you a wave. Don't wave back. But keep watching the window. If something should go wrong, you'll see

me or Androcles at that window again. If we scream for help, I want
you to run to Eco's house and tell him. Do you think you could find
your way to Eco's house from here? It's just up the Esquiline Hill."

Mopsus nodded mutely, his eyes wide at the gravity of his post.

"Good. Now keep your eyes on that window!"

I crossed the street with Androcles and entered the tenement. The
narrow hallway was deserted and, except for the crying baby, quiet.
The tenants, like most people in Rome, were out in the markets
searching for the necessities of life, which became harder to find
each day.

A stairway at one end of the hall led to the upper floors. I as-
cended and Androcles followed. "We shall be visiting a secret room,
Androcles, where we have no business being. I shall need you to keep
watch in the hall outside."

He mimicked his brother's grave nod.

"And I may need you for something even more important."

"What, Master?"

"I shall be searching for something. It may be well hidden and
hard to reach. A pair of tiny hands could turn out to be very useful."

"My hands are smaller than Mopsus's," he boasted, holding them
up for me to see.

"So they are."

We reached the landing of the third floor. The sound of the crying baby receded. The smell of cabbage grew stronger, mingled now
with other smells—onions, perfume, lamp oil, stale urine. What had
the daughter of Titus Aemilius thought of such a place?

We came to the top floor. The hallway was empty and dim. I motioned to Androcles to tread quietly.

I located the loose floorboard, just where Aemilia had described
it. Wedged in a narrow space beneath was the key. It was not one of
those stout keys with notches, to be inserted into a lock and given a
strong turn, but a thin bronze rod which curved eccentrically this
way and that, as if it might have been accidentally bent beneath a
wagon wheel. At one end there was a tiny hook.

Finding such a key is only half the trick in using it. The eccentric
shape allows it to slip through the equally eccentric passage inside

the keyhole. Once through, the hook at the end needs to find the eye it was fashioned for, which, unless the user has used that particular lock before, can require a considerable amount of trial and error.

I replaced the floorboard and stepped to the door. The lock was a bronze box bolted to the wood from inside. In such a neglected, insecure building, the elaborate mechanism seemed conspicuously out of place.

I slipped the key in, twisted it this way and that to negotiate the hole, then tried to imagine in my mind's eye what the hook needed to catch against. Up or down? Farther in or farther out? A jiggle or a twist? I tried various motions, then finally removed the key and started over. Again, I had no luck. My patience nearing an end, I pulled out and tried once more. This time, I seemed to locate a divergent keyhole. The key entered in a different direction. The hook caught on something. I held my breath, turned the key and pulled toward me. The lock gave a satisfying click. The door opened.

Behind me, I heard Androcles release a pent-up breath. I looked over my shoulder and nodded toward the stairs. "Stand watch on the landing," I whispered. "If anyone starts up, come quietly and let me know. Can you do that?"

He nodded and tiptoed toward the stairs.

I stepped inside and pulled the door not quite shut behind me. The room was even darker than the hallway. I found my way to the window at the southwest corner, which was covered with heavy winter drapes, made of a fabric far superior, I wagered, to anything to be found in the other apartments. I pulled them apart and opened the shutters. Above the rooftops, as Aemilia had said, I could see the sacred temples atop the Capitoline Hill. Mopsus stood across the street, leaning against a wall, his arms crossed, idly kicking his heels against the ground. He looked up at the sound of the shutters opening. I waved. He uncrossed his arms and started to wave back, then caught himself. He peered up and down the street, hardening his posture and trying to look formidable. I shook my head. If I had specifically asked him to look like an errant slave bent on getting into mischief, he could not have delivered a better performance.

I turned around and surveyed the room. It was sparsely furnished with a low sleeping couch and a little trunk against one wall. Perhaps it was nothing more than a love nest, after all. Lovers' needs were simple.

Atop the trunk there was a simple oil lamp, a vessel containing spare oil, and a small round mirror. I peered inside the lamp and the vessel and poured oil back and forth between them until I was satisfied that they contained nothing else. The mirror was of solid silver and had no secret parts. I glanced at my reflection. I saw a bearded man with furrowed brow but clear eyes, not yet entirely gray and youthful-looking for his years, a sign of the gods' favor. The fact that it was Aemilia's mirror made me uneasy. I put it aside.

The trunk was not locked. Inside I found a few pieces of clothing—a man's loincloth and tunic, a cloak that might have been worn by either sex. There was also a spare coverlet for the bed. At the very bottom, there was a small dagger. That was all.

The trunk appeared to contain nothing of significance. But remembering that Numerius Pompeius had carried confidential reports in his shoe, I looked at each item again. Satisfied that the dagger had no secret compartments, I used it to cut open the stitches of each garment. I had brought my own knife for the purpose, but this one looked sharper. I found nothing.

I examined the empty trunk. I used the dagger to undo the hinges and cut into the leather. I turned it over and rapped on the bottom, listening for the hollow echo of a hidden compartment. The trunk was nothing more than an ordinary trunk.

I turned my attention to the bed.

It was a fine piece of furniture—like the drapes, surely finer than anything to be found in the humble apartments down the hall or on the floors below. The frame was made entirely of ebony with ornately carved legs. Against the wall, an ebony sideboard inlaid with ivory ran the length of the frame from head to foot. Aemilia would have lain on the inner side, next to the board and the wall; Numerius would have lain on the outside, as men typically do. I once explained to Bethesda that this arrangement was so because the man protects the woman in sleep. She laughed and said it was because men needed to get up and pass water more often during the night.

But I imagined the lovers had done little sleeping in this bed. They would have met here in the day; it seemed doubtful that Aemilia could have escaped her parents' vigilance after dark. It was a bed for the waking hours, a bed for loving, not sleeping. The bed where their baby was made.

The thick mattress was covered with a linen sheet, haphazardly tucked at the corners. A woolen coverlet was thrown over it. Several pillows were scattered about. The bed had a rumpled, used look. Both Numerius and Aemilia were no doubt used to having their beds made by a slave, and either did not know how to do it themselves or did not care to. Keeping house was not how they spent their time in this room.

I pulled off the coverlet and cut open the stitches. There was nothing hidden inside.

I pulled off the linen sheet. It was too sheer to conceal anything. It gave off a faint odor. I held it to my nose and smelled jasmine, spikenard, the scent of warm bodies. For an instant I imagined it wrapped around Aemilia, clinging to her. I imagined the two of them lying side by side, with only the sheet to cover them. I shook my head to clear it.

The pillows and the mattress were the most likely places to conceal something. I pulled them off the bed and saw several pieces of parchment hidden beneath the mattress, atop the webbing of straps strung between the sideposts. If they were Aemilia's Greek love poems, copied out in her own hand, I had no desire to read them. But how could I determine what they were unless I examined them?

I looked at the first poem. The handwriting was self-consciously fancy, painfully childish. The words were not.

When I look at you I can no longer speak.
My tongue is broken. A thin flame runs under my skin.
I see nothing. My ears roar. Sweat pours down me.

A trembling seizes me all over.
I am greener than grass. I feel close to dying.
Somehow this can be endured, when I look at you . . .

Sappho, of course. What love-smitten teenage girl could resist the poet of Lesbos?

I forced myself to read the other poems, one by one. The words made my face flush hotly.

Finally, having read them all, I examined the pieces of parchment front and back. I walked to the window and held each one to the light, looking for signs of invisible lemon ink or perforations that could be a code, but saw nothing of the sort. The love poems were only that, bits of Sappho and my old friend Catullus copied out by a daydreaming girl to pass the hours between visits to her lover. Incriminating, to be sure, but only if shown to her parents.

Standing at the window, from the corner of my eye I noticed Mopsus down on the street corner. He waved at me. I glowered, shook my head, and refused to look back at him. I had specifically told him not to wave, which would only attract attention to us both. When I ignored him, he only seemed to wave more frantically. I determined to thrash him with my tongue when I was done. I stepped away from the window.

Beneath the bed I noticed a wide shallow bowl. I moved the bowl to the floor in the middle of the room. I knelt and dropped the poems into it. I reached into my tunic for the flint box I had brought for the purpose, and concentrated so hard on striking a spark that I didn't hear Androcles's footsteps in the hall outside. I gave a start when he pushed open the door and stuck his head inside.

"Master! There's a man coming up the stairs!"

I suddenly understood why Mopsus waved so frantically. I looked back to Androcles. "Come inside then, quickly!" I whispered.

Androcles slipped inside, then turned to shut the door. He was too late. The door caught on something. Androcles pushed hard, but to no avail. A man's foot was thrust into the breach. Androcles gave a little squeal of panic.

Fingers wrapped around the edge of the door. Androcles threw his whole body against it, but he was no match for the man on the other side. The door relentlessly began to open.

I dropped my flint box. I reached for the knife. I rose to my feet and braced myself, my heart pounding.

"Master, I can't stop him!" cried Androcles.

Slowly but steadily the door opened, until the sunlight from the window fell upon the quizzical, artificially darkened face of my old friend Tiro.

XI

"A rather good view of the Capitoline," Tiro noted, gazing out the window. "I wonder how much an apartment like this lets for on the open market?"

After stepping inside and patting a startled Androcles on the head, Tiro had made a leisurely circuit of the room, noting the emptied trunk and stepping over the mattress and pillows strewn on the floor, and came to rest at the window.

"Tiro, what are you doing here?"

He lowered his gaze. "That boy down there, staring up at me as if I were a gorgon—isn't he one of yours, Gordianus?"

I walked to the window and waved to Mopsus to show that all was well. Visibly relieved, he pantomimed coming up to join us, but I shook my head and signaled that he should continue keeping watch.

"Androcles," I said, "go back to the head of the stairs and stand guard, as you did before. Perhaps we can avoid being surprised a second time."

"But, Master," Androcles protested, "isn't this the assassin you had us follow for you the other day?"

Tiro raised an eyebrow.

"I never told them any such thing. The boys have more imagination than common sense. Go, Androcles."

"But, Master—"

"I shall be perfectly safe. At least, I think I will be." It was my turn to raise an eyebrow at Tiro. Once Androcles was out of the room, I repeated the question I had asked him before. "What are you doing here?"

He tapped his nose. "The same thing you are, I imagine. Following my nose."

"Following me, you mean."

"Perhaps."

"Do you make a habit of trailing after me every time I leave the house?"

"No more often than you follow me, I imagine."

"Why today, then?"

"Because yesterday Numerius's young lover paid you a visit."

"How do you know they were lovers?"

"I know all sorts of things."

"And how did you know she came to see me yesterday? Were you watching my house, or were you following her?"

He shook his head. "Gordianus, you can't expect me to tell you everything, any more than I expect you to tell me all you know. Still, I think it might serve both our interests if we were to pool our knowledge. About Numerius, I mean."

"You're looking for the documents he told you about, aren't you?"

"Aren't you, as well, Gordianus? Since we're looking for the same thing, why not help each other find it?"

I didn't answer.

Tiro stepped to the middle of the room and knelt beside the bowl with Aemilia's poems. The flint box lay beside it. "You were about to burn these before I arrived," he observed. "What are they?"

"Nothing to interest you."

"How can you be sure of that?"

I sighed. "They're erotic poems copied out by a lovesick girl.

Aemilia told me they were here. She asked me to burn them. I see no reason to do otherwise."

"But they might not be what they seem."

"They're not what either of us is looking for, Tiro."

"How do you know that?"

"I know!"

"But you'll let me take them, won't you? What harm could there be in that, Gordianus? I'll burn them myself, once I've had a chance to thoroughly examine them. No one else will ever see them."

"No, Tiro!"

We looked at one another for a long moment, neither willing to look away. At last he rose to his feet and stepped away from the bowl. "Very well, Gordianus. I can see that you won't be swayed. What obligation do you owe to this girl?"

I didn't answer, but knelt by the bowl and recommenced striking the flint. A spark flew into the bowl. The dry parchment ignited. The flame was tiny at first, then spread along the edge of the parchment. I watched the words catch fire: *A thin flame runs under my skin. I see nothing . . .*

I looked up to see the glow reflected off Tiro's swarthy features. "Nothing is as fascinating as fire, don't you think?" he said, smiling faintly. "After the flames, nothing is left but a bit of ash, which crumbles to nothing if you touch it. Where does the flame come from? Where does the parchment go? No one knows. Now it will be as if the girl never copied those poems, and Numerius never heard her read them. Numerius might as well never have existed."

"But he did. And Aemilia loved him." Inside her a part of Numerius still existed, I thought, at least for a while. The baby, too, soon would be ashes.

Tiro made a scoffing noise. "She loved him? Perhaps. But did he love her?"

"He was determined to marry her, despite Pompey's wishes. Aemilia was certain of that."

"Was she? No doubt she imagined all sorts of things, lying on that bed with him after an hour of making love, gazing out the window at the temples on the Capitoline. No doubt he told her all sorts of lies—whatever he needed to tell her to keep her coming back to meet him here."

"A life spent with Cicero has made you a stodgy moralist, Tiro."

"Nonsense! But when I see a love nest like this, and I've seen just how young and tender the girl was, it's no mystery what sort of young man Numerius must have been. A perfect specimen of his generation—selfish, without morals, out to take whatever he can, with no thought to the consequences. If it weren't for his kinship to Pompey, he'd have been just the sort to join Caesar."

I looked at Tiro steadily. "You make him sound the sort of man that no one should regret killing."

Tiro gave me a sour look. "Don't mock me, Gordianus. And don't accuse me of murder, even in jest."

"I wasn't."

"I'm only saying that if Numerius really loved the girl, he'd have done the right thing and taken her for a wife, with or without the Great One's blessing, instead of taking her for a lover in a squalid hole like this."

"Tiro! Have you forgotten the love affair that you were carrying on behind Cicero's back when I first met you? You were a slave then, and she was the daughter of your master's client, and the consequences could have been terrible for both of you—not to mention for any child that might have resulted."

"Unfair, Gordianus! I was young and stupid—"

"And Numerius wasn't?"

Tiro stared at the ashes in the bowl.

"'Every man likes to remember youthful indiscretions, but no man likes to be reminded of them.'" I said quietly.

"Ennius," said Tiro, recognizing the quotation. He managed a weak smile. "You're right. We're not here to pass judgment on Numerius. We're here to discover his secrets. Shall we work together, Gordianus, or not?"

"There are two knives," I said, holding up the one I had brought and offering him the one I had found in the trunk.

"I brought my own," he said, "but this one looks sharper." Together we set to cutting open the pillows and the mattress.

They contained at least one surprise. Instead of common straw or wool, they were stuffed with swan's down, mixed with enough dried herbs to faintly scent the whole room; I had been wondering where the smell came from. Numerius had not been one to stint himself of luxury when it came to lovemaking.

Each time we cut into a pillow, feathers came bursting out. Soon the room was adrift in white fluff. Bits of down floated in the air like snowflakes. The absurdity of it made us both laugh. The tension between us leaked away. Perhaps it would have been otherwise if we had found what we were seeking, but as we sifted and searched it quickly became evident that nothing was hidden among the stuffing.

"I've searched everywhere I can think of," I told Tiro. "Why don't you have a look yourself, starting with the trunk. Perhaps you'll notice something I've overlooked."

He carefully examined every item in the room, including the bedposts, searching for hollow chambers. Together we examined every floorboard, looking for one that might be loose. We ran our hands over the plastered walls and poked at the ceiling. We found nothing.

"If there ever were some documents regarding a plot to kill Caesar, they aren't here," said Tiro, sticking out his tongue to blow a bit of down from his upper lip.

"Nor were they hidden at Numerius's house. His mother told me she made a thorough search for just such material and found nothing."

"Yet Numerius told me he was 'sitting on something enormous'—something so dangerous it could get him killed."

"Which it did," I said, lowering my eyes.

Tiro walked about the room, stirring up eddies of swan's down. "So I'm no closer to finding what I was looking for, and you're no closer to discovering who murdered Numerius and getting your son-in-law back from Pompey. Listen, Gordianus—I'm leaving Rome tomorrow. Come with me."

I cocked an eyebrow.

"Why not?" he said. "I'm sick of traveling alone."

"Surely you'll take a bodyguard for the road."

"Yes, one of those idiots at Cicero's house."

"The older one's brighter," I said. "Not quite as stupid, anyway."

"Fortex, you mean?"

"If that's his name."

"Fortex won't make much of a traveling companion. I could have better conversations with my horse. You're good company, Gordianus."

"You want me to go with you simply to keep you amused, Tiro? Someone has to look after my family."

"You've got that cyclops from Pompey at your front door, haven't you? And your son Eco can look in from time to time."

"Perhaps. Still, what reason have I to leave Rome?"

Tiro looked at me gravely. "You want to get your son-in-law back, don't you? There's not much time left for that, Gordianus. Pompey's withdrawn to Brundisium, with his back to the sea. Caesar is pursuing him. It can only be a matter of days now. If you have any intention of bringing Davus back to Rome . . ."

"I see your point. What about you, Tiro? Why are you leaving Rome?"

"I received a message from Cicero today. He wants me to stop at his villa in Formiae on my way and carry some letters to Pompey—"

"Formiae? Cicero is still down the coast?"

"Yes."

"But Pompey ordered all loyalist senators to rendezvous at Brundisium."

"Yes. Well . . ." Tiro's expression became guarded.

"Don't tell me Cicero is still vacillating! Is he waiting for the war to be over before he takes sides?"

"It's not like that, Gordianus; not as bad as you make it sound. Cicero sees himself as—how to put it?—uniquely positioned to play a special role. What other man of his eminence can still communicate with both sides?"

"Cicero is still in contact with Caesar?"

"Cicero and Caesar never stopped corresponding. Pompey knows that. Cicero hasn't misled him. Now that the crisis is entering a new stage, Cicero may be in a position to act as go-between, as peace-maker. In order to do that, he must maintain a delicate balance—"

"Nonsense! Cicero simply hasn't the nerve to throw his lot with Pompey. He detests Caesar, but he fears that Caesar may win, so he secretly cozies up to both sides. He's the worst sort of coward."

Tiro grimaced. "Who's being the stodgy moralist now, Gor-dianus? We all find ourselves in a situation not of our choosing. Every man has to steer his own course. It'll be a lucky man who comes out of this alive without a bit of tarnish on his con-science."

I had no answer for that.

He took a deep breath. "Well then, Gordianus, will you come with me to Brundisium or not?"

On the way home, I bought the Egyptian basket ringed with hip-popotami as a gift for Bethesda. I needed something to soften the news that I was leaving Rome. As it turned out, it was a wise choice for a gift, since a reed basket can be thrown across the room and not break.

Unlike her mother, Diana seemed to receive the news with en-thusiasm. Anything that might result in the return of Davus was a welcome development. But that night, as I packed a saddlebag with things I would need for the journey, Diana came into the room. She spoke without looking at me.

"I think it's a brave thing you're doing, Papa, going off like this. The countryside must be terribly dangerous."

"No more so than the city these days, I imagine."

She watched me fold a tunic. I did such a poor job that she felt obliged to take it from me and fold it herself.

"Papa, I know that you're doing this for me. Even though . . . I mean to say, I know that you were never . . . pleased . . . by my marriage. Yet now you're willing to . . ." She fought back sudden tears. "And I worry that I may never see either of you again!"

The folded tunic came undone in her hands. I put my arm around her. She reached up to touch my fingers on her shoulder. "I don't know what's wrong with me, Papa. Every since Davus left . . ."

"Everyone's nerves are as frayed as a beggar's cloak, Diana. What do you want to bet that Cicero breaks out in tears twice a day?"

She smiled. "I doubt that Caesar does."

"Perhaps not. But Pompey may. There's a picture for you: Davus yawning outside the Great One's tent, and Pompey inside, crying like a baby and tearing his hair."

"Like a scene from Plautus."

"Exactly. Sometimes it helps to think of life as a comedy on a stage, the way the gods must see it."

"The gods can be cruel."

"As often as not."

We were silent for a while. I felt a great sense of peace, standing next to her with my arm around her.

"But Papa," she said quietly, "how will you manage to get Davus from Pompey? If you haven't discovered who killed Numerius, Pompey will never let him go."

"Don't worry. I have a plan."

"Do you? Tell me."

"No, Diana."

She shrugged my arm from her shoulder and stepped away. "Why not, Papa? You used to tell me everything."

"You don't need to know, Diana."

She pursed her lips. "Don't tell me your plan, then, Papa. Perhaps I don't believe you have one."

I took her hands and kissed her forehead. "Oh, I assure you, daughter, I do have a plan." And I did—although using it might mean that I would never come back from Brundisium alive.

PART TWO

MARS

XII

Horses were hard to come by. The best had been taken by those who fled the city in the first wave of panic or requisitioned by Pompey's forces. Tiro promised to meet me outside the Capena Gate before dawn the next day with fresh mounts, but what could possibly be left in the stables? I had visions of myself atop a swaybacked nag with knobby joints and a hide worn to leather, but I underestimated Tiro's resourcefulness. I found him waiting for me with Fortex, the bodyguard, both of them mounted. A third horse stood idly by, munching at the grass between two moss-covered funeral shrines alongside the road. All three beasts were as sleek and fit as any rider could wish.

We set out at once. The sun was no more than an intimation of fiery gold not yet cresting the low hills to the east. Patches of darkness lingered like vestiges of Night's trailing shroud. In such uncertain light, there was something eerie about that stretch of road, flanked on either side by so many tombs of the dead.

The Appian Way itself is as smooth as a tabletop, with polygonal paving stones fitted so tightly that not a grain of sand could be passed between them. There is something reassuring about the solid immutability of a Roman road. Meto once told me of venturing on a reconnaissance mission into the wild woods of Gaul. Alien gods seemed to peer from gnarled roots. Lemures flitted among shadows. Unseen creatures scurried amid moldering leaves. Then, in a place where he never expected it, Meto came upon a road built at Caesar's instigation, a gleaming ribbon of stone cutting through the heart of the forest, letting in fresh air and sunlight.

The Appian Way is surrounded not by wilderness but by tombs for miles along either side. Some monuments are large and elaborate, like miniature temples. Others are no more than a simple marker, an upright stone pole with a bit of engraving. Some fresh-scrubbed and beautifully tended, surrounded by flowers and shrubbery. Others have fallen into disrepair, with columns knocked askew and cracked foundations choked by weeds.

Even in broad daylight, there is something melancholy about a trip down the Appian Way. In that tenuous predawn light, where unsettled spirits seemed to lurk in the shadows, the road beneath our feet meant more than Roman order and ingenuity. It was a path by which the living could traverse the city of the dead. Every clop of our horses' hooves against the stones was a note of reassurance that we were just passing through.

We came to the shrine of Publius Clodius, set among those of his ancestors. The last time I had traveled any great length on the Appian Way, it had been to investigate the murder of Clodius. He had been the darling and the hope of the urban rabble. His assassination sparked riots in Rome; a mob with torches made the Senate House his funeral pyre. Desperate for order, the Senate had called on Pompey, and the Great One had used emergency powers to instigate what he called judicial reforms. The result had been the prosecution and exile of a great many powerful men who now saw in Caesar their only hope to ever return. The ruling class was irreparably fragmented, the rabble more disaffected than ever. In hindsight, was the murder of Clodius on the Appian Way the true beginning of civil war, the opening skirmish, the first casualty?

His shrine was simple, as befitted a patrician with pretensions to the common touch. Atop a plain pedestal sat a ten-foot-tall marble stele carved with sheaves of wheat, a reminder of the grain dole that Clodius established. The sun cleared the hills. By the growing light I was able to see that the pedestal was littered all about with humble votive offerings—burnt tapers and plugs of incense, bouquets of sweet herbs and early spring flowers. But there was also a pile of something that looked and smelled like human excrement, and a graffito smeared in the same stuff on the base of the pedestal: CLODIUS FUCKED HIS SISTER.

Tiro wrinkled his nose. Fortex barked out a laugh. We rode on.

A little farther, on the opposite side of the road, we passed the Pompeius family plot. The tomb of Pompey's father was a gaudy, elaborate affair. All the gods of Olympus were crowded into the pediment, as if jealous of the honor, painted in lifelike colors and surrounded by a gilded border that glimmered red in the rays of the rising sun. The tomb looked recently painted and refurbished but lately neglected; weeds had grown about the base in the time since Pompey and his household had fled south. Otherwise, everything seemed perfect, until I noticed that heaps of horse dung, easy enough to collect on the road, had been deposited on the bronze roof. By midmorning of a sunny day, as this promised to be, travelers would smell the shrine to the elder Pompey long before they saw it.

Fortex snickered.

"Outrageous!" muttered Tiro. "When I was young, men fought for power just as viciously as they do today, but nobody would have dared to desecrate a tomb, not even as an act of war. What must the gods think? We deserve whatever misery they thrust upon us. Here, you! Climb up there and get rid of that stuff."

"Who, me?" said Fortex.

"Yes. Do it at once."

Fortex made a face, then dismounted, muttering, and looked about for something to use as a shovel.

While we waited, I let my horse wander idly along the edge of the road, looking for tender grass amid the tombs of the Pompeii. I shut my eyes, feeling the warmth of morning sunlight on my eyelids and enjoying the casual, uncontrolled movements of the beast beneath me. Behind me I heard the slave climb onto the brazen roof, then the sound of scraping, followed by the soft impact of dung hitting the road.

I must have dozed. The moment slid out of ordinary time. When I opened my eyes, before me I saw the tomb of Numerius Pompeius.

It was a simple stele of the ready-made sort, engraved with a horse's head, symbol of death's departure. It was a little way off the road, behind a row of more conspicuous tombs. Compared to its neighbors, it was small and insignificant. I would never have noticed it, passing by on the road. How strange that the horse should have brought me directly to it, and that the first thing I should see when I opened my eyes were the words newly chiseled in the narrow, five-line space reserved for personalizing the monument:

NUMERIUS POMPEIUS
GIFT OF THE GODS
WHO JEALOUSLY RECLAIMED HIM
AFTER TWENTY-THREE YEARS
AMONG THE LIVING

Those words would have come from his mother. Having no one else to blame for his death, Maecia blamed the gods. I felt a twinge of shame.

I looked down. It was not so inexplicable after all that my mount had wandered to this spot. At the foot of the stele someone—Maecia, of course—had planted flowers, not yet budding. The horse found the tender foliage to his liking and had already eaten most of it to the ground.

I pulled on the rein and scolded him. At the same moment I saw a movement from the corner of my eye. A figure emerged from behind a nearby monument.

My heart lurched inside my chest. The shadows had lifted with the dawn, but something uncanny seemed still to lurk amid the tombs. Perversely, it seemed somehow appropriate that the lemur of Numerius would emerge from the underworld to confront me just as birds began to sing and the whole world stirred to life.

But the ragged creature who emerged from behind the monument was not a lemur. Nor were the others, three at least, who quickly joined him. I wheeled my horse about in the difficult space between the crowded monuments. "Tiro!" I shouted. "Bandits!"

Certain stretches of the Appian Way are notoriously unsafe. The area around the tomb of Basilius, situated far beyond the city wall and marking the true beginning of the countryside, is especially dangerous; I myself had been ambushed there once and kidnapped. But we had not gone nearly that far, and I had never heard of bandits this close to the Capena Gate. How desperate men were these, and how little order was left in Rome, that they should dare to attack travelers practically within shouting distance of the city! It was our own fault. Tiro should never have sent our single bodyguard on a fool's errand to shovel horse dung. I should never have shut my eyes and allowed my horse to wander. The bandits saw us lower our guard and decided to strike.

I frantically attempted to guide my mount back onto the road. Just a moment before, I had been scolding him for eating Maecia's flowers. Now he balked, confused. A hand gripped my ankle. I kicked and lost my balance. I swayed, nearly fell, and grazed my head against a stone obelisk. Another hand gripped my foot. I turned and saw an ugly, gap-toothed face glaring up at me. There is a certain look a man has when he's worked himself up to kill, if necessary. I saw that look in his eyes.

An instant later, a scrap of dung, sun-hardened to make a suitable missile, struck the man square between the eyes. He gave a squeal and released his grip on me. Finally sure of himself, my mount galloped between the monuments and onto the road.

Tiro was wheeling about, a long dagger in his hand. Fortex gave a whoop, leaped off the roof of the shrine, and mounted his horse in a single fluid motion. One of the bandits came up behind him. The startled horse kicked the man in the chest. He flew through the air like a thrown doll, struck his head against the wall of the shrine, and crumpled lifeless to the ground.

They came at us from both sides of the road, a gang of ten men at least, maybe more. In the next instant they might have swarmed over us and pulled us from our horses. But they seemed to have no leader, and the sight of one of their number lying dead caused them to hesitate. As one, the three of us turned our horses and set off with a great clattering of hooves.

Some of the bandits ran after us. One of them managed to grab Tiro's ankle. I saw a glint of steel, felt drops of blood strike my face and heard a scream that rapidly receded. I turned my head. The stricken man stood clutching his arm. Several of his companions kept running after us. None of them seemed to have weapons, except stones, one of which struck Fortex's mount on the rump. The beast neighed and lurched, but never slowed its pace.

One by one the men gave up the chase. I watched them grow distant and dwindle, like the Capena Gate beyond them, like the shrines of Clodius and the elder Pompey. The stele of Numerius Pompeius was lost amid so many others.

Alongside me, Fortex suddenly laughed and gave a whoop. A moment later, Tiro broke into a grin and did the same. What excuse had they for joy? What had just occurred could be read as an omen, and a very bad omen at that. Only moments into a journey of many days, we had let down our guard and very nearly lost out lives. The gods had pointed me to the tomb of Numerius Pompeius and then unleashed a desperate horde upon us. It had been a grim episode, ending in bloodshed and death.

But the exhilaration was contagious. A moment later I began to laugh and whoop along with them. It was the morning of a new day, the sun shone brightly across the fields, and we were alive! Not only alive, but putting Rome behind us—leaving behind Numerius's mourning mother and his pregnant lover, leaving behind my weeping daughter and scolding wife, leaving behind the glum shopkeepers and the daily panics in the Forum, shaking off the chilly gloom of the city and galloping into the future with the bracing wind in our faces.

I knew that such a feeling of freedom couldn't last; it never does. But I knew, too, that it might be the last time I ever tasted such exhilaration. I urged my horse to gallop even faster. I drew ahead of

Tiro and Fortex, until I had the illusion of being alone on the road, a single rider, invincible, unrestrainable. I threw back my head and cried out to heaven.

~

Past the tomb of Basilius we slackened our pace to rest the horses. As the plain began to slope upward into the foothills of Mount Alba we came to the village of Bovillae, and passed the spot where Clodius had been killed. The terrain grew hillier, the way less straight. We passed the road leading up to Clodius's fortresslike mountain villa, never to be finished now, the place where I first met Mopsus and Androcles.

In the town of Aricia we obtained fresh mounts at the local stable, where Tiro produced an official document, a diplomatic courier's passport signed by Pompey himself and stamped with the Great One's seal ring. The piece of parchment entitled the bearer to exchange horses at no charge, by order of the Senate's Emergency Decree. While Tiro haggled over the quality of horses the stabler offered in exchange, I heard my stomach growling and noticed there was a tavern across the way. Crossing the road, I looked toward the hills and caught a glimpse of the villa of Senator Sextus Tedius, where the secret of Clodius's death had been revealed to me. Over stale bread and mutton stew, I struck up a conversation with a local freeholder. I asked him what old Senator Tedius was up to.

"Gone off to fight with Pompey," the man said.

"You must be mistaken," I said. "Sextus Tedius is far too old and feeble. The man's a cripple."

"No mistake, citizen," said the man, laughing. "He's left his spinster daughter in charge of the villa and gone off to war. I know that for a fact, because before he left, he called everyone together at the town forum and made a long speech saying we all ought to do the same, and shame on any man who stayed behind. And us no more than farmers, and the planting season almost on us! Who does he think feeds the soldiers? Crazy old coot!" The man shook his head and lowered his voice. "Maybe things will be different when it's Caesar in charge. What do you think, citizen?"

Past Mount Alba, the way sloped steadily downward. As twilight was falling, Tiro led us off the main road to a trading post called Forum Appii on the edge of the Pontine Marshes. I thought he intended to seek accommodations for the night; the courier's passport entitled its bearers to room and board as well as fresh horses. But we rode past several inns and didn't stop until the road ended at the terminus of a broad canal, where a cluster of buildings included warehouses, stables, a tavern, and a boarding platform for the canal barge.

Tiro explained that the canal ran through the marshes with an elevated road alongside it. The barge was a long, flat vessel with a waist-high railing all around. It was pulled by a team of mules on the road, guided by boatmen with stout poles.

"There's a pen for livestock at the back of the barge, so we can bring the horses with us," Tiro explained. "We'll pay our fare, get settled on board and set out at nightfall. We'll eat dinner at our leisure and travel while we sleep. In the morning we'll be almost to Tarracina, rested and ready to push onto Formiae. It's the most civilized way in the world to travel."

It sounded reasonable enough. There were only a few drawbacks that Tiro failed to mention, such as the exorbitant price of bread and wine at every nearby tavern (provisions sold on the barge turned out to be even more expensive, and doubled in price after it started moving); the crammed conditions (the ticket seller kept loading more and more passengers until the head boatman finally drove away some of the latecomers, saying they might swamp the vessel); the incompetence of the mule driver (who took an hour to hitch up his team after the last passenger was boarded); the near impossibility of eating amid the combined smells of swamp and barnyard (the animals were penned at the rear, and the wind was at our backs); the invisible, buzzing insects (gnats in the nose, midges in the eyes); the torturous sleeping conditions (everyone side by side and head to toe, like corpses laid out after a battle, except that corpses do not fart, snore, or drunkenly sing all night); and the sheer perversity of the boatmen, who seemed to think it amusing if they could jolt everyone awake every few minutes by banging the barge against the side of the canal, and even better if they could get us well and truly snagged, which meant an hour of hammering, banging, and yelling back and forth in the darkest hour of the night.

I managed to get about an hour of sleep that night. When we docked the next morning, I stumbled off with everyone else to bathe at a spring in a nearby grove sacred to the nymph Feronia, patron goddess of freedmen. The water revived me a little. Then we were off again.

At Tarracina we rejoined the Appian Way. I felt the pains of the previous days' ride in my buttocks and thighs, and so did Fortex, I think, for I kept seeing him wince and scowl. Perhaps he was simply testing ferocious faces, in case we encountered more bandits. Tiro, well broken in to the rigors of travel, was in high spirits. In a matter of hours he would see Cicero.

We arrived at Formiae that afternoon. Tiro, not wanting to be observed, avoided the town and the main road to Cicero's villa. Instead we took an alternative route through uncleared woodland. The road dwindled to a bridle path, the path to a trail, the trail to a faint trace amid briars and brambles. Twilight was falling. Shadows gathered in the woods. I feared we might become lost, but Tiro knew the way. Just as the sun was sinking, we emerged from the woods into a vineyard. Beyond the vines I caught glimpses of a handsome villa with white walls and a red roof.

There was a little covered porch along the back of the house, where a man in a long white tunic sat with a scroll on his lap. He was turned sideways in his chair with a hand raised, instructing a young slave where to hang a lamp so that he might continue reading. The slave saw us approaching through the vineyards. He gave a shout and pointed. The man turned about and rose with a start. The scroll tumbled to his feet and unfurled.

I had never before seen such a look of panic on any man's face, nor such a complete transformation when he recognized his visitors. He smiled and laughed and strode out to greet us, leaving the slave to gather up the scroll.

We had arrived at Cicero's retreat.

XIII

After the travails of the night barge, the simple accommodations at Cicero's villa seemed luxurious beyond measure.

I suspected that our host and his family, left to themselves that night, would have eaten only casually; but for our arrival, a formal dinner was hastily prepared. We dined on couches in a spacious room off the central garden, and Cicero gave me the place of honor to his left. Cicero's wife, Terentia, seemed to be in a foul mood and said little, except to give orders to the serving girls. Young Marcus, not quite sixteen, had been out hunting all day with the manager of the estate and ate ravenously; the years of my increasing estrangement from Cicero had coincided with the boy's growth to manhood, and I would hardly have recognized him. Tullia's appetite was as voracious as her younger brother's, and Cicero made a joke of it, saying his daughter was eating for two; her pregnancy was beginning to show, and Cicero seemed rather pleased to show her off. A grandchild is a grandchild, his expression seemed to say, even if the marriage had taken place behind his back and the father was a dissolute wastrel and a partisan of Caesar. Every time I looked at the girl, with her beaming face and gently swollen belly, I thought of Aemilia back in Rome.

The food was simple, but better than anything I had eaten for quite some time in Rome, where fresh meat and spices were hard to come by. Young Marcus had killed two rabbits that day, and they provided the main course. There was also asparagus stewed in raisin wine, and a chickpea soup heavily spiced with black pepper and dill weed.

The talk was simple as well, mostly about our journey. Marcus was especially eager for details of the ambush outside the city. Tiro described the skirmish and praised Fortex, who was off eating in the kitchen. "The man saved Gordianus's life, I have no doubt."

"It's true," I said. "One of the wretches was about to pull me off my horse, when your man Fortex threw a piece of hardened dung from the roof of the shrine. He must have been, what, at least thirty feet away? Struck the bandit right between the eyes."

Young Marcus laughed and clapped his hands. Cicero shrugged. "The slave did no more than he should have. He's a bodyguard, after all. When I bought him, I was assured he had quick reflexes and ex-cellent aim. I made a wise purchase."

After the sleepless night on the barge and the long day's ride, I was exhausted. As soon as the dessert of aniseed cakes with raisins had been offered to everyone, I excused myself. A slave showed me to my room and helped me change into a sleeping tunic. I fell onto the bed and was asleep almost at once.

As happens sometimes on a journey, my sleep was easily dis-rupted. I suddenly woke, needing to pass water and having no idea what time it was. My little room was pitch-dark and I assumed I had slept for hours. But when I opened my door, hoping for a bit of stray moonlight to help me locate my chamber bowl, I saw light from an open door across the garden. I heard low voices. Someone was still up.

I found the chamber bowl and relieved myself. I went back to bed, but was no longer sleepy. After a while I got up and opened my door again. The light still shone from the room across the way. I heard quiet laughter.

I stepped out of my room, under the shadow of the colonnade. I peered across the moonlit garden. The room opposite mine was evidently Cicero's study; by the flickering light of the brazier within I could see a pigeonhole bookcase stuffed with scrolls. One voice was Cicero's, the other Tiro's. The two of them were up late talking, probably sharing a bit of midnight wine. All their lives they had been master and slave, then statesman and secretary, now spymaster and spy. No doubt they had a great deal to catch up on.

The night was still. Cicero's trained orator's voice carried like a bell on the crisp air. I distinctly heard my name. Tiro said something in response, but his voice carried less clearly and I didn't catch it. They both laughed, then were silent for a while. I imagined them sipping from their cups.

When Cicero spoke again, his tone was serious. "Do you think he knows who killed Numerius?"

I strained to hear Tiro's reply, but caught only a mumble.

"But he must know something," said Cicero. "Why else is he going all the way to Brundisium with you to see Pompey?"

"Ah, but *is* he going to Brundisium?" said Tiro. "Somewhere between here and there . . ."

"Is Caesar," said Cicero. "And with Caesar, Gordianus's son, Meto. I see your point. What *is* Gordianus up to?"

"Does it really matter?" I heard the shrug in Tiro's voice.

"I don't like surprises, Tiro. I've had far too many over the past year. Tullia's marriage to Dolabella . . . Caesar crossing the Rubicon . . . this unsavory business with Numerius Pompeius. No more nasty shocks! Especially not from Gordianus. Find out what he knows, Tiro."

"He may know nothing."

"Gordianus always knows more than he lets on. He's hiding something from you, I'm sure of it."

I heard footsteps and drew back into the shadows. A slave crossed the garden, carrying something in each hand, and went into the study.

"Good, the extra lamps!" Cicero exclaimed. "Light yours, Tiro, and I shall light mine. Every year that passes, my eyes grow weaker . . . There, now we have light enough to read. Have a look at this latest letter from Pompey. Nothing but a long rant against Domitius Ahenobarbus for losing Corfinium . . ."

The glow from the open doorway was strong enough now to dispel the concealing shadows of the colonnade. I stepped back into my room so as not to be seen by the departing slave. I lay on the bed and closed my eyes, thinking to rest for just a moment before going back to listen, and slept until noon of the following day.

I woke to the smell of roasting pork.

An hour earlier, another guest had arrived at Cicero's villa, accompanied by a sizable retinue. Cicero had ordered a pig butchered to feed the lot of them. After I splashed my face with water and dressed, I found my way to the roasting pit behind the house where a crowd of men passed a wineskin and watched the carcass as it was slowly turned on a spit. They appeared to be a ragtag bodyguard of freedmen and slaves. Their tents, pitched outside the house, were tattered and patched and their stacks of mismatched weapons and armor looked to be of poor quality.

Some of the men were playing trigon in a clearing by the vineyard. Young Marcus was among them, laughing and monopolizing the leather ball. An enthusiastic athlete and hunter was quite the opposite of what I would have expected of Cicero's son. I wondered if his father approved of his consorting with such lowly types.

I found Tiro and asked him what personage worthy of Cicero's hospitality had arrived accompanied by such a shabby retinue. Before Tiro could answer, I saw the visitor emerge from the little bathhouse connected by a covered walkway to the main building. He wore nothing but a large towel wrapped around his waist. His florid face and fleshy arms were flushed from the heat. His rust-colored beard and the wiry hair on his chest sparkled with beads of water. He disappeared into the house.

"But that can't be . . ." I began.

Tiro nodded. "Lucius Domitius Ahenobarbus."

"But I thought Caesar captured Redbeard at Corfinium."

"Captured him yes, but couldn't hold him. Or so Domitius tells it." Tiro lowered his voice. "Personally, I suspect Caesar simply let him go as a gesture of clemency. But Domitius has his own version of events. Several versions, actually. According to Cicero, in the hour since he arrived he's already told three different tales of his hairbreadth escape. I'm sure he wouldn't mind telling yet another, if you care to listen. But don't ask him about his botched suicide. He's liable to burst into tears."

I looked at Tiro sidelong, unable to tell whether he was joking.

"And whatever you do, don't mention that I'm here," he went on.

"Domitius isn't privy to the secret of your return to Italy?"

"No. We want to keep it that way, for now."

"Why don't we resume our journey, then, and get away from here? I'm rested and eager to get started."

Tiro smiled and shook his head. "Cicero may have new instructions for me, after he's spoken with Domitius. We'll leave tomorrow. Get some more rest, Gordianus. Relax while you can. The way between here and Brundisium may be hard going."

A little later, Cicero and Domitius set out on a leisurely ride around the estate, to discuss their affairs away from prying ears. Tiro seemed to vanish. Young Marcus spent the afternoon playing trigon. As for me, I passed the day pleasantly enough in my host's study. Cicero had instructed his slaves to give me access to his library, but he also must have warned them that I might snoop, for a slave was always present in the room, adding columns on a wax tablet or scrolling through a ledger, keeping an eye on me. I would have preferred to rifle through Cicero's correspondence; instead I reread the first book of the *Gallic Wars*. Cicero's copy was personally inscribed:

> *To M. Tullius Cicero,*
> Who has expressed approval of the
> author's prose if not his politics.
> *G. Julius Caesar*

That night, while Domitius's bodyguards feasted outside and sang camp songs, I was again invited to the formal dining room, where I found myself demoted from the place of honor in favor of Domitius. Tiro was not present.

We dined on the choicest cuts of the roast pig, served with a rosemary gravy. There was more asparagus, marinated in herbs and olive oil, and fried carrots tossed with cumin seeds and dressed with a fish-pickle sauce that Cicero claimed had just been unearthed after fermenting for ten years in a clay jar buried in his cellar.

Domitius's mood was as changeable as a comet. He was boisterous and talkative one moment and sullen the next. He behaved as men will who have suffered a rapid series of shocks and reversals. He had boldly broken from Pompey to make a stand at Corfinium, then been betrayed to Caesar by his own men. He had screwed up the courage to kill himself rather than face a humiliating death, then learned too late that Caesar intended mercy. He had wept in the face of certain death, then discovered that his physician had given him not poison but a narcotic to calm his nerves. He had been captured by Caesar, then just as abruptly had been released—for no matter how often or variously Domitius told the story of his "escape," the truth was evident.

"Barely escaped with my life!" Domitius said to me, pleased to have two fresh ears for the tale. "Oh, Caesar pretended that I was free to go, but he intended an ambush from the start."

"But why an ambush?" I asked.

"So that Caesar could spare himself the ugly business of executing his legal successor to the governorship of Gaul! He could claim that the perimeter guard mistook us for deserters and killed me by accident, or some such nonsense. He offered me a choice first. 'You're free to join with me, Lucius. Perhaps I could even post you to Gaul. With your family connections there, you could be of great value.' As if the decision were his to make! As if the Senate hadn't already appointed me governor! As if Gaul were his private kingdom, not the property of the Senate and people of Rome, to administer as *they* please, according to the law!"

Cicero, of course, had heard this earlier. Domitius sensed his waning attention and directed his words chiefly to me and to young Marcus, sparing hardly a glance for the women.

"I told the scoundrel no, absolutely not, that I would never serve under him at any time or in any capacity. 'Very well,' he said, in that cool, supercilious, oh-so-superior, oh-so-disappointed manner he affects. 'Run to Pompey, if you must. I'll even allow you to take bodyguards. No regular soldiers, though; I can't spare them. Choose a few from among the freedmen and slaves who've been attending your household in Corfinium. They'll have to make do with odds and ends; I need the best weapons and armor for my own men.' *My own men*—meaning the cohorts he stole from me, soldiers I recruited, trained, and equipped with my own money!

"So I found a few brave men willing to go with me. That night we barely eluded one of Caesar's scouting parties. He must have sent them after us. We hid in the brush alongside the road. They passed so close I could hear the breath in their nostrils."

"Why didn't you fight them?" asked Marcus eagerly.

"And give Caesar the satisfaction of tricking me into a battle I couldn't possibly win? No, I didn't play his game. That was always his way with enemies in the Senate. Pretend to want a settlement, negotiate the fine points until their eyes glaze over, and then—" He grabbed the carving knife from the serving platter and thrust it into the pork. "Stab them in the back!"

Cicero bit the head off a piece of asparagus and nodded in agreement. "No one has ever been more adept at political chicanery than Caesar."

Domitius lapsed into one of his moody silences. I saw his lips move, engaging in some internal debate or recrimination, and wondered what he was rehashing—the decision to stand at Corfinium, the betrayal of his men, the bungled suicide?

"But if you left Caesar to join with Pompey, why aren't you there?" asked young Marcus innocently. "You've come in the opposite direction." I saw his father wince.

"Join Pompey? Why should I do that?" said Domitius. "Without men to command, what purpose could I serve? Pompey can fend for himself."

"Does Pompey mean to make a stand at Brundisium?" asked Marcus. "Or will he sail across the Adriatic?"

Domitius managed a bitter laugh. "Every man in Italy would like to know the answer to that question, my boy. I'm afraid that the Great One is not in the habit of making his secret strategies known to my humble self. But we shall all know soon enough. Caesar moves with such speed, he'll be at Brundisium in a matter of days. Then Pompey will see what he's up against—and without me to help him! The fool should have joined me in Corfinium. That was the place to make a stand!"

Cicero shifted uneasily. "We've all been puzzled by Pompey's apparent lack of—"

"He plans to head east, of course," said Domitius suddenly. "That must be what he was planning all along. Well, let him. If he can lure Caesar into a trap in Greece or Asia, good for him. For myself, I intend to head for Gaul and carry out my duty to the Senate. Governor of Gaul they appointed me, and governor of Gaul I shall be."

"If you go by land, won't the way be blocked by troops loyal to Caesar?" asked Marcus.

"I intend to take ships, if I can find ships to hire, and sail directly to Massilia. The Massilians aren't like the rest of Gaul. Their city-state was founded by Greek colonists hundreds of years ago. They're remarkable people, not barbarians like their neighbors."

"But will they welcome you?" I asked.

"Of course they will. Their treaties are with the Senate, not with Caesar. The Massilians know Caesar! They've had to deal with him all these years, during his illegal tenure as governor. They've seen firsthand what Caesar is—a preening pretender, pompous, vain, covering himself with glory every time he managed to conquer another tribe of dimwits and toothless crones."

I cleared my throat. "I happened to be reading his memoir of the Gallic Wars today. You can't deny the man's—"

"What, his 'military genius'? Yes, I can deny it, and I do! That book is pure rubbish, nothing but nauseating self-glorification from start to finish, propaganda posing as history. He writes about himself in the third person—so insufferably pretentious—but did you ever see a book so full of vanity? No mention of the great men who came before him, who settled the southern coast of Gaul and built the roads that got him there, no bow to those in the Senate who voted against their better judgment to extend his command. You'd think he won the whole province in a dice game with Vercingetorix! I'll tell you this: any competent Roman commander, given the same resources and advantages that the Senate gave to Caesar, could have accomplished the same thing, and probably in less time."

This was too much even for Cicero. "I think, Lucius, we must give Caesar his due. In military matters, at least—"

Domitius scoffed. "Please, Marcus Tullius, you can hardly expect me to defer to *your* judgment of military matters!"

Cicero looked at him sourly. "Even so . . ."

I cleared my throat again. "Actually, you misunderstood me, Domitius. I wasn't going to say that you can't deny Caesar's military genius. I was going to say that you can't deny the man's *literary* genius."

"On the contrary, I can deny it, and I do!" said Domitius. "As a stylist he's completely inept, an amateur. His prose has no ornament, no style. It's as bald as his head! They say he dictates from horseback. Given the grunts he produces, I believe it!"

Cicero smiled. "Some find Caesar's lean prose to be elegant rather than undernourished. Our friend Gordianus can be excused for having a prejudice in the matter. Whatever virtues Caesar's writing may possess, some credit must go to the son of Gordianus."

Domitius looked at me blankly. "I don't follow you, Cicero."

"Gordianus's adopted son, Meto, is rather famous for his editorial services to Caesar. As important to Caesar, some say, as Tiro has been to me."

Comprehension dawned in Domitius's eyes. He smiled thinly. "Oh, I see, you're *that* Gordianus. Yes, I see." His smile became a leer. "But surely, Cicero, you don't mean to suggest that Tiro ever performed for you some of the services that one hears this Meto performs in private for his beloved commander?"

Terentia huffed. Young Marcus tittered. Tullia drew in a breath and looked at me sympathetically. Cicero actually blushed.

Had *everyone* in Rome heard and given credence to these rumors
about Caesar and my son? While I ground my teeth and considered
how best to answer Domitius, he moved to another subject.

"Very well, purely for the sake of argument, I'll concede that Caesar is the military genius his own prose makes him out to be, helped
along by his starry-eyed amanuensis. In that case, whatever shall become of our Pompey? Do you know, I almost hope that Caesar *does*
trap Pompey in Brundisium. Let him strip the Great One of his legions and give him the same slave's choice he gave to me. Pompey
would have to commit suicide. After all his blunders, there could be
no other honorable course. Then where would we be?" Domitius
laced his fingers beneath his chin and stroked his red beard. "The
Senate will need another champion—a savior from the West, not the
East. The right man could summon Pompey's troops from Spain and
rally the Gauls against their would-be king. Massilia would be the
ideal place to carry out such a plan, don't you think? Yes, rally Spain
and Gaul, then march directly into Italy—a second crossing of the
Rubicon, a second invasion of armed men, not to destroy the constitution and the Senate but to restore them. Given proper resources,
the right man could put that scoundrel Caesar on the run!" Domitius
fell to ruminating and peered into the middle distance.

"In the meantime, what shall I do about my triumph?" said Cicero. "Now *there's* a dilemma."

"Your triumph?" I said, puzzled by the sudden change of subject.

"Yes, the triumphal procession due to me for my successful military campaigns in Cilicia. In the normal course of things, I should
have been voted a triumph by the Senate directly upon my return. I
should have entered the city gates in a chariot with blaring trum-
pets! What's the point of being a provincial governor if there's no triumph at the end of it? But of course, this hasn't been a normal year.
I decided to forgo my triumph, in light of the crisis. But now . . .
well, I must celebrate it sooner or later. I can't postpone it forever.
But what if Caesar drives Pompey from Italy and then occupies
Rome? If I celebrate my triumph while Caesar is in command of the
city, it may be read as an endorsement of his tyranny. I suppose I

shouldn't return to Rome at all, not while Caesar's there. I should make a point of refusing to take my seat in the Senate . . ."

Cicero paused for a sip of wine. Terentia spoke up. "It was bad enough that you postponed your triumph, which may never happen now. But what about your son's toga day? Marcus turns sixteen this year. All the best families mark their sons' coming of age during the feast of Liberalia, just after the Ides of March. Will we be back in Rome by then to celebrate Marcus's majority, or not?"

From the way the children cringed, I sensed this was an ongoing family argument. Cicero released a heavy breath. "You know that would be impossible, Terentia. The Liberalia is only twelve days off. Why must you bring this up? You know how fervently I hoped for Marcus to celebrate the donning of his manly toga in Rome, with all the best people in attendance. But it cannot be. For one thing, the best people are scattered to the four corners of the earth. For another, I can't return to Rome with honor, not yet. And wherever we celebrate his toga day, arrangements can't possibly be made in time for the Liberalia."

"But the Liberalia is the proper day," insisted Terentia. "On the feast of Father Freedom, the priests carry the phallus of Dionysus from the fields into the city streets, and the young men in their manly togas follow behind, singing bawdy songs. It's a religious act, the symbol of a boy's emergence to manhood in the company of his peers."

"It's all right, Mother, really," said Marcus, turning red and frowning at his plate. "We've discussed this before. It doesn't have to be the Liberalia. Another day will do. And we can do it in Arpinum instead of Rome. It *is* the family's hometown."

"Hometown to your *father's* family, Marcus," said Terentia, with frost in her voice. "We can hardly expect your relatives on the Terentius side to trek all the way to Arpinum, with brigands and runaway soldiers stalking the highways. Besides, the villa at Arpinum is in no condition to receive visitors. The roof leaks, the kitchen's too small, and there aren't enough beds. At least here in Formiae I've managed to get the household up and running."

"Surely you're not suggesting that we celebrate his toga day here?" protested Cicero. "We've no family in the area. I scarcely know the members of the local town senate. No, if not Rome, then Arpinum."

"I don't see why we can't just go back to Rome tomorrow." Tullia sighed and looked to her mother for support. "Everyone else is. Your cousin Gaius returned, and my friend Aufelia and her husband are on their way back. Father's friend Atticus never left."

As the table talk degenerated into a family squabble, I waited for a pause in the conversation to excuse myself. Domitius, I noticed, paid no attention. He held an asparagus spear between his thumb and forefinger and seemed to be interrogating it. How pathetic the man seemed, with his delusions of military glory and his obsessive jealousy of Caesar. Yet he seemed to me no more pathetic than Cicero, the great orator reduced to agonizing over his postponed triumph and his son's toga day. How irrelevant, even ridiculous, they both seemed.

But as I lay in bed that night, kept awake by a disagreement between the fish-pickle sauce and my stomach, I wondered uneasily if I was not as deluded in my own way as Cicero and Domitius. What was the exact relationship between Julius Caesar and my son? Once, I had thought I understood it, but it appeared there might be a complicating factor which I had not accounted for. In such parlous times, I could not afford such a miscalculation. As we continued the journey, and grew closer to the camps of Caesar and Pompey, I could afford it even less.

Sleep finally came, and with it, nightmare. There was no narrative, only a series of wrenching horrors. I had misunderstood something and made a terrible mistake. Someone was dead. I was covered with blood. Bethesda and Diana wore shrouds and wept. The ground shook and the sky rained fire.

I woke drenched with sweat, and swore never to touch fish-pickle sauce again.

XIV

We set out before dawn. I was tired from lack of sleep and my stomach was out of sorts, but Tiro was in high spirits.

"I take it *you* didn't have the fish-pickle sauce last night," I said.

"Did Cicero break open a new jar? He must have been trying to impress Domitius. No, I ate simple fare. Nothing but millet porridge and roast pork off the spit."

"You ate outside with Domitius's men?"

"Of course. How else could I have gathered information from them? I posed as a freedman attached to the villa."

"You spied on Domitius? I thought he was Cicero's ally."

"I didn't spy on him. I simply talked to his men. They had a lot to say about the morale of Domitius's former troops, the size of Caesar's forces, the condition of the roads, and so on."

"What about the ambush Caesar supposedly set for Domitius after letting him go?"

Tiro smiled. "According to the men, there *was* an incident. A mail carrier passed them on the road just outside Corfinium."

"A mail carrier?"

"Yes, a lone man on horseback. Domitius panicked. He made his men hide in the bushes. They thought he might die of a heart attack. The ambush was entirely in his imagination!"

"Rather like the welcome that's waiting for him in Massilia, I suspect."

A sphinxlike expression crossed Tiro's face. "I wouldn't be too surprised if the Massilians welcome him with open arms. Open hands, anyway."

"What do you mean?"

Tiro slowed his mount and let Fortex ride ahead. "I appreciate your discretion last night, Gordianus. You said nothing to Domitius about me, even when my name was mentioned."

"I only did as you asked."

"And I thank you. I would appreciate it if you could be just as discreet about Domitius's visit to Cicero."

"Cicero wants it kept secret? Why?"

"He has his reasons."

I snorted. "Cicero won't join Pompey, he doesn't want it known that he's hosted Domitius—is he so fearful of offending Caesar?"

Tiro grimaced. "It's not that. All right, I'll tell you. Domitius didn't leave Corfinium empty-handed."

"He was stripped of his legions."

"Yes, but not of his gold. When Domitius arrived in Corfinium, he deposited six million sesterces in the city treasury. Most of it was public money he brought from Rome, for military expenses. Caesar could have seized it for himself, but I suppose he doesn't want to be seen as a thief. He returned the entire amount to Domitius when he set him free."

I sucked in a breath. "You mean Domitius and that ragtag retinue are transporting six million sesterces?"

"In trunks, loaded in wagons. You see now why he was so suspicious of Caesar and so fearful on the road."

"What will he do with all that money? Return it to the treasury in Rome?"

Tiro laughed. "He'll use it to go to Massilia and win over the Massilians, of course. But you see why Cicero doesn't want his visit made public. If the money vanishes—and who knows what might happen in the coming days?—and the trail leads back to Formiae, someone might presume that Domitius left it here with Cicero, for safekeeping. These are desperate times. That kind of rumor could draw cutthroats like grasshoppers to the green leaf. Whole households have been slaughtered for considerably less than six million sesterces, Gordianus. Cicero isn't ashamed of playing host to Domitius, and he isn't fearful for himself. But he has his family to think of. Surely you can understand that."

That day we rode forty-four miles and reached Capua. The next day we covered thirty-three miles and stopped at Beneventum. At various stables along the way Tiro exchanged our horses, always producing his courier's passport signed by Pompey. Some stablers honored it without question. Others treated us with barely concealed contempt and tried to give us inferior mounts. One stabler refused to deal with us at all. He took a long look at the document, gave us a cold stare, and told us to move on. Tiro was furious. "Do you realize the penalty for flouting a document issued under the Senate's Ultimate Decree?" he asked the man. "The penalty is death!" The stabler swallowed hard but said nothing. We went in search of another stable.

After a good night's sleep in Beneventum, Tiro decided that we should leave the Appian Way and strike out on an old mountain road that cut directly west to east across the Apennines. "A shortcut," Tiro called it. He insisted that we exchange our horses for a wagon and a slave to drive it. The stabler in Beneventum wrinkled his nose when he saw Pompey's seal on the document. He tried to resist the trade, but Tiro was in no mood to haggle. At last the man gave us a wagon with a canvas top and a toothless slave to drive it.

The wagon seemed unnecessary to me. Saddlebags were adequate for our provisions, and our progress on steep, winding roads would be faster on horseback. As we set out that morning, I said as much to

Tiro. He shook his head and pointed toward the dull gray clouds that wreathed the mountaintops. Later that day, his judgment was confirmed. A few miles into the foothills, the sky opened and poured rain, then sleet, then hail. While we sat in the covered wagon, bundled in dry blankets, the miserable driver shivered and sneezed and urged the horses on.

The storm grew worse, until at last we had to stop at a little inn beside the road. We spent the night there—and the next three fretful days as well, as the storm continued to howl and bluster. Recriminations were pointless, but I still felt obliged to suggest to Tiro that we would have done better to stay on the Appian Way. He said the same storm would likely have trapped us no matter what route we took, and we were lucky to have found a snug place to pass the time. To combat the tedium, the innkeeper had a small library of well-worn scrolls (trashy Greek novels and dubious erotic poetry) as well as a supply of board games. After three days, I decided I could die happy if I never read another story of shipwrecked lovers. I envied Fortex and the wagon driver, who both seemed content to sleep day and night in the stable, like hibernating bears.

Occasionally, over a game of Circus Maximus or Pharaohs Down the Nile, I sensed that Tiro was trying to draw me out, following Cicero's instructions to discover my intentions and any secrets I might know about the death of Numerius Pompeius. As subtly as I could, I always deflected him and changed the subject.

At last, the storm passed. A full day of travel brought us to the eastern slopes of the mountains. We slept that night at an inn nestled amid rocky bluffs and pine forests. The following morning, watching the sunrise from the window of our room on the upper floor, I glimpsed a smudge of silver and blue in the distance that Tiro declared to be the Adriatic. It was our eleventh day out of Rome.

The sky was cloudless. We set out with the wagon uncovered. After an hour or so, descending through a narrow mountain pass, we encountered the soldiers.

We heard them first. The low booming of marching drums echoed up through the folds of the mountain. Tiro told the wagon driver to stop. I listened closely. Along with the drums I heard the stamp of feet and a muffled clatter of armor. Tiro and I left the driver and Fortex in the wagon. We climbed to the top of a rocky knob and gazed down.

Thousands of men were marching up from the coastal plain. Their helmets in the morning sunlight merged into a glittering ribbon that snaked sinuously up the mountainside, over crests, through saddles, around bends, filling the width of the road as water fills a river channel.

"Caesar's men, or Pompey's?" I said.

Tiro squinted. "I'm not sure. I know the insignia of every cohort and legion, but they're not close enough for me to tell."

"They soon will be, at the speed they're marching. There must be thousands of them! The column goes on for miles. I can't see the end of it." I looked back at the wagon. "I suppose we'll have to pull off the road as best we can and wait for the whole army to pass. That could take all day."

Tiro fretfully shook his head. "What does it mean? They don't have the look of a defeated army, that's for sure. Too disciplined. Too many of them! If they're Pompey's men, they can't have reached the mountains without encountering Caesar. That can only mean that Caesar's been defeated. Pompey's crushed him, and now Pompey and the senators who fled are heading back to Rome. The crisis is over—*if* this is Pompey . . ."

I nodded, wondering what that would mean to Davus, to Meto. The tramping and clattering grew louder moment by moment, booming and bouncing across the rarefied mountain air until it seemed to emanate from the empty sky like constant thunder.

"And if they're Caesar's men?" I asked.

Tiro shook his head. "I don't know. Maybe Pompey escaped from Brundisium before Caesar could reach him, and now Caesar has turned back, empty-handed. Or did Caesar trap him there, annihilate his forces, and then turn back toward Rome? But there *can't* have been time enough for a siege. It makes no sense. These *must* be Pompey's men . . ."

He sucked in a breath. "Numa's balls!" Tiro cursed so rarely that I stared at him in wonder. His face was ashen. "Of course! Not Pompey's men, and not Caesar's either!"

"Tiro, you're making no sense."

"There, do you see those advance scouts riding ahead of the rest? See the band of polished copper around their helmets?"

I squinted. "I can't quite—"

"I'm sure of it: a copper band. And the officers will have copper disks on their breastplates, showing a lion's head. Domitius owns copper mines. These are his cohorts, the men who betrayed him in Corfinium."

"Coming after Domitius to claim lost pay?" I suggested.

Tiro was not amused. "Perhaps they've turned against Caesar. But no, surely they'd be marching to join Pompey, if that were the case." He looked frantically back at the wagon, where the driver and Fortex stared up at us, perplexed. "Infernal Pluto! There's no way we can hide the wagon—the road's hemmed by boulders and trees, and we haven't passed a branch road for miles." He shook his head. "I should have traded the driver and wagon for horses this morning. On horseback, we might have had some chance to hide ourselves."

"Does it matter? We could simply be innocent travelers crossing the mountains."

"On this road, Gordianus, there are no innocent travelers."

He seemed close to panic. I tried to calm him. "We'll hide among the rocks, Tiro. The driver can stay with the wagon and tell them he's traveling alone."

"The driver would tell them everything at the first rattle of a sword."

"Take the driver with us, then."

"And leave an abandoned wagon by the side of the road? That

would be even more suspicious. They'd be sure to search for us then, and they'd find us in minutes. How would that look—four men with something to hide, skulking in the woods?"

"You're right. We have no choice but to stay with the wagon. When the advance scouts arrive, we'll wave and smile and remark on what fine weather we're having."

Tiro took a deep breath. "You're right. We must simply brazen it out. You'll be the master and I'll be your slave. Why shouldn't you be heading for Caesar's camp? You have a son under his command."

"Yes, that's the story, all the better because it's partly true. First, I suggest we leave this hilltop. Peering down at them like this—it makes us look like spies, don't you think?"

He managed a crooked smile. "Start back without me. I need to relieve myself."

"Go ahead. Don't be shy."

He winced. "No, Gordianus, it's not my bladder. A fright like this—it goes straight to my bowels."

Tiro hurried into the woods. I cast a final look at the endless stream of men pouring up the mountain, then scrambled down the hillside and rejoined the others.

Tiro arrived at the wagon just before the first scout on horseback came through the pass. The soldier rode slowly toward us, warily scanning the trees and boulders behind us. He stopped several paces away.

He noted the iron ring on my finger. "Who are you, citizen? What business do you have on this road?"

"My name is Gordianus. I'm traveling from Rome. Are you one of Caesar's men?"

"I'll ask the questions, citizen. Who are these others?"

"The driver comes with the wagon. I hired both from his master, at an inn on the other side of the mountains. We weathered a nasty storm, let me tell you. May the gods grant you fairer skies than we had."

"And these others?"

"Slaves. That one's a bodyguard, as you can tell by the look of him. A good thing I brought him along. We weren't a mile out of Rome when some bandits attacked us; would have killed us if they had the chance, I'm sure. But we haven't had a bit of trouble since."

"And the dark one?"

"Another slave. A philosopher. His name is Soscarides."

The scout looked at us disdainfully. He was the sort who had little use for civilians. "You still haven't stated your purpose for being on this road."

I looked at the copper band around his helmet and cleared my throat. He and his fellows had once been loyal to Domitius. Now he had sworn allegiance to Caesar—or so we presumed. What if we were wrong? What if Domitius's troops had turned on their new master? Caesar might be dead, for all we knew, and these troops might be marching back to Rome with his head on a stake. But I had to give the man an answer. I thought of the gamblers in the Salacious Tavern back in Rome, casting dice and crying "Caesar!" for luck, and I took a deep breath.

"I have a son in Caesar's service, on his personal staff. Soscarides here was the boy's tutor when he was young. Call me soft, but I can't stand the worry any longer—can't stand waiting idly in Rome for news. So here I am."

"You're looking for Caesar, then?"

"Yes."

The man looked at me sternly for a long moment, then came to a decision. He smiled." Just keep following the road then, citizen. You'll find him." His tone changed as completely as his face, like an actor putting aside a mask.

"At Brundisium? That's the rumor along the road."

He smiled but didn't answer. He was ready to be friendly, but not that friendly.

A second scout rode up. The two of them withdrew to the far side of the road and conferred, casting glances at us. The second scout rode on. The first returned. "You might as well get comfortable, if you can. You'll be here for a bit. Some troops will be marching past."

"Are there many?"

He laughed. "You'll see. I'll stay here with you until the head of the column arrives. No need for you to answer the same questions for my commander. He'll decide whether or not to cut your heads off." He grinned to let me know it was a joke.

I glanced at Fortex, who snorted to show that he wasn't impressed. Tiro looked calm—philosophical, even. The driver looked nervous.

The column came up through the pass. We saw horsehair-crested helmets first, then the officers who wore them, mounted atop magnificent chargers. They were followed by drummers. The steady tattoo of the marching beat reverberated between the steep hillsides. The officer wearing the helmet with the most elaborate crest signaled to the others to proceed while he broke from the column and cantered over to the wagon. A lion's head roared from the copper disk on his breastplate.

"Report!" he said to the scout, who saluted him crisply.

"A traveler from Rome and three slaves, cohort commander. The man's name is Gordianus."

The officer looked at me keenly. "Gordianus? Why does that sound familiar?"

"He says he has a son on Caesar's personal staff."

"Of course! Gordianus Meto, the freedman. I met him in Corfinium. So you're Meto's father, are you? You don't look a thing like him. But of course you wouldn't, would you? I'm Marcus Otacilius, cohort commander. What in Hades are you doing here?"

"I'm eager to see my son. Is he well?"

"Well enough when I last saw him."

"He's not with you, then? Is this not Caesar's army?"

"This is Caesar's army, yes. Every man you see has sworn allegiance to Gaius Julius Caesar. While Caesar tends to business down on the coast, he's dispatched these cohorts to Sicily, to secure his interests there."

It was exactly the sort of strategic decision that Caesar would make: not to immediately test the loyalty of troops acquired from a hostile general by throwing them into the chase after Pompey, but to post them elsewhere.

"My son is with Caesar, then? Where are they?"

Otacilius hesitated, then nodded to the scout. "Ride on. I'll handle this."

The scout saluted and galloped toward the head of the column. Soldiers poured through the pass in endless rows and proceeded up the mountain, winter cloaks thrown behind them like capes, scale armor glinting across their chests.

The officer smiled. "I don't suppose there's any harm telling you what Caesar's up to. He's already—"

The driver suddenly jumped from the wagon, spun about, and pointed at us. "They're lying!"

Otacilius's horse cantered skittishly, startled by the sudden movement. Even before he gave a signal with his hand, two rows of men broke from the passing column. In the space of a heartbeat, the wagon was circled by a ring of spears.

Otacilius regained control of his mount. He looked from me to the toothless driver. "What is this about?"

"They're lying!" The driver pointed at Tiro. "That one's up to something. My master back in Beneventum told me to keep an eye on him. He carries some sort of document with the seal of Pompey the Great."

The officer looked at me coolly. "Is this true?"

I felt hackles rise on the back of my neck. I opened my mouth, wondering how to answer.

Tiro spoke up. "Master, may I speak for myself?"

"Please do, Soscarides."

He addressed the officer. "That worthless driver is the liar! He and I have been quarreling ever since my master hired him from the stabler in Beneventum. He's got a grudge against me—thinks I have it too easy because I stayed dry while he was wet and miserable driving through the mountains. I think the cold must have settled in his brain. Give him a few lashes and see if he sticks to his tale!"

The driver's mouth formed a toothless circle of outrage. "No, no! They're all Pompey's men, I tell you. My master said so. He didn't like giving them the wagon, but he had to, on account of that document the lying one carries. Search him if you don't believe me!"

The officer looked genuinely distressed. He and I shared a bond of friendship, through Meto—but only if I was telling the truth about being Meto's father. "What do you have to say about this document . . . Gordianus?"

I looked at Tiro. "By Hercules, Soscarides, what is the slave talking about?"

Tiro looked back at me calmly. "I have no idea, Master. Let the officer search me, if it pleases him."

"I shall have to search you all, I'm afraid."

Otacilius confiscated our weapons first. Tiro and I each carried a dagger, and Fortex carried two. We were forbidden to leave the wagon while the soldiers sorted through our saddlebags. They found nothing of interest. Then we were made to stand in the wagon and strip off our garments, layer by layer.

"Our loincloths as well?" I asked, trying to play the outraged citizen.

"I'm afraid so," said Otacilius, wincing. He turned his head and caught some of the troops sniggering as they passed by. "Eyes straight ahead!" he barked.

I stood naked and held up my empty palms. "As you can see, cohort commander, I have nothing to hide. Nor do the two slaves."

Otacilius looked appropriately chagrined. "Return their clothing. What do you say to this?" he barked at the driver, who quailed in speechless confusion.

I felt better with my loincloth covering me. I pulled my tunic over my head. "I only hope, cohort commander, as compensation for this embarrassment, that you'll lend me adequate men . . . and appropriate utensils . . . to see that the lying driver is appropriately punished."

"No!" the man wailed. "Return me to my master in Beneventum! Only he has the right to punish me."

"Nonsense!" I said sternly. "You were let to me along with the wagon. While you're in my service, I have every right to chastise you."

"Actually, for deceiving an officer of the Roman army in time of military crisis, this slave is liable to be executed by military law, and his master fined, at the very least," said Otacilius coldly. I felt a stab of pity for the cringing driver, who was now the one ringed by soldiers with spears. If only he had kept his mouth shut!

"No, wait!" He lunged desperately toward Otacilius. One of the soldiers gave him a vicious poke with his spear. A blossom of blood stained his shoulder. He clutched the wound and wailed. "Up on that knob! The two of them climbed up there before the troops arrived, spying on you!"

"There's no crime in curiosity," said Otacilius.

"But don't you see? That's when they must have hidden the document, or destroyed it. They saw you coming, and they got rid of it. Go look up on that hill! You'll find it there!"

Tiro rolled his eyes in disgust. "The lying slave will have you searching every stretch of road from here back to Beneventum, if you listen to him. Stupid lout! Perhaps if you stop lying and tell the truth, the cohort commander will at least allow you a quick and merciful death."

Otacilius worked his jaw back and forth and stared at me. I played the affronted citizen and stared back at him. I realized that he had not given back our daggers. That meant he had not made up his mind about us.

At last he called another row of troops from the column. "You men, go search that hilltop. Bring back anything you find that a traveler might have left there—any sort of bag or pouch, and any scrap of parchment, no matter how small or burnt."

Surely they would find nothing, I thought. Tiro had been with me atop the knob. He hadn't mentioned the courier's passport, and I hadn't seen him hide it. The only sign of a human that the soldiers were likely to come across, I thought ruefully, was the deposit left by Tiro when he stole away to relieve himself . . .

I suddenly realized that Tiro had not lingered behind on account of his nervous bowels. He had gone off to dispose of the document.

Parchment burns easily. Parchment could also be torn, ground underfoot, chewed, even swallowed. But had Tiro destroyed it beyond trace, or merely hidden it, thinking to retrieve it after Caesar's troops passed by? I avoided looking at him, fearful that my expression might give me away. Instead I watched the soldiers scramble up the hillside. At last I could stand it no longer. I glanced in Tiro's direction. In the instant our eyes met, I knew as surely as if he had spoken that he had not obliterated the document, but had only hidden it. My heart sank. I drew a deep breath.

Perhaps, I thought, the soldiers would be content to search the bare hilltop. But I knew it was a vain hope; these men were trained to follow tracks, watch for signs of passage, ferret out hiding places. Their commander had ordered them to search and retrieve. That was what they would do.

Tiro, Fortex, and I stood in the wagon and waited. The driver clutched his wounded shoulder and sobbed. Row after row of soldiers marched past. I felt the suspense one feels in the theater, awaiting a reversal of fortune.

At last the soldiers came scrambling down the hillside. They had found not one artifact, but several. What Roman road is without litter? There was part of a cast-off shoe, chewed on by some animal with pointed teeth. There was a bit of ivory which appeared to be a broken strigil, used for scraping oneself clean at the baths. There was a tattered scrap of cloth which might once have been a child's soiled, discarded loincloth. The most valuable find was an old Greek drachma, the silver tarnished black.

"We also found this, cohort commander. It was rolled up tight and stuffed between some rocks on the far side of the hill." The soldier handed a piece of parchment to Otacilius, who unrolled it. His face grew long.

"A courier's passport," he said quietly. "Issued by authority of the Ultimate Decree. Signed by Pompey himself. Stamped with his seal ring." Otacilius peered at me above the parchment. "How do you explain this, Gordianus? If, in fact, you *are* Gordianus . . ."

XV

Row after row of soldiers marched past. Face after face peered sidelong at us, some scornful, some merely curious. A few even looked at us with pity. We must have made a sorry sight: four men with arms bound behind their backs, tethered to one another by their ankles, being led down the mountain in single file along the side of the road by a cohort commander on horseback. A foot soldier followed behind, using his spear for a prod.

The wagon driver was hindmost in the group. The wound at his shoulder had rendered him faint and weak. He had a hard time keeping up. The footpath alongside the paved road was rough and uneven. Occasionally he stumbled, sending a jerk through the tether that connected our ankles, making Fortex trip forward into Tiro, who tripped forward into me. The foot soldier would prod at the stumbling slave with his spear; the slave would let out a yelp. The soldiers marching past would laugh, as if we were performing a roadside mime show for their amusement.

Otacilius peered at me over his shoulder occasionally, his face inscrutable. Another tether connected the two of us, one end tied around my throat, the other wound around his forearm and clutched in his fist. Despite my best efforts to keep up and maintain some slack in the tether, my neck was soon wrenched and sore, the flesh chafed and raw. I was lucky to still have a head connected to my shoulders.

We might have died within moments after Otacilius discovered our lies. We were an unexpected anomaly encountered on the road, a hindrance to the army's progress, a problem to be disposed of. He might have had us all executed where we stood. As soon as the passport from Pompey was produced, I braced myself for that possibility. To avoid the horror of it I let a great tide of recriminations flood my thoughts. If only Tiro had had the sense to destroy the passport, rather than hide it. If only we had stayed on the Appian Way instead of taking Tiro's "shortcut." If only we had dragged the driver into the woods and cut out his tongue before the first scout arrived. If only we had left the wagon behind that morning, and the driver with it . . .

The list of regrets circled endlessly in my mind as we trudged downhill, the monotony interrupted only by the occasional stumble by the driver, followed by more stumbling up the line and a jerk at the tether around my throat, then the squeal of the driver as he was poked, and the laughter of the soldiers passing by.

"Who are those wretches?" said one soldier.

"Spies!" said another.

"What will they do to them?"

"Hang them upside down and flay them alive!"

That elicited a squeal of terror from the wagon driver, who stumbled again. The humiliating sequence repeated itself. The passing soldiers howled with laughter. Not even the most stumblebum troupe of Alexandrian mimes could have put on a funnier show.

What *did* Otacilius intend to do with us? The fact that he hadn't yet killed us offered some hope. Or did it? He assumed we were spies. Spies knew secrets. Secrets might be valuable. Therefore we might be valuable. But I suspected that the Roman military in regard to spies, like the Roman judiciary in regard to slaves, recognized only one credible means of obtaining secrets: through torture.

We had been spared our lives, but toward what end? We were being led down the mountain, toward the rear of the army, but for what purpose? I found it easier to scroll mentally through endless recriminations and regrets than to contemplate those questions.

"Gordianus," Tiro whispered behind me. "When we arrive, wherever they're taking us—"

"Silence!" Otacilius looked over his shoulder and glared down at us. A crueler man might have given a wrench to the tether around my throat for good measure, but I saw that his gaze was clouded by doubt. If I was the man I claimed to be, then I was the father of a personal confidant of Caesar, a man Otacilius knew. On the other hand, I had lied about the courier's passport, which linked us directly to Pompey, and if the wagon driver was truthful, Tiro was not my slave Soscarides, but the actual leader of our little traveling party. Had I lied about being Meto's father, as well? Otacilius faced a dilemma. His soldier's instinct was to pass the dilemma along to someone higher up.

It occurred to me that I might possibly escape with my neck intact if I kept doggedly proclaiming my identity—but only if I betrayed Tiro. How else to explain the passport? Once he was known to be Tiro, higher ranking officers could probably be called forward to identify him, despite his disguised appearance; as Cicero's secretary, Tiro was well known in the Forum. What would be done to him? Would he be released, as Domitius had been released, and sent back to Cicero unharmed?

I doubted it. Tiro was not Domitius. He was a citizen and a member of a senator's household, but only by dint of having been manumitted by Cicero. What would be done to a former slave traveling incognito as a spy, who had brazenly lied to a Roman officer? I couldn't believe that he would simply be set free.

This vexing train of doubts and apprehensions served at least to keep my mind off the more and more frequent stumbling from behind, the tug of the tether at my neck, and the raucous laughter of the marching soldiers. I was weary and thirsty. My head buzzed as if there were a swarm of bees inside it.

Down and down we trudged, until at last we arrived at a broad, high meadow that overlooked the coastal plain and the glimmering Adriatic in the distance. The meadow appeared to be the site of the previous night's camp. A single large tent was still standing. We passed the staging area where the last cohort was assembling in ranks to begin the march up the mountain.

In my dazed state, I wondered how many soldiers I had seen in the last few hours. If the army consisted of Domitius's entire force from Corfinium, they amounted to thirty cohorts in all, with six hundred men in each cohort, and I had passed every one of them. Now I knew what a body of eighteen thousand armed men looked like. How many men did Caesar have in Italy, that he could spare so many troops for Sicily?

Otacilius led us toward the tent, where a team of camp-strikers had begun to pull up stakes. A young officer in splendid armor stepped out, carrying under his arm a helmet with an elegant horse-hair crest. There was no copper disk with a lion's head on his breast-plate. He was not one of Domitius's men, yet Otacilius was quick to jump from his horse and salute him as a superior.

"Numa's balls!" I heard Tiro mutter behind me.

I peered at the officer more closely. It must have been fear and fatigue that kept me from recognizing him at once, for there was no mistaking his curiously brutish yet babyish face. His profile was the brute: seen from the side, his dented nose, jutting chin and craggy brows made him look like an angry boxer. Seen straight on, his full cheeks, gentle mouth, and soulful eyes made him look like a homely poet. At every angle between, his face was a mixture of contradictions. It was a face women found fascinating, and men trusted or feared instinctively.

Otacilius conferred with him in a low voice. I heard my name spoken. The man looked toward me. His eyebrows registered surprise, then shock. He shoved Otacilius roughly aside and strode toward us, casting aside his helmet and drawing his short sword from its scabbard. He grabbed my shoulder and put the blade to my neck. I sucked in a breath and closed my eyes.

An instant later, his bearish arms were around me, crushing me to his barrel chest. The tether that had been around my throat lay on the ground, cut in two.

"Gordianus!" he bellowed, pulling back to give me the full effect of his homely features at close quarters.

"Marc Antony," I whispered, and fainted to the ground.

~

I heard voices, and gradually realized that I was in an enclosed space—not a room exactly, but a shelter of some sort, full of soft light.

"A citizen his age, led by his neck on a forced march!"

"The prisoners had to be bound, Tribune. Standard procedure for suspected insurgents and spies."

"It's a wonder you didn't kill him! That wouldn't mark an auspicious beginning for you in Caesar's army, cohort commander—killing Gordianus Meto's father."

"I only followed regulations, Tribune."

I realized I was in a large tent, and remembered the tent in the meadow from which Antony had emerged. I lay on a hard pallet with a thin blanket over me.

"He's waking up."

"A good thing for you! You're dismissed, Marcus Otacilius. Go back and rejoin your cohort."

"But—"

"The sight of you is likely to send him straight to Hades! You've made your report. Get out."

There was a rustling noise, a flicker of light from a parted tent flap, and then the face of Marc Antony abruptly loomed over me. "Gordianus, are you all right?"

"Thirsty. Hungry. My feet hurt."

Antony laughed. "You sound like any soldier at the end of a hard march."

I managed to sit up. My head whirled. "I fainted?"

"It happens. A forced march, no food or water—and from the marks on your neck, it looks like that fool Otacilius half-strangled you."

I felt my throat. The flesh was tender and bruised, but not bleeding. "For a moment, up at the pass, I thought he was going to execute me."

"He's not *that* big a fool. We'll talk about it later, after you've had something to eat and drink. Don't get up. Sit on the cot. I'll have something brought to you. But eat quickly. The tent needs to come down. I intend to set out within the hour."

"What about me?"

"You'll come with me, of course."

I groaned. "Not back up the mountain!"

"No. To Brundisium. Caesar needs me, to close in for the kill."

Antony's company consisted of a hundred mounted soldiers. He had been dispatched by Caesar to escort the troops bound for Sicily as far as the foot of the Apennines, then to rejoin the main force. His contingent was kept small so that he could move swiftly. Every man was a battle-hardened veteran of the Gallic Wars. Antony boasted that his hand-picked century was the equal of any two cohorts.

He invited me to ride alongside him at the head of the company. The slaves were allowed to ride in the baggage wagon. Fortex he presumed to be my personal bodyguard. Tiro he failed to recognize, even at close quarters. This surprised me, because there was no man in Rome whom Antony hated more than Cicero, and I feared that he might recognize Cicero's secretary even disguised, but Antony accepted the explanation that Tiro was Meto's old tutor Soscarides with hardly a glance. 'Antony isn't simple,' Meto had once told me, 'but he's as clear and plain to read as Caesar's Latin.' Apparently he expected others to be equally transparent.

As for the wagon driver, the poor slave had arrived at the meadow exhausted and feverish from his shoulder wound, too delirious to answer questions or to speak for himself. He was loaded into the baggage wagon along with Tiro and Fortex. I found it convenient to pretend that his delirium preceded our encounter with Otacilius. "The wretched slave caught a fever coming over the mountains," I told Antony as we rode out. "I think he must have been out of his wits from the moment he woke up this morning. All that nonsense he told the cohort commander—he was raving."

"Still, he was right about that courier's passport, wasn't he?" Antony looked ahead, showing me his fierce boxer's profile.

"Ah. Yes. That's a bit embarrassing. I told my man Soscarides to hide it until the troops passed. Foolish of me, perhaps, but I thought I might save myself some trouble. Instead, I was caught lying. I can't blame the cohort commander for being suspicious of me after that."

"But Gordianus, how in Hades did you ever get your hands on such a document? Signed by Pompey himself!"

I decided to evade, rather than lie. "I don't know how else I could have obtained fresh horses at every stop along the way. I was able to take advantage of it . . . thanks to Cicero." That was not a lie, exactly. "I stayed at his villa at Formiae for a couple of nights."

"That piece of cow dung!" Antony turned to face me. His features straight on had grown as fearsome as his profile. "Do you know what I'd most like to see come out of all this? Cicero's head on a stake! Ever since the bastard murdered my stepfather, putting down Catilina's so-called conspiracy, he's made a career of slandering me. I don't know how a fine fellow like yourself can stay friends with such a creature."

"Cicero and I aren't exactly friends, Tribune . . ."

"You needn't explain. Caesar is the same. Every time the subject of Cicero comes up, we argue. He tells me to stop ranting. I ask why he coddles such a scorpion. 'Useful,' he says, as if that won the argument. 'Some day, Cicero may prove useful.'" Antony laughed. "Well, he proved useful to you, I suppose, if he gave you that courier's passport from Pompey! But it landed you in trouble in the end, didn't it? You rode up one side of Italy, but you had to walk down the other! You're lucky Marcus Otacilius brought you straight to me, or you might very well have lost your head. But you've always been lucky, to live as long as you have. Imagine, the father of Gordianus Meto suspected of spying for Pompey! The world has become a strange place."

"Perhaps stranger than you think," I said under my breath.

"Well, we shall sort everything out when we reach Brundisium." He seemed relieved to be done with the subject, but his words left me unsettled. What remained to be sorted out, if Antony had accepted my story?

There was the problem of the wagon driver, of course. What would happen when his delirium receded? And what if Tiro were recognized? How could I explain my complicity in his masquerade as Soscarides? Betraying Tiro now was out of the question. He could not possibly fall into worse hands. I could all too easily imagine Antony taking out his hatred of Cicero against Cicero's right-hand man.

"You look pensive, Gordianus." Antony reached over and squeezed my leg. "Don't worry, you shall see Meto soon enough! After tonight, we'll have three days of hard riding to reach Brundisium. If your luck holds, we should arrive just in time to witness Pompey's last stand!"

⁓

We camped that night half a mile off the road, in a shallow valley amid low hills. Antony pointed out the site's defensibility.

"Is there really any danger of attack, Tribune?" I asked. "The mountains are to our right, the sea to our left. Behind us is Corfinium, securely garrisoned by Caesar's men. Before us is Brundisium, which I presume to be surrounded by Caesar's main force. I should think we're as safe as a spider on a roof."

"Of course we are. It's all my years in Gaul. I can never pitch camp without thinking something unseen might be lurking in plain sight."

"In that case, could I have my dagger back? The one that Otacilius confiscated? He took daggers from my slaves, as well."

"Certainly. As soon as we've made camp."

The men shucked off their armor and set to work pitching tents, digging a pit for the latrine, kindling a fire. I went in search of the baggage wagon. A small knot of men surrounded it, looking down at something on the ground, talking.

"The fever must have taken him."

"It can happen that quickly, with a wound like that. I've seen stronger men bleed less and die faster."

"He was just an old slave, anyway. And from what I heard, a troublemaker."

"Ah, here's the tribune's friend. Let him through!"

The crowd parted for me. I stepped closer and saw the body of the wagon driver on the ground. Someone had crossed his arms over his chest and closed his eyes.

"He must have died during the day," explained a soldier who stood over the body. "He was dead when we came to unload the wagon."

I looked about. "Where are the others? The two slaves who were in the wagon with him?"

Tiro and Fortex stepped into sight. Neither said a word.

The soldiers were summoned to another duty and dispersed. I knelt beside the body. In death, the slave's face was even more haggard than in life, his cheeks sunken around his toothless mouth. I had never even asked his name. When I wanted something from him, I had simply called him "driver."

I rolled him over. Besides the wound at the shoulder, there were several others, where he had been poked and prodded during the march, but they appeared to be superficial. His shoes were thin, his feet blistered and bloody. The tether had worn the skin around his ankles. There appeared to be faint bruises around his throat as well; in the fading light it was hard to tell. Instinctively, I felt my own throat, where the tether had chafed it. But there had been no tether around the slave's throat.

Tiro and Fortex stood over me. I looked up at them. I spoke in a low voice. "He was strangled, wasn't he?"

Tiro raised an eyebrow. "You heard the soldiers. He died of fever, from his wound. He was old and weak. The march down the mountain killed him. That was his own fault."

"These discolorations at his throat—"

"Liver spots?" said Tiro.

I stood and looked him in the eye. "I think he was strangled. By your hand, Tiro?"

"Of course not. Fortex is trained for that type of thing."

I glanced at Fortex. He wouldn't meet my gaze.

"It had to be done, Gordianus," whispered Tiro. "What if he had recovered, and started talking again?"

I stared at him.

"Don't judge me, Gordianus! In times like these, a man has to do things against his own nature. Can you say that you wouldn't have done the same?"

I turned away and walked toward the campfire.

XVI

Antony never questioned the untimely death of the wagon driver. He was used to seeing men die suddenly, from wounds that did not appear fatal. He had other things on his mind.

The next morning, the soldiers threw the body into the latrine pit and covered it. The death of a slave merited no more ceremony than that.

As we rode out, Antony's only comment was that I might contact the slave's owner when I had the chance, to let him know what had become of his wagon and driver. "If you suspect he's the litigious type, you could offer him a token settlement; the slave obviously wasn't worth much. And since the owner was honoring your courier's passport, technically you don't owe him anything. Let him sue Pompey!" Antony laughed, then shook his head. "Civilians always suffer losses in wartime—property ruined, slaves running off. In a place like Gaul, the locals have to patch things up for themselves. Here in Italy it'll be different. Once things get back to normal, there'll be a flood of litigation—suits for damages, pleas for reparations, petitions for tax relief. The courts will be jammed. Caesar will have his hands full."

"So will advocates like Cicero," I said.

"If Cicero still has his hands," said Antony.

The coastal road was mostly straight and flat, but not in the best condition. Winter storms had damaged some sections, dislodging stones and washing out the foundation. Normally, such damage would have been repaired promptly by gangs of slaves working under a local magistrate, but the chaos in the region had prevented that. The recent passage of so many men, vehicles, and horses—first Pompey's army, then Caesar's—had aggravated the situation. But despite the mud and the muck, we traveled well over forty miles that day, and did the same the next day and the next.

I had traveled with Antony a few years before, from Ravenna to Rome, and again found his company enjoyable. He was a notorious carouser, whether the arena was a battlefield in Gaul, a wild party on the Palatine, or the floor of the Roman Senate. He had plenty of stories to tell, and he enjoyed hearing mine, as long as they involved scandalous women, political chicanery, or trials for murder, or best, all three together. I hardly saw Tiro, who traveled in the baggage wagon and stayed out of Antony's sight.

It was in the hour before twilight of the third day—one day after the Ides of March, one day before the feast of the Liberalia—that we arrived in the vicinity of Brundisium. We were spotted by lookouts posted atop a low hill east of the road. A centurion rode out to greet Antony. The man was flushed with excitement.

"Tribune, you've arrived just in time!"

"For what?"

"I'm not sure, but the men posted on the other side of the hill are whooping and cheering. Something's happening down in the harbor."

"Show us the way!" barked Antony. I hesitated to follow, uncertain of my place now that we had reached the theater of battle. Antony peered back at me. "Aren't you coming, Gordianus?"

We rode to the top of the low hill, where several tents had been pitched and a sizable contingent of soldiers had been posted as lookouts. Toward the north, in the direction we had come, the site commanded a sweeping view of the beach and the coastal road for miles. The centurion had seen us approaching for hours.

Toward the south, the site overlooked the city, the harbor, and the sea. The centurion led us to a vantage point with an unobstructed view. "They say this was the very spot where Caesar stood, when he planned the siege," he said proudly.

The walled city of Brundisium is situated on a peninsula surrounded by a semicircular harbor. A narrow strait links this protected harbor to the Adriatic Sea. The easiest way to visualize the city, as it might appear on a map, is to hold up your right hand and form a reverse letter C. The space enclosed by your forefinger and thumb represents the peninsula upon which the city is built. Your forefinger and thumb represent the northern and southern channels of the harbor. Your wrist represents the strait through which ships must sail to reach the sea.

From our vantage point, the city on the peninsula appeared as a cluster of tenements, warehouses, and temples crowded within high walls. Pompey's soldiers were clearly visible on the towers and parapets, their helmets and spears glinting in the westering sun. Along the landward western wall, which ran between the north and south channels of the inner harbor, the besieging army of Caesar was encamped. The force appeared to my eye enormous. Row upon row of catapults and ballistic machines had been assembled, along with several siege towers on wheels, which rose even higher than the city walls.

But I saw nothing to cause a commotion among the watchers on the hillside. The siege towers and war machines were unengaged. No smoke rose from the city, and I saw no sign of fighting along the wall.

"There!" Antony pointed away from the city, toward the entrance to the harbor and beyond. A fleet of large ships was approaching from the open sea. Several had already reached the harbor entrance and appeared to be maneuvering to sail through in single file. I found this curious, as I had sailed in and out of Brundisium myself in the past, and knew that the harbor entrance was deep and wide enough for several ships to sail abreast, yet these were apparently endeavoring to enter one at a time, keeping as close to the center as possible.

As the first ship entered the straits, I saw the reason for such a course. The sight was so strange, I had trouble believing my eyes. At the narrowest part of the entrance to the harbor, great piers of some sort had been built out from both promontories, extending far into the water. This breakwater very nearly met in the middle, or so it appeared at a distance, almost closing off the entrance to the harbor. Short towers had been built at intervals along both arms of the structure, and these were equipped with catapults and ballistic machines.

"By my ancestor Hercules, what are we seeing?" muttered Antony, as puzzled by the sight as I was. He turned his head and scanned the other soldiers watching along the hillside. A bearded little fellow was standing atop a boulder nearby, viewing the scene intently with his arms crossed, mumbling to himself. Antony called out to him. "Engineer Vitruvius!"

The man blinked and looked in our direction.

"Engineer Vitruvius! Report!"

The man scrambled down from the rock and came running. He saluted Antony. "Tribune, you've rejoined us!"

"You state the obvious, Marcus Vitruvius. What's not so obvious is what we're witnessing down there. What in Hades is going on?"

"Ah!" Vitruvius looked toward the harbor, but was so short that the tops of some trees down the hillside blocked his view. "If we may retire to higher ground, Tribune . . ."

We followed him back to the boulder. He scrambled atop it, crossed his arms, and gazed down at the harbor. "Now, Tribune, if I may explain the situation . . ." His tone was typical of the condescending manner of builders and engineers even when dealing with superiors, if those superiors know less than they do of construction and mathematics.

Vitruvius cleared his throat. "Seven days ago we arrived outside Brundisium. Caesar moved at once to encircle the city and the harbor, placing the greatest part of his six legions before the city wall but also securing the promontories north and south of the harbor entrance. Our commander hoped to trap not only Pompey but also the two consuls and the many senators with him, so as to force immediate negotiations and a settlement of the crisis."

"But . . ." prompted Antony.

"A bad sign: our advance intelligence indicated that Pompey had assembled a considerable fleet, yet there were only a few ships in the harbor. Where had the fleet gone? Alas, before we arrived, Pompey had already sent the consuls, senators, and a substantial part of his army across the Adriatic to Dyrrachium, out of harm's way. Always seeking peace, our commander endeavored to negotiate directly with Pompey. The Great One sent back word that no lawful settlement could possibly be concluded in the absence of the consuls. Hence, no negotiations.

"Our intelligence from within Brundisium—Pompey has treated the locals with contempt and they're eager to help Caesar—informed us that Pompey kept twenty cohorts with him. Not to hold the city indefinitely—how could he, with only twelve thousand men against three times that number?—but long enough for his fleet to reach Dyrrachium, unload the first round of passengers, then return to Brundisium to pick up Pompey and his men.

"Our commander, having pursued Pompey this far, had no intention of allowing him to slip away. He came to me. 'They must be stopped, Engineer Vitruvius! We must prevent Pompey's ships from reentering the harbor when they return, or if they manage to do so, we must prevent them from leaving. But I have no ships of my own, and my men cannot march on water. This strikes me as an engineering problem, Marcus Vitruvius. Can you blockade the harbor?' I said I could. 'Then make it thus, Engineer Vitruvius!'"

The little man waved his arm in the direction of the harbor. "You can see the result from here. We began by building great breakwaters of earth and stone on either side of the harbor entrance, where the water is shallow. Unfortunately, as the work progressed and we reached deeper water, it became impossible to keep the earthworks together. At that point we built a raft, thirty feet square, at the end of each breakwater and moored each raft with anchors at all four corners to keep them still in the waves. Once these platforms were in position, we added more rafts, joined them firmly together and covered them with a causeway of earth, so that they were as steady as an actual breakwater, even though they float atop the waves. If you squint, you can see that screens and mantlets have been put up all along both sides of the causeways to protect the soldiers coming and going. On every fourth raft we constructed a tower two stories high, to defend against attacks by sea. The goal, of course, was close off the harbor completely."

Antony grunted. "All this was your idea?"

Vitruvius beamed. "Actually, if you believe the Greek historians, Xerxes the king of Persia did something like this when he bridged the Hellespont and led his army from Asia into Europe. I've always wondered how such a feat was accomplished. I suspect he must have used a similar technique, anchoring rafts and linking them together."

Meto had often told me of great feats of engineering conjured by Caesar in his battles against the Gauls. Under Caesar's command, men bridged rivers and chasms, dug vast trenches and canals and tunnels, and constructed great towers and siege engines. But an attempt to close off a harbor was something new.

Antony nodded, clearly impressed. "What was Pompey's response to all this construction? Don't tell me he watched idly from the city walls once he realized what was happening."

"Of course not," said Vitruvius. "After he stopped gaping in wonder, the Great One commandeered the largest merchant vessels remaining in the harbor and outfitted them with siege towers, three stories tall. The ships have been making sorties out to the harbor entrance every day, trying to break up our rafts. They've managed to slow the work, but not destroy it. It's been a daily spectacle, watching our towers on the rafts and their towers on the ships fire missiles and fireballs and arrows back and forth. Blood on the water . . . trails of reeking smoke . . . explosions of steam!"

Antony frowned. "But the blockade remains unfinished. The channel is still open."

Vitruvius crossed his arms and assumed the impregnable expression of every builder whose project has fallen behind deadline. "Alas, we simply didn't have time to finish, especially with Pompey's ships hectoring us. But the idea was sound! Given another five days, or even three—" Vitruvius shook his head. "And now the fleet has returned. Those are Pompey's ships you see, lining up to enter the harbor. And there! See the commandeered merchant vessels with their towers, sailing out from the city to harass our men on the rafts and run interference for the incoming ships!"

As the sun dropped behind the hills to the west, we watched the sea battle unfold. One by one Pompey's transport ships slipped through the gap in the breakwater and ran the gauntlet. Boulders flew through the air, hurled by catapults on the rafts. Most missed the mark and landed in the water, creating prodigious splashes. Some struck masts or prows, shredded sails and sent splinters flying. One catapulted stone landed squarely on the deck of a ship and appeared to break through, at least to the rowers' deck below, but the ship failed to sink.

At the same time, atop the towers on the rafts, men loaded giant missiles into ballistics engines and sent them flying toward the ships. The missiles looked to me like arrows carved from entire tree trunks, and the machines to hurl them were like enormous bows with winches on either side to set the tension. Some of the missiles were set afire before they were shot, and went hurling through the air streaming flames and smoke. The aim of the ballistics engines seemed more accurate than that of the catapults. They caused more damage to the incoming ships, yet still failed to sink any.

Meanwhile, the fighting vessels from the city returned the fire, hurling missiles and stones at the rafts and even attempting to board them, as they might an enemy ship at sea. Caesar's men on the rafts managed to repel these attacks, but in so doing were distracted from their own assaults on the transport ships. Unceasingly, soldiers ran back and forth on the causeway atop the rafts, toting fresh missiles to the ballistics engines and rolling boulders to the catapults. Archers on both sides choked the air with arrows, and the waves grew congested with a flotsam of spent missiles and bodies.

From a distance, all this commotion seemed utterly chaotic, a great stirring together of earth, sea, fire, and smoke. Yet at the same time, it appeared to be an orderly if hectic operation carried out by purposeful men using every ingenious device and method they could conceive and construct for the purpose of mutual destruction. It was thrilling to watch, as a lightning storm is thrilling. The battle proceeded with compelling inevitability. We seemed to be watching a single vast machine of many parts which, once set into motion, no power on heaven or earth could prevent from completing its manifold operations.

As the sun went down and the reek of smoke and steam thickened, the battle became increasingly obscure. It appeared that every one of Pompey's transport ships would win through to the harbor. At the same time, Caesar's rafts had withstood the assault against them and remained in place.

At last, only one transport ship remained outside the harbor entrance. The wind had risen, and the vessel was having difficulty maneuvering. There was a lull in the battle. I sensed the energy of both sides flagging. The operation of the catapults and ballistic machines grew more sporadic. The constant hail of arrows ceased. Perhaps both sides had run low on ammunition, or perhaps the increasing darkness made it difficult to take aim.

Then there occurred one of those incidents which prove the madness of battle, which give the lie to any vision of warfare as an orderly operation. One of Pompey's assault vessels shot an incendiary missile from its catapult. To carry flammable material on board a ship must have been terribly dangerous, and none of the ships had hurled such a fireball before. Why did the captain hurl it then? As a flippant parting gesture? To use up the last of his ammunition before the close of battle? Or was it a calculated, last-ditch attempt to destroy the rafts?

Whatever the intention, the result could not have been what the captain intended. The fireball greatly overshot the rafts. Like a comet it flew over the heads of Caesar's men, descended in a precipitous arc, and crashed onto the deck of the last of Pompey's transport ships waiting to enter the strait.

Why did the ship catch fire so quickly and so completely, when its sisters had not, despite similar fireballs hurled by Caesar's catapults? Perhaps the flaming ball of pitch landed on a cache of something flammable. Perhaps it was the action of the rising wind. Whatever the cause, with stunning rapidity the whole ship was engulfed in flames, from the waterline to the top of the sail. Flaming bodies leaped off the deck. Even on the hillside, we heard the screams of the rowers trapped below the deck. Their cries were drowned out by the triumphant cheering of Caesar's men along the breakwater, who jumped up and down in their excitement.

Then their cheering abruptly ceased. Out of control, buffeted by the wind, the flaming ship suddenly listed toward the nearest stretch of Caesar's rafts, heading for the very tower which had been the intended target of the fireball. The men in the tower poured out like ants from a hill. Moments later, the ship crashed into the line of rafts. The mast shattered from the impact and fell onto the breakwater. The fleeing soldiers were trapped beneath the sail, which descended on them like a fluttering sheet of flame.

Soldiers who had previously carried ammunition along the causeway now relayed buckets of seawater as they desperately tried to douse the fire and keep it from spreading. Pompey's assault ships might have taken advantage of the confusion, but they had already turned away from the enemy and retreated toward the city, escorting the transport vessels safe within the harbor.

Night fell. The battle was over.

XVII

We made camp and dined that night with the man stationed at the overlook. I had thought Antony would be as eager to report to Caesar as I was to find Meto now that we had at last reached Brundisium. But Antony was not a man to be stinted of his supper, even if it consisted of nothing more than a soldier's ration of gruel, or of his wine at the end of three hard days of riding.

We ate on the hillside beneath the open sky, seated on little canvas folding chairs. The wind died. The sea and the harbor grew as still as a black mirror, reflecting the mantle of stars overhead. The flames of the ship wrecked against the breakwater gradually died down. Within its high walls, the compact little city of Brundisium seemed to glow from the bottom up, as if the ground itself were illuminated. One by one, runners lit torches atop the towers and along the parapets, until the whole course of the wall was outlined like a coiled serpent. Outside the landward wall, Caesar's army was dotted with hundreds of twinkling campfires. Beyond the besieging army, farther west, the foothills of the Apennines brooded in darkness, the ridgeline faintly aglow with the last intimations of light from the setting sun.

"Today we saw a battle!" said Antony, who seemed greatly cheered, despite the fact that Pompey's fleet had won through.

"And tomorrow, we'll likely see a siege," noted Vitruvius. Antony had invited him to dine with us to continue explaining the feats of engineering involved in construction of the breakwater. Now Vitruvius fell to cataloguing, for my benefit, the various engines and strategies that might be deployed when Caesar threw his forces against the defenders of Brundisium—scaling ladders, wheeled siege towers, battering rams, sappers who would dig under the foundations to weaken the walls, soldiers who would advance in tortoise formations surrounded by shields and bristling with spears.

I fell to wondering about Davus. Where was he, at that very moment? Did Pompey still keep him among his personal bodyguards? That was my hope, but who knew where he might have ended up, thanks to Pompey's whim or simple expediency. Perhaps Davus was guarding the city walls, striding even now among the tiny figures illuminated by the torches along the parapets, heavily cloaked for the night watch and anxiously counting the hours to dawn. Or perhaps he had taken part in the sea battle that day, manning one of Pompey's assault ships. Davus couldn't swim, Diana had said. Nor could I, for that matter. What terror could be greater than being trapped aboard a ship deliberately sailing toward danger? The sight of wounded men struggling in the waves that day had horrified me more than anything else, more even than the flaming transport ship. Had Davus been among those tiny figures, flailing and screaming amid the flotsam of the battle?

And what of Meto? I saw again the flaming sail descending on the fleeing soldiers. Could my son have been among them? It seemed unlikely. Caesar kept him close at hand. Probably, at that moment, he was encamped with the main part of the army outside the city walls, dining in the commander's private mess, taking careful notes as Caesar discussed with his lieutenants the next day's strategy.

Who was in greater danger, Davus or Meto? To judge from the

surface of things, anyone would have said Davus, I suppose. I was not so sure.

Long after his bowl of gruel was empty, Antony kept holding up his cup for more wine. Once he was properly drunk, he insisted that Vitruvius and the centurion of the night watch join him in a round of bawdy songs. Most were simply vulgar, but one was actually rather funny, about a mincingly effeminate officer who'd rather be at home trying on his wife's dresses, but who turns out to be the bravest fighter of all. So much for military humor, I thought. Men need a bit of nonsense to divert them, and wine to wash it down, after witnessing carnage such as we had seen that day.

Antony was still singing lustily when I took my leave and went to the officers' tent, where I had been allotted a space. I fell on my pallet but couldn't sleep, fretting over Meto and Davus and wondering what the next few days would bring. When I set out from Rome, I thought I had a plan. Now, worn down by the journey and faced with the realities of the situation, it seemed to me that whatever vague notion I had in mind had vanished like morning mist. I was out of my element. I felt tiny and insignificant, overwhelmed by the forces around me. Now that the critical moment was fast approaching, I did not feel as brave as I had hoped.

The flap rustled. Someone stole into the tent and moved uncertainly among the cots. I heard a whisper: "Gordianus?"

It was Tiro. I rose from my bed, wrapped my blanket around me, and ushered him outside.

"Can't you sleep, either? Isn't the baggage wagon comfortable enough?"

"Lumpy," growled Tiro. "Fortex and I take turns dozing. I'm still not convinced that Antony hasn't recognized me."

"Antony hasn't even looked at you. Nobody notices slaves, unless they're young and beautiful."

"Still, each night, I expect to be strangled in my sleep."

I thought of the wagon driver, strangled in his delirium, but said nothing.

"What happens tomorrow, Gordianus?"

"I don't know. If I'm lucky, I'll see Meto."

"And Caesar as well?"

"Perhaps."

"Take me with you."

I frowned. "I thought you came all this way to see Pompey, not Caesar."

"So I did. This is my exit from Italy, Gordianus. I intend to be on Pompey's ship when he sets sail for Dyrrhachium."

"You never told me that."

"You didn't need to know. But before I go, as long as the opportunity presents itself, I should like to have a peek inside Caesar's tent."

"So that you can assassinate him?"

"Don't joke, Gordianus. I only want to have a look. One never knows what might be useful later."

"You want me to help you spy on Caesar?"

"You owe me a favor, Gordianus. Could you have traveled all the way from Rome this quickly, without me?"

"Could you have survived the last four days without me lying for you, Tiro? I think we're even."

"Then do this for me as a favor, and I'll do a favor for you. Isn't it your intention to get into Brundisium, to retrieve your son-in-law from Pompey?"

"If I can."

"How do you plan to get inside the city walls, with Caesar's army on one side and Pompey's on the other?"

"I'm not sure," I admitted.

"I can get you inside, alive and in one piece. You'll come with me and Fortex. But in return for that favor, I want you to take me along when you see Meto—and Caesar."

I shook my head. "Impossible. Caesar is even more likely than Antony to recognize you. Caesar has dined in Cicero's house! He must have seen you many times, and not just taking shorthand in the Senate."

"Seen me, yes, but never really looked at me. You said it yourself, Gordianus: nobody notices slaves."

"Caesar notices everything. You're risking your head, Tiro."

"Perhaps not. What if he does recognize me? Caesar is eager to be known for his clemency."

"Clemency for senators and generals, Tiro, not for freedmen and spies."

"I'll take my chances. If anyone asks who I am, you'll say I'm Soscarides, Meto's old tutor."

"And what about Meto? Is he supposed to go along with the lie as well?"

"Do this for me, Gordianus! If you want to get into Brundisium before your son-in-law is dead on the ramparts or sailing off to Dyrrhachium, do me this favor."

"I'll sleep on it," I said, suddenly very weary. I yawned. When I opened my eyes, Tiro had disappeared. I returned to the tent.

Despite my worries, despite the horrors I had witnessed that day, sleep came swiftly, but not without dreams. It was not flames or drowning water, or mountain passes and forced marches I dreamed about. It was the girl Aemilia, Numerius's lover. I saw her with a baby in her arms, smiling and content. I felt a great sense of relief and stepped closer to have a look, but stumbled against something at my feet. I looked down to see the body of Numerius, which some-how was also the body of the wagon driver, a garrote twisted tight around his throat. Aemilia's baby had vanished. She shuddered and wept. The front of her gown was soaked with blood between her legs.

I woke with a start. Antony loomed above me, his eyes bloodshot.

"Dawn, Gordianus! Time for me to report to Caesar, and for you to see your son. Piss if you need to. Then round up those two slaves of yours and we're off."

~

Before we rode down to the main camp, Antony wanted a last look at the breakwater from the hill. There were clouds overhead, but the horizon was clear. The rising sun in our eyes and its scintil-

lating reflection on the water made it difficult to see, but the wreck-
age of the flaming ship appeared to have been removed during the
night. Men were busy repairing the damage to the breakwater, and
construction continued. "Vitruvius is down there now," said Antony.
"He told me last night that he hopes to add another raft to each end
of the breakwater by the end of the day, to further close the gap. The
ships that sailed in yesterday will have a harder time sailing out!"

We rode down onto the plain. Antony was attended by a small
staff of officers. I was accompanied by Tiro and Fortex, for whom
horses were found. The camp was like a city, probably more populous
than the city being besieged and surely more orderly, with its row
upon row of precisely spaced tents. Some of the soldiers stood in lines
awaiting morning rations. Others, already fed and outfitted for battle, were marching off to man the trenches and earthworks and siege
machines below the city walls.

I was astounded by the speed with which Caesar had been able to
move such vast numbers of men and equipment. Ten days before, the
plain outside Brundisium had been empty; now it was home to
thirty-six thousand men, every one of whom appeared to know exactly where he should be and what he should be doing at that moment. Thirty days before, not one of these men had been within two
hundred miles of Brundisium, and Domitius still held Corfinium.
Sixty days before, Caesar had only just crossed the Rubicon. The
scale and swiftness of the operation was awesome. I pitied the Gauls
who had confronted such a force. I despaired for Pompey.

We passed a guarded checkpoint, where Antony vouched for me.
As we drew closer to the center of the camp, he fell back beside me.
I saw him cast a wary glance at Tiro and Fortex, as if seeing them for
the first time.

"You *are* sure, Gordianus, that you can vouch for your two
slaves?"

I barely hesitated. "Of course. Why do you ask?"

"No reason, really. It's only, ever since we crossed the Rubicon—
before that, actually—there's been a rumor . . ."

"What sort of rumor?"

"A plot. To assassinate Caesar. Wild talk, of course."

I felt a chill up my spine. "Does Caesar take it seriously?"

"Caesar thinks he's immortal! But what man isn't made of flesh and blood?" He groaned from his hangover and massaged his temples. "It's only—you see, every time I vouch for you, I'm vouching for your slaves as well. Of course, you're above suspicion, Gordianus. That goes without saying. But the slaves who travel with you—"

"I take complete responsibility for my slaves, Tribune." I kept my eyes straight ahead.

"Of course, Gordianus. I meant no offense." He gave me a firm slap on the back, then rode up to rejoin his men. He didn't give Tiro and Fortex another look.

I steadied myself with a deep breath, then looked sidelong at Tiro. It seemed to me that he clutched his reins too tightly, but his face betrayed no expression. He had overheard, of course; Antony was not the sort to lower his voice for the benefit of slaves. I thought of Daniel in the lion's den, a tale Bethesda told, handed down by her Hebrew father. Was that how Tiro felt, riding into Caesar's camp, led by a tribune who would gladly flay him alive? Yet here he was, despite his fear. I wondered if I could summon as much courage in the coming hours.

We came to a large tent, more elaborate than the others, made of red canvas embroidered with gold and decorated with pennants. Messengers on horseback waited in a line outside the entrance. As we approached, a soldier stepped out of the tent, conveyed an order to the first messenger, and the man was off. Meanwhile, another messenger came riding up, dismounted, and rushed into the tent.

"Morning reconnaissance," explained Antony. "Intelligence reports come in, orders go out. It's a beehive in there."

"Perhaps I should wait outside."

"Nonsense. Just mind that you don't get trampled." He climbed off his horse and offered me a hand. "Leave your slaves outside."

I looked at Tiro and shrugged. I had done my part. He was not to see the inside of Caesar's tent after all. But I underestimated his persistence.

Tiro jumped from his horse. "Please, Master! Let me come with you."

"You heard the tribune, Soscarides."

"But you brought me all this way to surprise Meto, to see the look on his face. If you talk to Meto first and let it slip that I'm here, where's the surprise? And the longer you wait, the more hectic the day may become. Even an hour from now, if there's to be a battle—"

"The tutor is right," said Antony. "'Swiftly done is best done.' Who said that, tutor?" He looked at Tiro keenly.

"Euripides," said Tiro.

Antony frowned. "Are you sure? I once heard Cicero say it on the floor of the Senate House."

Tiro's face stiffened. "No doubt, Tribune. But Euripides said it first."

Antony laughed. "Spoken like a true tutor! I suppose you're not a spy or an assassin, after all. Bring him along, Gordianus. Give Meto a surprise."

"Yes, Master, please," said Tiro.

"Either that, or have the slave beaten for his insolence," suggested Antony. He wasn't joking.

I glowered at Tiro and seriously considered the option. I could see wheels spinning behind his eyes. "The date!" he suddenly said.

Antony looked at him quizzically.

"It's two days past the Ides," said Tiro. "Liberalia day!" I remembered Cicero and his wife arguing over the upcoming Liberalia and their son's toga ceremony. "You can't beat a slave for speaking his mind on the feast day of Father Freedom, Master. Letting slaves speak freely is part of the holiday." Tiro looked quite pleased with himself.

"Is it Liberalia already?" Antony grunted. "I always lose track of holidays during a military campaign. We count on augurs to watch the calendar and make the proper sacrifices, and leave it at that. Well, I celebrated the god of the grape in my own way last night, and I'm all for parading a giant phallus through the camp and singing bawdy songs, though I doubt we'll have time for it. But the slave's right, Gordianus, you should indulge him. We must court the favor of all the gods, including Dionysus."

Tiro looked at me archly. I looked back at him coolly. "Very well, Soscarides, come along. Fortex, you'll stay here with the horses."

Inside the tent, messengers rushed about and the crowd of officers buzzed with conversation, but the scene was more orderly than I expected. Antony's metaphor was fitting: not the frenzied scramble of a stirred antbed, but the steady swarm of a beehive.

Most of the officers appeared to be about Antony's age, in their early thirties or younger. A few I recognized, though I was more used to seeing them in senatorial togas. Outfitted in armor, they looked like boys to me. Their faces were radiant with excitement. I thought of the crippled old senator, Sextus Tedius, dragging himself off to make a stand with Pompey. The contrast was devastating.

A flash of red caught my eye. Through the crowd I glimpsed a bald head, singular amid so many full heads of hair, and spotted the king bee himself. Caesar was in the process of being strapped into a gilded breastplate even more elaborate than the one Antony wore. The flash of color was his cape. Caesar was famous for his red cape, which he wore on the battlefield so that he could always be seen, by his own men and those of the enemy as well. Even as he was being dressed, he appeared to be listening to three messengers at once. His deepset eyes stared straight ahead. He nodded occasionally, absently brushing his fingers over his brow, combing forward the thin hair at his temples. His expression was composed, determined, attentive but aloof. On his thin lips there was the faintest intimation of a smile.

I was ten years older than Caesar, and by habit still thought of him in terms of his early reputation in the Senate, as an aristocratic, radical young troublemaker. He was a troublemaker still, but now in his fifties. To the ambitious, vibrant young men in that tent, he must have seemed a father figure, the brilliant man of action they all aspired to emulate, the commander who would lead them into the future. What appeal could musty relics like Pompey and Domitius hold for such young men? Pompey's conquests were all in the past. Domitius's glory was secondhand, inherited from a dead generation. Caesar embodied the moment. The fire in his eyes was the divine spark of destiny.

I looked about. Tiro stood behind me, taking in everything, but Antony had disappeared. I spotted him across the tent embracing another man in nearly identical armor. When they relaxed the embrace, I saw that the man in Antony's arms was his fellow tribune Curio. The two had been lifelong friends. More than friends, some said. When their boyhood attachment became the stuff of gossip, Cicero had urged Curio's father to separate them, saying Antony was corrupting Curio. Antony was banned from Curio's house, but it did no good; he sneaked into Curio's bedroom through the ceiling. So the story went, and Antony had never denied it. Now they were seasoned soldiers, and in the last year both had been elected tribunes. When the crisis came, they fled from Rome together to join with Caesar before he crossed the Rubicon.

The tent seemed full of such men, all bursting with energy and passion, all projecting the bright invincibility of youth. They made me feel old and very unsure of myself.

I turned about, seeking the face I longed to see. I gave a start. Meto stood before me, a look of utter consternation on his face.

My son did not looked pleased to see me.

XVIII

"Papa, what are you doing here?"

Like the officers around us, Meto looked like a boy to me, though he was now almost thirty and had streaks of premature gray at his temples. He had the eyes of a scholar, but the weathered hands and rugged brow of a seasoned campaigner. The scar across his face, which he had received at the age of sixteen fighting for Catilina, had almost been erased by the winds and rain and burning sun of Gaul. As always when I saw him after an absence of months, I looked him quickly up and down and whispered a prayer of thanks to Mars that his body appeared whole and his limbs intact.

I felt such a flood of emotion that I couldn't speak. I reached for him. He was stiff for a moment, then returned the embrace. Remembering the boy he had once been, I was amazed at his strength. When he pulled back, he was smiling ruefully.

"What are you doing here, Papa? You must have been traveling for days. The danger—"

"I'm here for Davus."

"Davus?"

"He's with Pompey. At least I hope he still is, and not already across in Dyrrhachium . . . or . . ."

"With Pompey? Don't tell me Davus ran off to fight with his old master! We former slaves are entirely too sentimental." There was a bitterness in his voice I was not used to hearing.

"No. Pompey took Davus with him by force."

"By force?"

"Pompey claimed he had a legal right—something to do with the transfer of ownership and the terms of Davus's manumission. Legal or not, there was no way I could stop him."

"But why should Pompey steal Davus from you?"

"Partly for spite. Partly to have a hold over me."

Meto's face stiffened. "Is the rest of the family all right? Eco, Bethesda, Diana? The children?"

"I left them all in good health."

"Thank the gods. What does Pompey want from you?"

I looked at the crowd pressed close around us. I was acutely aware of Tiro standing silently behind me, straining to hear everything. It was impossible to say all I wanted to say. I lowered my voice. "The day before Pompey left Rome, a kinsman of his was . . . killed . . . in my house."

"And Pompey accused you of the crime?"

I shook my head. "No, no! But he held me responsible. He charged me with finding the killer. I told him I couldn't. I tried to refuse. But Pompey was in a state. On a whim, he took Davus to coerce me."

"Poor Diana!" whispered Meto.

"That's why I've come to Brundisium. To get Davus back, while I still can."

"How?"

"I'll find a way. What about you, Meto? I've been sick with worry for you—"

Meto suddenly pulled back. Tiro had taken a step closer, and Meto seemed to notice him for the first time. "Is this man with you, Papa?"

"Yes."

"One of your slaves? I don't know him."

"Let me explain—"

"Wait a moment . . ." Meto stared hard at Tiro. "By Hercules, it's—"

At that moment I felt a slap on my shoulder, and gave such a start I thought my heart had bounded from my chest. It was Antony.

"Here they are, father and son, off whispering and conspiring among themselves," he said.

I blinked. Beside Antony I saw a blur of gold and crimson, surmounted by the serene countenance of Julius Caesar.

"Gordianus! When did we last meet? In Ravenna, I think. You were investigating the murder of our friend Publius Clodius. You were then in the employ of Pompey, as I recall."

He always remembered me, which always surprised me, since he knew me chiefly as Meto's father and the two of us had never had a conversation of real significance. Meto had told me that Caesar's memory for names and faces was part of his charm. He could meet a foot soldier in the heat of battle, exchange no more than a few words, and years later greet the man by name and ask for news from his hometown.

"Imperator," I said, with a deferential nod.

"The slave with him is an old tutor of Meto's," explained Antony.

Meto raised his eyebrows, but said nothing.

Caesar glanced past my shoulder at Tiro. I held my breath. His expression registered no change. His eyes reconnected with mine. He raised an eyebrow. "I hope you're not *still* in the employ of Pompey, Gordianus. Antony tells me that you've been traveling on a diplomatic passport signed by the Great One himself."

I took a deep breath. "That document came to me by way of Cicero, not directly from Pompey. Despite appearances, Imperator, I assure you that the Great One and I are hardly even on speaking terms."

Caesar flashed a wry smile. "That rather describes my own relationship with Pompey at the moment. You're an intrepid man, Gordianus, to have journeyed all this way, and a good father, if you did it to inquire after Meto. But I assure you, I take good care of him.

He's as dear to me as he is to you. I suggest you return now to the lookout where you camped last night, out of harm's way. Observe developments from a safe distance. This could turn out to be a very interesting day. In particular, watch the rooftops of the city."

"The rooftops, Imperator?"

"The citizens of Brundisium are angry at the way they've been treated by Pompey's troops. Pompey never did learn to discipline his men properly. As a result, there are townspeople quite willing, even eager, to let us know when Pompey begins his nautical retreat. They will signal us from the rooftops. That will be the moment we strike. There's nothing harder to manage than a tactical withdrawal from a besieged city, even by ship. When he turns his back and begins to flee, that will be the moment of Pompey's greatest vulnerability. The gods willing, he shall not escape me."

I nodded and felt a trickle of sweat run down my spine, feeling the presence of Tiro close behind me, listening to every word. In his enthusiasm, Caesar himself was telling me secrets, treating me with complete trust, while a spy I had brought into his tent stood close enough to touch him. I felt lightheaded, as I had at the end of the forced march down the mountain when I fainted at Antony's feet.

"Are you well, Gordianus?" said Caesar. "Take a day of rest. But no rest for me! The signal to attack may come at any moment. Come, Antony. Meto, bring your stylus and wax tablets."

I cleared my throat. "Perhaps, Imperator, my son might stay behind for just a moment. I've come a long way to see him. We've barely had time to talk—"

"Not today, Gordianus." Caesar smiled at Meto and put his arm around him, then reached up to tug at his earlobe affectionately. I thought I saw Meto stiffen at the man's touch. Caesar seemed not to notice. "Today, your son is mine, every hour, every minute. My eyes and my ears, my witness, my memory. He must see all, hear all, record everything. Later, there'll be time to talk. Come, Meto." He slipped his arm from Meto's shoulder.

The tent rapidly began to empty, like a swarm leaving the hive. Meto followed Caesar for a few steps, then hung back. He looked over his shoulder at Tiro, then at me. He frowned. "Papa, what's going on?"

"I wanted to ask you the same question," I said.

"Meto, come on!" Antony barked.

My son gave me a last, cryptic look, then departed with the rest. I wished I had given him one more embrace.

~

"I suppose you're quite pleased with yourself," I said to Tiro. Along with Fortex, we were making our second circuit of the camp on horseback. Tiro was all eyes and ears, taking in every detail.

As we had left Caesar's tent, one of his aides handed me a copper disk stamped with an image of Venus. The man told me I could show it as a passport to anyone who questioned us. The disk signified that I was a guest of the imperator himself, allowed to come and go and move freely about the camp, as long as I stayed out of the way. The disk was even good for obtaining rations at the mess tent.

Had it been up to me, we would have spent no more time in the camp than it took to leave it. I was eager to get into Brundisium. Once Pompey began his nautical retreat and the siege commenced, everything would be in chaos. Any hope of finding Davus could slip away in an instant. I wanted to know Tiro's plan. But Tiro insisted on taking full advantage of Caesar's hospitality first. "You traveled on Pompey's passport," he said with a smile. "Now I shall travel a bit on Caesar's."

"Tiro, we must get inside the walls, quickly."

"Indulge me, Gordianus. Today is Liberalia, you know!"

"I should like to indulge you by sitting you down on one of those giant phalli the priests of Dionysus carry."

Fortex yelped at the idea. Tiro hooted. He was in high spirits, almost giddy. Why not? He had carried off his charade with spectacular success. He had slipped through Antony's hands unscathed, slipped in and out of Caesar's tent undetected, and had even garnered valuable information from the lips of the imperator himself. Now he was skimming a last bit of intelligence, observing the numbers and dispositions of Caesar's troops and siege machines.

After some morning cloudiness, the sky had cleared. An offshore wind was rising. It was a perfect day for sailing. At any moment Pompey might begin his retreat. The transport ships might be loading at that very moment. "What will be the use of all this information you're gathering, Tiro, if we wait too long to get into Brundisium? Pompey may leave without you—or he may become trapped, for lack of what you might have told him."

"You're right, Gordianus, we must be getting on. But first, something to quiet the rumbling in my belly. Who knows what sort of rations Pompey's troops have been reduced to inside the city? I suggest we eat at Caesar's expense, and slip into Brundisium with full stomachs."

"Where's the mess tent, then?" I grumbled.

"Three up and two over." Tiro had memorized the layout of the camp.

We were given steaming millet porridge sweetened with a dollop of honey. I even found a few raisins in my portion. Fortex grumbled at the lack of any meat.

"Meto tells me that a soldier fights best with grain in his belly," I said. "Too much beef bloats a man, makes him sluggish, turns his bowels to mud. Once, in Gaul, Caesar's troops ran out of grain. For days on end they had nothing to eat but cattle requisitioned from the natives. They hated it, to the point of becoming mutinous. They demanded their porridge!"

"Your son must be a remarkable person," said Tiro.

"Why do you say that?"

"Meto was born a slave, wasn't he?"

"So were you, Tiro."

"Yes, but I was educated and groomed to be Cicero's companion from early on. I had the life of a scribe. There's room for a slave to prove himself in that kind of position, to show off his natural talents and rise in the world. But Meto was born a slave to Marcus Crassus, wasn't he? A bad man to have for a master. Crassus may have been the richest man in the world, but he never knew the true value of anything."

I nodded. "Meto wasn't even in Crassus's household, properly speaking. He was an errand boy in one of Crassus's villas on the coast, in Baiae. That's where I first met him, during the slave revolt of Spartacus. There had been a murder, presumably by some runaway slaves. Crassus intended to kill every slave in the household in retribution, including Meto. Imagine, slaughtering an innocent child in the arena!"

"Roman justice is sometimes hard," agreed Tiro.

"Crassus wasn't entirely pleased with the way things turned out. When it was all over, he sent Meto off to an estate in Sicily. Do you know what Meto was doing, when I finally tracked him down? He was a scarecrow. It was terrible for him. Endless days in the hot sun, the buzz of insects in the grain, the hungry crows always coming back, the foreman beating him if any of the crop was eaten. He had nightmares about it for years afterward. Perhaps he still does."

"I should think by now he's seen enough horrors as a soldier to drive out that nightmare and replace it with others," observed Tiro. "What made him want to become a soldier?"

"Catilina." I saw Tiro wrinkle his nose at the mention of the radical insurgent who had been Cicero's enemy. "When he was sixteen, he fell in love with Catilina, or the idea of Catilina, and ran off to fight for him. I was there, too, at the battle of Pistoria, when Catilina's dreams ended. Meto and I survived, by the favor of the gods. That taste of battle was more than enough to satisfy any curiosity I ever had about warfare and slaughter, but Meto wanted more. He needed another leader to follow, more battles to fight. It has something to do with being born a slave, I think. I freed him. I made him my son, and never treated him as anything less than my own flesh and blood. But he never quite felt a sense of birthright, a sureness of belonging. The night before his toga day, when he was sixteen . . ."

I caught myself. Why I was speaking so candidly? The mood of an army camp on the brink of battle has a way of loosening a man's tongue. "On the eve of his toga day, Meto had the nightmare—the scarecrow nightmare. I told him that was all in the past. He knew that, but he didn't feel it. Becoming my son, becoming a citizen—it all felt unreal to him. In his heart, he was still a frightened, helpless slaveboy. It wasn't until he went off to Gaul and found favor with Caesar that he seemed finally to put his beginnings behind him. He found the place where he belonged, and the leader he was looking for. And yet, now—" I stopped myself from going further. "I don't pretend to understand him, Tiro, not completely. But I am his father, as surely as if he came from my seed."

"You love him very much," said Tiro quietly.

"More than anything else. Too much, perhaps."

XIX

"I'm not a swimmer," I said.

After eating, we had returned to the lookout post on the hill north of the city. Tiro, Fortex, and I sat on horseback, surveying the view. It was much as I had seen it the day before, except that the harbor was now crowded with moored transport ships, and the harbor entrance had been pinched a bit tighter, thanks to new rafts hastily added to the end of each breakwater. Tiro had said he wanted a final look at the lay of the land and the disposition of Caesar's forces, but I was beginning to suspect that he had no idea of what to do next and was searching for a way to get inside the city walls.

Lacking the wings of Daedalus, this could be done in only two ways: by land or by water. Entry by land would require getting past the front line of Caesar's heavily manned trenches, traversing the no man's land before the city wall, and then penetrating or scaling the wall itself. We could hardly do any of this in secret. Long before we crossed the front line, the attackers would order us to stop or be killed as defectors. Even if we crossed the no man's land alive, the defenders might fire upon us long before we could explain ourselves, and they could hardly be expected to open the gates or let down ladders even if they wanted to help us.

That left the possibility of approaching Brundisium by water. The city wall that fronted the harbor was shorter and less heavily guarded than the landward wall, but scarcely less formidable to three men without wings. Outside this wall, a narrow road ran along the waterfront and gave access to the port situated at the tip of the peninsula, but the entire length of this road had been covered with a veritable thicket of spikes and caltrops to make passage impossible and discourage even small boats from landing. There was only one point of possible ingress: the port itself, where gates in the walls opened onto a wide boardwalk and several large quays projected into the water. The gates to the port were open and there seemed to be a great deal of activity on the quays, but as yet there was no sign that the ships moored there were being readied for departure.

"What did you say, Gordianus?" mumbled Tiro, gazing intently at the prospect.

"I said, I'm not a swimmer. I've always been a city boy, you know. Born and raised in Rome."

Tiro blinked. "People swim in the Tiber all the time. Upstream from the Cloaca Maxima, anyway."

"No, Tiro. People splash in the Tiber, and float across on planks, and in dry years they wade across. That's not the same as swimming across a harbor with arrows falling around you."

"Who said anything about swimming?" said Tiro. "Do you see those little fishermen's huts down there, on our side of the channel? Just a stone's throw away, facing the city across the harbor?"

I nodded. The huts were few and spaced well apart. I hadn't even noticed them in the twilight of the previous day, distracted by the battle at the harbor entrance.

"The huts looked abandoned," said Tiro. "No signs of life. The fishermen have all retreated inside the city walls. But they left their boats behind. They're only skiffs, too small to be of any use to Caesar, so they've just been left there, pulled up on the sandy beach. I can see five or six of them from here. We have our choice. I have my eye on that one with the white sail. Less visible than, say, the one with the orange sail."

"Do you know anything about sailing a vessel like that?"

"You might be surprised by the things I know, Gordianus."

"Once we're out in the harbor, what then?"

"We sail directly for the quay. The channel can't be more than a quarter of a mile across."

"What if the current's against us? What if Caesar's men come after us?"

"Then Fortex shall have to row harder," said Tiro.

Fortex rubbed his jaw.

"And you may have to swim," added Tiro.

I didn't like the sound of that.

We were halfway down the hillside, our horses picking their own path through the bramble, when a voice called out from the ridge behind us.

"You can't go down there! It's off-limits!"

It was the centurion in charge of the lookout. Tiro turned and waved. He held a hand to his ear, flashed a stupid grin and shrugged, as if to say he couldn't make out what the man was saying. "Ride on," he whispered. "Look straight ahead. Ignore him. Head directly for the skiff. Faster!"

We urged our mounts down the hillside and reached the narrow beach. Behind us, I heard the galloping footfall of a horse.

"How many?" said Tiro, keeping his eyes ahead.

Fortex glanced over his shoulder. "Just the one."

"Good. He thinks we're harmless, then. We'll allow him to go on thinking that as long as possible. You know what to do, Fortex."

At the strip of beach between the hut and the skiff we dismounted. The centurion was closing on us. I drew close to Tiro.

"What do you mean to do to him?"

"What do you think?"

"Does it have to be like this?"

"We made a bargain, Gordianus. You took me into Caesar's tent, and I'm to get you into Brundisium. Do you want to come along or not? This is war. Did you think there'd be no bloodshed? Just be glad it's not *your* blood about to be spilled."

"It's murder, Tiro. As surely as the death of that wagon driver was murder."

"Murder is a legal term, Gordianus. It doesn't apply to slaves, and it has no meaning on a battlefield."

"Perhaps we can simply knock him unconscious . . . drag him into the hut . . ."

Tiro made a face. "You muddied your mind reading those Greek novels while we sat out the storm in the mountains. All hairbreadth escapes and happy endings! This is the real world, Gordianus. There's only one sure way to get rid of this fellow. Fortex will see to it. It's what he's trained for. Now smile; we have company."

The centurion rode up. He dismounted and walked toward us. There was a spring in his step; the short, brisk ride had exhilarated him. His smile was a little disdainful, but not hostile. I was only an ignorant civilian after all, a sheep that needed herding, not a wolf. He addressed me and ignored the others. "No civilians are allowed along the shoreline."

I held up the copper disk. "But Caesar himself gave—"

"The imperator has issued explicit orders regarding the shoreline. *No exceptions.*" He raised his voice, apparently thinking I might be a little deaf.

"I . . . only wanted to have a look at this quaint fisherman's hut."

The centurion shook his head and smirked a bit. I was like a doddering grandfather who had to be indulged, but only to a point. He took no notice of Fortex, who circled behind him.

Blood pounded in my ears. In a matter of seconds it would be done. The young centurion, all flushed and smugly smiling, would be gripped from behind. Fortex would slit his throat—a flash of steel, a spurt of blood. His eyes would widen in shock and then go blind. A living man would become a corpse while I watched.

Beyond the centurion's shoulder, I had only a partial view of Fortex, but from his movements I could see that he was stealthily drawing his dagger. Tiro stood off to one side, playing the dutiful, retiring slave, holding his breath.

I reached for the centurion's shoulder and drew him toward me. Fortex, uncertain, held back.

"Do you have a grandfather?" I said.

"Two," said the centurion.

"I thought so." I walked him away from the skiff, away from Fortex, and toward the hut. "Is one of them a little deaf? A bit doddering?"

"Both of them, actually." He grinned crookedly. I had made him think of home, far away.

I nodded. "Well, young man, I'm neither doddering nor deaf. I can hear you perfectly well. My eyes are good, too. The reason I rode down here was because I saw someone go into this hut."

He frowned. The hut was crudely built, with a thatched roof. The thin door hung on rusty hinges. "Are you sure?"

"Absolutely. I saw a man in rags skulking down here on the beach, behaving suspiciously. I saw him go into this hut. I thought I should come to investigate."

"You should have called me at once." The centurion rolled his eyes, exasperated.

"But I know how busy you must be. It hardly seemed worth bothering you. Probably it's the owner of the hut, come back to fetch something."

"A looter, more likely." The centurion drew his sword. He walked up to the door and pulled it open with such force that the top hinge broke. "You, inside, come out!" He took a step closer, peering into the darkness. I followed behind, pulling my dagger from its scabbard. With one hand I knocked his helmet forward, over his eyes. With the other I raised the dagger and struck him hard with the pommel at the base of his skull. He fell in a heap at my feet.

I sheathed my dagger. "Make yourself useful, Fortex. Pull him inside the hut. And don't harm him!"

I stepped back and scanned the ridge. "I don't think anyone up

there could have seen that, do you, Tiro? The hut shielded me from
view. Besides, they're all too busy watching the city and the harbor
entrance. I've managed to buy us a little time, but before long they'll
miss him, or start wondering about our horses on the beach. What
are you waiting for? Pull the skiff into the water and let's get going!"

Tiro looked chagrined. "Gordianus, I—"

"You should read more Greek novels, Tiro, and less of that insipid
poetry Cicero produces."

Within moments we were in the skiff and away from the beach.
Tiro unfurled the white sail. Fortex pulled hard at the oars. I sat in
the prow, shivering. I had wet my feet getting into the boat. The water was colder than I expected.

I watched the shoreline. The centurion suddenly appeared at the
doorway of the hut, looking dazed and rubbing the back of his head.
I waved to him and returned the smug smile he had given me earlier.
He staggered out of the hut, shook his fist, and yelled something I
couldn't make out.

Fortex laughed. "I should like to have cut his throat. I've never
killed a centurion. Ah well, perhaps another time."

The wind was with us. So was the current. We skimmed across
the smooth water. The shoreline receded and the walls of the city
loomed higher. Our course was a bit ragged—Tiro was not quite the
sailor he made himself out to be—but despite some zigzagging we
kept heading in the general direction of the port. It seemed almost
absurdly easy, considering how daunting the task of getting into
Brundisium had appeared to me the previous night.

The other skiff was upon us so quickly that it seemed to materi-
alize from thin air. Tiro was busy with the sail. Fortex was rowing with
strong, steady strokes. It was I who saw the skiff first, but not until
it was almost within arrowshot of us. It was a long sleek boat, larger
than ours, with two rowers and two archers, both of whom already
held their bows aloft with arrows notched, aimed in our direction.

I looked to see where the skiff had come from, and noticed a strip
of shoreline directly across from the port. A considerable contingent
of soldiers was gathered there, along with a few small boats. Another
skiff was heading out to join the first in pursuing us.

I nudged Tiro and pointed. Just as he turned to look, one of the bowmen released an arrow. We both flinched, but the arrow fell well short, into the water. It was a test shot to gauge the wind and measure the distance. The second bowman released a shot that came substantially closer. Meanwhile, with two rowers to our one, the skiff steadily gained on us.

"By Hercules, Tiro, can't you keep to a straight course?" I shouted. "If you keep zigzagging back and forth, they're bound to catch us before we reach the quay!"

Tiro made no answer. Perversely, it seemed to me, he veered off course, heading directly toward the city wall, instead of continuing at a more oblique angle toward the port. The skiff gained on us rapidly. I heard a noise like a hornet's buzz and ducked. An arrow flew over my head and tore into the sail, where it snagged and caught, the shaft flapping against the taut canvas. We were at their mercy, with no way to defend ourselves. I gazed at the cold water, bracing myself for the moment we would have to abandon the boat, debating whether drowning was preferable to death by arrows.

Suddenly I heard shouting above our heads and looked up to see soldiers manning the harbor wall. I saw the strategy of Tiro's navigation, to bring us close enough to the wall to put our pursuers in range of arrows from the city's defenders. The fact that we were pursued by Caesar's men was enough to bring Pompey's soldiers to our defense.

With a whoosh like carrion birds taking flight, a hail of arrows descended from the wall. Some fell closer to us than to the pursuing skiff. The water was dotted with little vertical splashes. None of the arrows struck a target, but the point was made. Caesar's men stopped closing in on us.

Tiro sailed parallel to the wall, heading for the quay. The pursuers likewise turned and sailed parallel to us, keeping their distance, trying to edge close enough to shoot us with their arrows without being shot themselves by the archers on the wall. I lay back and crouched as low in the boat as I could, not only to avoid arrows but to give Tiro room to move as he struggled with the sail.

I heard a scream from the other boat and saw that one of the archers had been struck by an arrow in his shoulder. He lost his balance and fell into the water. I hoped our pursuers would turn about, but they left the man's rescue to the boat that followed behind them.

We drew closer and closer to the port. A crowd had gathered on the quay to watch, cheering like spectators at a race. Gazing up from the bottom of the boat, I caught glimpses of the archers who trotted along the parapet, keeping up with us. They hooted and laughed whenever they paused to notch an arrow, take aim, and fire. They were above harm, in no danger of return fire from our pursuers. To them the exchange was a lark, a diversion. How different it felt to me, hunkering down in the boat, watching arrows fly overhead.

A hornet's buzz was followed by a splintering crash, and I felt something tickle my nostrils. An arrow had pierced the side of our boat and stopped just short of splicing my nose.

Suddenly the skiff gave a lurch. We abruptly slowed and angled about. My first thought was that Tiro had been struck and had lost control of the sail, but he was still upright, almost on top of me. Then I saw Fortex. He still gripped the oars, his knuckles fish-belly white, but he had stopped rowing. His eyes were open. His lips trembled as if he wanted to speak, but all that emerged from his mouth was a bloody cough. An arrow had pierced his neck clear through. The metal point protruded from one side, the feathered shaft from the other.

Tiro was frantically working the sail and unable to see what had happened. "Row, Fortex!" he yelled. "Row, damn you!" The oars, dipped in the water and held rigidly in place by Fortex's grip, acted as rudders, causing us to spin. Tiro cursed. A moment later the boat struck something with an impact that rattled my teeth. Tiro tumbled overboard. The splash stung my eyes and sent cold water up my nostrils.

I heard cheering, and realized it was the quay we had struck. I blinked and peered over the bow. Our pursuers had kept up the chase until the last possible moment. Now they turned about and headed back. A final, double volley of arrows followed after them, as the archers on the wall were joined by more archers firing from the quay.

I had reached the port of Brundisium, unscathed.

XX

Everyone in the crowd around us seemed to have an opinion.

"He'll probably die if you pull out that arrow."

"He'll die for sure if you leave it in!"

"Are you certain he's still alive?"

Fortex lay flat on his back on the boardwalk, his eyes open and unblinking, his beard thickly matted with coughed-up blood. More blood coated the shaft of the arrow protruding from either side of his neck. His body was absolutely rigid, every muscle quivering with tension. His fingers remained curled in a white-knuckled grip. It had been a struggle to pry them from the oars. It had been a greater struggle to lift him out of the boat and onto the quay. The front of the tunic was smeared with blood.

I stood at his feet, gazing down, unable to take my eyes off him. Tiro stood beside me, shivering and soaking wet.

"What do you think, Gordianus?"

"He's your man, Tiro." We were in Pompey's domain now. I saw no point in maintaining the charade that Tiro was my slave.

Tiro replied in a whisper, his teeth chattering. "The merciful thing might be to put him out of his misery."

Fortex gave no sign that he heard. His wide-open eyes stared up at heaven. The tension in his body was excruciating to witness, as if every muscle were defiantly clenched. Was it fear, or bravery, or simple animal instinct that caused him to hold on so desperately to life?

We had called for a physician, but none had come. I looked at the arrow and wondered what we should do about it. If we cut off one end, the shaft could be removed. But would that only cause more bleeding? Perhaps the arrow was the only thing preventing his jugulars from spurting fountains of blood onto the boardwalk.

It was impossible to watch him quivering in silent agony and do nothing. I made up my mind to remove the arrow. I reached for my dagger. I gritted my teeth, trying not to envision the mess I might make of it.

Before I could move, the crisis ended. The tension in Fortex's body abruptly subsided. His fingers uncurled. His eyes rolled upward. A sigh escaped his lips, like a low note from a flute. He crossed his own Rubicon and departed for the River Styx.

The crowd relaxed with a collective murmur of relief. People went about their business. A living man with an arrow through his neck was something to see. A dead man was not.

"Funny," said Tiro, "how sometimes a man lives precisely as long as he needs to, and no more."

"What do you mean?"

"Fortex. It was his task to get me safely to Pompey. If he'd been shot a minute sooner, we'd never have made it to the quay. You and I would have died in the boat with him. Instead it happened just so, and here we are. As if the gods decreed it."

"You believe every man has a destiny, then? Even slaves?"

Tiro shrugged. "I don't know. Great men have a destiny. Perhaps the rest of us have one only insofar as we cross their paths and play a part in their destinies."

"Is that what makes you so brave, Tiro? Belief in destiny?"

"Brave?"

"On the mountain, facing Otacilius. In Antony's camp. In Caesar's tent. In the boat, standing up to work the sail, with arrows whizzing past your nose."

Tiro shrugged. I looked past him, to the gates that opened from the boardwalk into the city. A determined-looking centurion and a company of soldiers were marching directly toward us.

"This journey we've taken together, Tiro—did I facilitate your destiny, or did your facilitate mine?"

"It would seem to have been mutual."

"And the role of Fortex was simply to get us here?"

"What else?"

"I wonder if Fortex would have seen it that way. What about that nameless wagon driver?"

"He got us over the mountains, didn't he? It all worked out for the best."

"Not for him. Still, if you're right, the gods have seen us safe thus far. If they intend for me to accomplish what I came for, then I shall live a little longer, at least. I shall try to be as brave as you've been."

Tiro gave me a puzzled frown, then stepped forward to meet the soldiers. The centurion asked his name.

"Soscarides. I expect you've been briefed to look for my arrival."

"Quite a show, from what the archers tell me." The centurion was a grizzled veteran with a big homely face and a tight little smile.

"I'm to report directly to the Great One himself and to no one else," said Tiro.

The centurion nodded. "Who's the dead man?"

"A slave. My bodyguard."

"And this one? Another slave?"

Tiro laughed. "Hold up your hand and show your citizen's ring, Gordianus. Centurion, this man is also known to the Great One. He'll come with me."

The centurion grunted. "Well, you can't report to the imperator as you are—you soaking wet, and this one with blood all down his tunic. I'll see what we can do about a change of clothes."

"There's no time," said Tiro. "You must take us to Pompey at once."

"Castor and Pollux, hold your horses!" The centurion scanned the loiterers on the boardwalk and pointed to a well-dressed civilian. "You there! Yes, you, and your friend. Both of you, come here!" When the two men hung back, the centurion snapped his fingers. Soldiers ran and fetched them by force.

The centurion looked the two men up and down. "Yes, you both look about the right size. And your clothes aren't too shabby. Strip!"

The men's jaws dropped. The centurion snapped his fingers. The soldiers assisted the men in taking off their clothes.

"Not so rough!" yelled the centurion. "Don't tear the tunics. Which one do you prefer, Soscarides?"

Tiro blinked. "The yellow, I suppose."

"Good enough. You who were in the yellow, take off your loin-cloth as well. Go on! My friend Soscarides here is wet to the balls and needs a dry one." He turned to Tiro and me. "Go on, fellows, take off those things you're wearing and put on your new clothes."

I pulled my bloody tunic over my head. "What is this pre-dilection these military types have for making other men strip?" I said to Tiro under my breath, thinking of our humiliation by Ota-cilius on the mountainside. Caesar had said that Pompey's men had alienated the citizens of Brundisium. I could see how.

The centurion looked at our feet. "Shoes, too!" he shouted at the two hapless civilians. They both gave a start, then obediently knelt and began untying the straps at their ankles.

"I can bear to let my own shoes dry on my feet," said Tiro, stand-ing naked for a moment as he exchanged his wet loincloth for the dry one.

The centurion shook his head. "Take it from me. I've marched men to the Pillars of Hercules and back. I'm an expert on feet. You'll be glad of having a pair of dry shoes, once things start moving."

"Moving?" said Tiro, slipping the yellow tunic over his head. It was an excellent fit.

The centurion squinted at the westering sun above the city sky-line. "Sun's sinking. Where do the hours go? Once it's dark, things will start to move, fast and furious. Believe me, you'll be glad you're wearing clean clothes and dry shoes! Remember me then, friend

Soscarides, and say a prayer for the centurion who looked after you as sweetly as your own dear mother!"

~

To slow the progress of Caesar's men once they entered the city, Pompey had barricaded all the major streets at various points and had also laid traps. These were trenches dug across the width of a street, lined across the bottom with sharpened stakes, covered with wicker screens and concealed by a thin layer of earth. Our progress to the city center was necessarily restricted to a course which meandered through secondary streets and alleyways. The centurion led the way while his soldiers formed a cordon around Tiro and me.

Officially, the townspeople had been confined to their homes, but in fact they were everywhere in the streets, yelling, frantically rushing about, wearing expressions of thinly suppressed panic. If Caesar's camp had seemed a beehive abuzz with orderly movement, then Brundisium was an antbed turned by the farmer's plow. I came to appreciate the calm determination of our centurion, who seemed unfazed by it all.

We finally emerged from the maze of narrow byways into the city forum, where civic buildings and temples faced an open square. Here there was at once a greater sense of order and a greater sense of chaos. Centurions shouted commands and troops stood at rigid attention in the square. At the same time, weeping women and ashen-faced men thronged the temple steps. From their open doors I caught the smell of burning incense and myrrh, and heard the echo of prayers wailed not in Latin but in the strange ululating language of the Messapians, the race that settled the heel of Italy at the beginning of time and built the city of Brundisium. The Messapians fought against Sparta in ancient days. They fought against Pyrrhus, who conquered them for Rome. The seafaring, cosmopolitan people of Brundisium worship all the deities worshiped in Rome, but they also pay homage to their own gods, ancient Messapic deities unknown in Rome, with unpronounceable names. Those were the gods they called on in their moment of despair, when the fate of their city hung in the balance.

We came to the municipal senate building on the east side of the forum, where Pompey had made his headquarters. The centurion told us to wait on the steps while he went inside. His soldiers maintained their cordon around us. Whether they were protecting us or holding us prisoner, I wasn't sure. Exhausted, I sat on the cold, hard steps. Tiro joined me. The atmosphere of the city under siege had dispirited me, but seemed to have stimulated Tiro.

"If Pompey can pull this off," he said, "he'll truly be the greatest military genius of the age."

I frowned. "Pull what off?"

"A successful retreat from Brundisium. He's already sent part of his army to Dyrrhachium, along with the consuls and the greater part of the senate. Now comes the tricky part. With Caesar ready to scale the walls and throw all his might against the city, can Pompey manage an orderly, organized retreat, through the streets, onto the ships, and out the harbor entrance? The tactical challenge must be staggering. The risk is enormous."

"I see what you mean. How and when does the last defender climb down from the parapet, cede his ground to the invader, and board the last departing ship? It could turn into a stampede."

"Which could turn into a rout." Tiro gazed about the forum, with its jarring mixture of rigid military order and barely contained religious panic. "Then there's the unknown, uncontrollable element of the civilian population. We know they've had their fill of Pompey. But can they be certain that Caesar won't slaughter them for harboring his enemy? The locals are liable to split into factions, divided by old grudges. Who knows how they'll take advantage of the chaos? Some may unbar the gates and lead Caesar's men safely around the barricades and traps, while others may throw stones at them from the rooftops. Some may panic and try to board Pompey's ships. The sheer numbers of them could jam the streets and make escape impossible. A commander is judged by his success at surmounting challenges. If Pompey can get all his men safely out of Italy to fight another day, he'll have earned anew his right to be called Great One."

"Do you think so? It seems to me he could have better demonstrated his genius by avoiding such a trap in the first place."

"Pompey did as well as any man could, considering the situation. No one foresaw that Caesar would dare to cross the Rubicon. That took Caesar's own lieutenants by surprise. I think he surprised even himself, committing such hubris."

"And the disaster at Corfinium?"

"Pompey had no control over that. He told Domitius to fall back and join him, but Domitius let vanity run away with his common sense, of which he has little enough to start. Compare Domitius to Pompey: in every decision since the crisis began, Pompey has acted strictly from reason. He's never shown a trace of vanity or foolish pride."

"Some would say he hasn't shown much nerve, either."

"It takes nerve to look an enemy in the eye and fall back step by step. If he can see this orderly retreat through to the end, Pompey will have shown that his spine is made of steel."

"And then what?"

"That's the brilliance of it! Pompey has allies all through the East. That's where his greatest strength lies, and where Caesar is weakest. While Pompey rallies those reinforcements, from his stronghold in Greece he can blockade Italy and cut off all shipping from the East, including the grain harvest from Egypt. Let Caesar have Italy, for the time being. With Egypt closed to him and the East rising against him, with starvation looming in Italy and Pompey's troops in Spain at his back, we'll see how long Caesar can last as king of Rome."

It was just possible, I thought, that everything Tiro said made sense. Did Caesar have any inkling of such a scenario? I thought of the infinitely confident man I had seen that morning, but perhaps that was only a part of his genius as a leader, never to show doubt or betray the nightmares that haunted him in the dark.

Perhaps it would all go Pompey's way, in the end. But that could happen only if he successfully escaped from Brundisium. We had come to a nexus in the great contest. In the next few hours, Pompey would cast a throw sufficient to let him play another round, or lose the game altogether.

The centurion returned. "The Great One will see you." I started to get up, but he laid a hand on my shoulder. "Not you. Soscarides."

I reached for Tiro's arm. "When you see Pompey, ask him to grant me an audience."

"I'll do my best, Gordianus. But in the midst of a military action, you can hardly expect—"

"Remind him of the task he gave me in Rome. Tell him—tell him I know the answer."

Tiro raised an eyebrow. "Perhaps you should tell me, Gordianus. I can pass the news on to Pompey, and ask for Davus to be set free. That's what you want, isn't it?"

I shook my head. "No. I'll reveal the truth about Numerius's murder only to Pompey, and only if he releases Davus first. If he wants to know what happened to Numerius, he must agree to those terms. Otherwise, he may never know."

Tiro frowned. "If I tell him all this, and it's only a ruse to gain you an audience—"

"Please, Tiro."

He gave me a last dubious look, then followed the centurion inside.

The sun dipped beyond the western hills. A chilly twilight descended on the forum, bringing a curious sense of calm. Even the shrill ululations from the temples seemed oddly comforting.

Torches were lit and passed among the troops. I understood now why Pompey waited for nightfall to make his exit. In the darkness, the barricades and pitfalls in the streets would be doubly dangerous. While the besiegers backtracked and stumbled over each other, Pompey's men, drilled in the escape route, would be able to circumvent the hazards and quickly reach the ships.

The centurion returned.

"Soscarides—?" I said.

"Still with Pompey."

"No message for me?"

"Not yet."

There was a clanging of brazen doors and a commotion at the top of the steps. I got to my feet. A large group of officers poured out of the building and onto the porch. The centurion and his soldiers sprang to attention.

Pompey walked at the head of the group, dressed in full armor plated with gold. The precious metal glistened and shimmered, reflecting the light of the torches in the square below. Under his arm he carried a gold-plated helmet with a yellow horsehair plume. Below the neck, thanks to the muscular torso molded upon his breastplate, he appeared to have the physique of a young gladiator. The illusion was belied by a pair of spindly legs which gold-plated greaves could not disguise.

I looked for Tiro in the retinue, but didn't see him. Nor did I see Davus.

"Great One!" I shouted, hoping to get his attention. I reacted as any citizen in the forum might, petitioning a magistrate. But this was not Rome, and the man before me was not Pompey the politician, obliged to ingratiate himself with every Marcus who could vote; this was Pompey the Great, Imperator of the Spanish Legions, the man who believed in carrying swords, not quoting laws.

"Quiet!" snapped the centurion. He remained at attention. His glaring eyes demanded the same of me.

Pompey halted at the top of the steps. The officers fanned out behind him. A trumpeter blew a fanfare for attention. I was no more than twenty feet away. Pompey looked tired and haggard. His eyes were puffy and bloodshot. But the soldiers in the square below must have seen a very different Pompey, a powerfully built, golden-sheathed, almost godlike figure, a statue of Mars come to life.

"Soldiers of Rome! Defenders of the Senate and the people! Tonight you will carry out the exercise for which you've been drilled over the last few days. Each of you has a role to play. You all know what to do. Act quickly and efficiently, obey the orders of your centurions, and there will be no problems.

"The enemy has been frustrated at every turn. A handful of veteran archers and slingers have successfully kept him away from the city walls. He has no ships. His efforts to block the harbor have proven futile. Typically, his ambition oversteps his ability. In the long run, he shall be sorry for it."

There was a murmur of laughter among the troops in the square. I had always been blind to whatever charm Pompey possessed, but these men seemed to appreciate it. Perhaps one had to be a military man.

"We are about to leave Italy and cross over the sea," Pompey continued. "Some of you may feel misgivings about this. Do not. We are moving forward, not falling back. Rome lies across the water now. We go to join her. A city is made of men, not buildings. We go to where the true heart of Rome resides, with the duly elected consuls. Let the enemy take over empty buildings if he wishes, and invest himself with whatever empty titles his imagination can devise. I think perhaps he has dwelled for too long north of the Rubicon, among primitive barbarians who worship kings. Having conquered those petty monarchs, he thinks he should become one himself. He should remember instead the fate of every despot who ever raised arms against the Senate and the people of Rome."

A murmur among the troops swelled into a cheer. Pompey cut it short by raising his hands. "Soldiers! Remember the first order of the day: *Silence!* The enemy's ear is pressed to the city gates. We must carry out this operation with an absolute minimum of noise. It starts now. Cohort commanders, begin evacuation!"

He gave a gesture to the officers behind him, like a circus master signaling the commencement of a race. As they moved forward, Pompey stepped back, withdrawing from the sight of the troops in the square like a golden deus ex machina disappearing at the theater.

The ranks of his retinue were thinned by the dispatch of the cohort commanders, and I was now able to spot Tiro, who walked to Pompey's side. The Great One's personal bodyguards closed around him. Among them I saw a lumbering hulk with a familiar gait. Even before he turned to show the profile of his boyish face, I knew it was Davus.

I tried to catch Tiro's eye, but he was busily conferring with Pompey. Suddenly I saw him gesture in my direction. Pompey nodded and turned. He looked straight at me, then stepped past his bodyguards and walked directly to me. The centurion beside me snapped to attention.

"I heard you shout at me earlier, Finder." Pompey sounded tired and irritable.

"Did you, Great One? You gave no sign."

"A trained orator lets nothing distract him. Tiro says you have news for me."

"Yes, Great One."

"Good. Centurion, don't you have evacuation orders?"

"Yes, Imperator."

"Then off with you!"

"Imperator, I should tell you that this man is armed. He's carrying a dagger. Shall I disarm him?"

Pompey managed a weary smile. "Worried about an assassination attempt, centurion? Killing people is hardly Gordianus's style. Is it, Finder?"

He didn't wait for me to answer, but dismissed the centurion and his men with a curt wave. "Come along, Finder. I suppose you'll want to say hello to that son-in-law of yours, since you dragged yourself across half of Italy to find him. I can't imagine why. I never met a fellow so thick. Hard to imagine that I once paid good silver for him."

I drew a deep breath. "And my report, Great One?"

He made a face. "Not here. Not now. Can't you see there's a fire at my feet? Save your report until we're safely on the water!"

XXI

"I can't believe it! I just can't believe it!"

"Davus, not so hard—you're squeezing the life out of me . . ."

"Sorry." Davus released me and stepped back. I reached up to rub my cheek, where the links of his mail shirt had pressed a tattoo into the soft flesh. Outfitted all in leather and steel, the sight of him was as overpowering as the hug he had just given me. Yet the broad grin across his face made him look as harmless as a child.

"I just can't believe it," he said again, laughing. "You came all this way, over the mountains and everything. How on earth did you get inside the city?"

"It's a long story, Davus. I'll tell you another time."

One of Pompey's officers gave a shout. He raised his arm and pointed at a tall building across the square. Up on the rooftop, some-one was running back and forth, waving a torch.

Pompey squinted. "By Hades, you were right, Tiro. Damn these townspeople! That's a clear signal to Caesar to commence his attack. Scribonius, order an archer to shoot that man down."

The officer who had pointed stepped forward. "He's out of range, Imperator."

"Then send someone up there."

"The way to the roof will almost surely be blockaded, Imperator. Is it really worth our time—"

"Then send some archers onto a neighboring rooftop and shoot at him from there!"

"Imperator, the evacuation has begun. By the time our archers—"

"I don't care! Look at that ape, waving his torch, laughing at us. The men in the square can see. The brave soldiers manning the wall can see! Terrible for morale. I want that man's head. And bring me his hand, as well, with the torch still in it!"

Scribonius summoned archers, but in the next moment Pompey's order was rendered moot. All around the city, civilians appeared on rooftops. Some waved torches. Others danced in the flickering torch-light like celebrants at a festival. Pompey was furious.

"Damn these people! When I retake Brundisium, I shall burn the city to the ground. I'll sell every man, woman, and child into slavery!" He paced back and forth, gazing westward. Above the rooftops we could see the towers flanking the city gate. "Engineer Magius, has the gate been sufficiently blocked?"

Another officer stepped forward. "You know it has, Imperator. There are tons of rubble piled against it. No battering ram will budge it. The only way Caesar's men can get into the city is by climbing over the walls."

"Scribonius, will the line of archers and slingers along the parapet hold?"

"Every one's a seasoned veteran, Imperator. They'll hold."

At that moment, we heard the first sounds of battle carried across the cold air. There was only shouting at first, then the eerie echo of steel clanging against steel, and the dull boom of a battering ram.

The square below rapidly emptied. The last of the soldiers filed out in silence, heading for the ships. The forum grew dark except for glowing patches of light from open temple doors. I found myself wishing I understood Messapic. It seemed to me that the ululations from the temples had gradually changed tenor, from songs of terror and lamentation to songs of deliverance. The chants mixed with the distant sounds of battle.

There was a signal for Pompey's retinue to commence evacuation. Suddenly, everyone around me was moving down the steps. The officer called Scribonius handed Davus a torch and told him to follow as rear guard.

We headed toward the port by a different route than the one the centurion had taken earlier. This street was wider and the way more direct. I wondered that it hadn't been blockaded and said as much to Davus, who told me to wait and see. At the first intersection we came to, the engineer Magius called a brief halt. He and a few other men gripped some ropes hanging from the buildings on either side. In an instant, tons of rubble poured into the street behind us. An ingenious system of pulleys had been installed, connected to wooden sluices and caches full of debris stored in the upper floors of the buildings facing the street.

The same operation was repeated at the next intersection, and the next. Magius was blockading the street as we passed.

At other places, Magius gave a signal for caution and led the company in single file along one side of the street, keeping close to the wall. Trenches with spikes had been dug across the street and covered over. Only Magius knew exactly where they were and on which side to bypass them. The traps were impossible to see. In the darkness, the dirt spread above the wicker blinds blended imperceptibly with the rest of the street.

Now and again I heard faint, echoing sounds of battle from behind us, shouts and screams mixed with the chanting from the temples. The darkness of the narrow streets, the flickering torchlight, the man-made avalanches of rubble, the unseen traps beneath our feet, all seemed like elements from a mad dream. Images of the day flashed through my overwrought mind: arrows crisscrossing in the blue sky above my head—the cold, still water of the harbor, promising death—Fortex on the quay quivering with tension, gripping invisible oars and staring agape at the boatman Charon coming for him across the River Styx.

I seemed to be trapped in a waking nightmare. Then I chanced to look at Davus beside me. He was grinning from ear to ear. For him, it was all a grand adventure. I gripped his arm.

"Davus, when we arrive at Pompey's ship, you'll stay behind."

He furrowed his brow.

"Davus, I have the information that Pompey wanted. About Numerius. But I shall give it to him only if he agrees to leave you behind."

"Leave me behind?"

"Listen, Davus, and try to understand! I shall be going with Pompey, but you shall not. It's the only way I can make this work. We'll leave you behind on the pier. As soon as the ship casts off, you must take off all your armor. Do you understand? Keep your sword to protect yourself, but strip down to your tunic and throw everything else in the water. There must be nothing to identify you as one of Pompey's men. The townspeople are likely to kill you out of spite, if Caesar's men don't kill you first."

"Stay behind?" Davus still didn't comprehend.

"Don't you want to go back to Rome? Don't you want to see Diana and little Aulus again?"

"Of course."

"Then do as I say! For a while, the city will be in chaos. But you're a big man; no one will bother you unless they have a reason. Don't pick any fights. Try to pass as one of the townspeople, at least until you can hand yourself over to Caesar's men."

"Hand myself over? They'll kill me."

"No, they won't. Caesar is doing everything he can to appear merciful. You won't be harmed, as long as you throw down your sword and don't resist. Demand to see Meto. And if Meto should be—if for any reason you can't find Meto, ask for Marc Antony, the tribune. Tell him who you are. Ask for his protection."

"What about you, father-in-law?"

"I shall take care of myself."

"I don't understand. You'll end up with Pompey over in Greece. How will you get home?"

"Don't worry about me."

"But Diana, and Bethesda—"

"Tell them not to worry. Tell them . . . I love them."

"This isn't right. I should go with you, to protect you."

"No! The whole point is to get you away from Pompey and back to Rome. Don't spoil all my efforts now, Davus. Do as I tell you!"

Suddenly there was a tremendous crash ahead of us. Rubble poured into the street. For a moment I thought Pompey had been struck, but he emerged from the dust cursing and coughing. Someone had set off one of Magius's barricading devices in an attempt to ambush us.

Pompey's men immediately swarmed over the rubble, looking for the culprits. Shrieks of laughter were followed by shrill screams. The soldiers returned with their squirming prisoners: four boys. The soldiers restrained them by twisting their arms behind their backs and clutching fistfuls of hair. The oldest looked about the same age as Mopsus. The others looked even younger. I was amazed they had the strength to pull down the rubble. Their success was a testament to Magius's engineering.

For Pompey, this was the final straw. He walked up to the oldest boy and slapped him across the face. The boy's defiance crumbled. He looked terrified. Blood trickled from his nose. He started to weep. So did his companions.

Pompey snapped his fingers. "Bodyguards! Come! Executing partisans isn't a job fit for soldiers."

Davus responded at once. I gripped his arm, but he pulled free. I hissed his name. He looked back at me and shrugged, as if to say he had no choice.

"Tie their arms behind their backs and lay them on the rubble," ordered Pompey. Davus held up his torch while the other bodyguards ripped apart the boys' tunics and used the strips to bind them.

"Gag them," Pompey ordered. "I don't want to hear any screams for mercy. Then cut off their heads."

The boys' weeping abruptly turned to shrieks. More cloth was ripped, and the shrieks were abruptly muffled.

"We'll execute them on the spot and leave them as an example. Let the people of Brundisium see the price for betraying Pompey the Great. Let them think about that, while they await my return."

It happened so swiftly it seemed unreal. In seconds, the boys were stripped to their loincloths, bound and gagged and ready to be beheaded. Tiro drew back into the shadows, keeping his eyes down. Davus hung back. Pompey noticed.

"Davus! You'll cut off the head of the ringleader."

Davus swallowed hard. He glanced in my direction, but quickly lowered his eyes. He handed his torch to a soldier and slowly drew his sword. He shifted nervously from foot to foot.

"Great One, no!"

Pompey turned to see who shouted. "Finder! I should have known."

"Great One, let the boys go."

"Let them go? They very nearly killed me!"

"It was a prank. They're boys, not soldiers. I doubt they even know you were at the head of the retinue."

"All the worse. How should that have looked in Rome? Pompey the Great killed by accident, by a gang of street rats pulling a prank! They'll pay with their heads."

"But how would that look in Rome? Boys, mere children, their heads cut off and left for their parents to find. If these were barbarians in the hinterlands, yes—but this is Italy. We could as easily be in Corfinium. Or Rome."

Pompey bit his lower lip. He stared at me for what seemed a long time.

"Put away your swords," he finally said. "Leave the boys as they are, bound and gagged. Let the people see that they were captured, and spared. If Caesar can show mercy, so can I. By Hades, let's get out of this godforsaken place!"

Davus's shoulders slumped forward in relief. Pompey gave me a last furious glance, then held out his arms to his bodyguards, who helped him over the pile of rubble. Davus fell back to resume his post as rear guard. He helped me pick my way step by step over the debris. The last of the barricades and traps was behind us. We pressed on toward the port, saying not another word to each other.

~

As soon as we passed through the city gates and onto the board-walk, one of the soldiers gathered up all the torches, ran to the quay-side, and threw them into the water. The port was clearly visible to Caesar's forces ringing the harbor. Darkness was as vital as silence to the success of Pompey's operation.

The quay was lined with men waiting to board their assigned ships. We hurried past them, heading for the end of the quay.

The uncanny quiet was suddenly broken by cheering that began ahead of us and spread down the length of the quay. I thought at first that Pompey's arrival had been noticed, and the cheer was for him. Then I heard a shout: "They're through! They've made it!" The first of the transport ships to cast off had passed safely beyond the break-waters at the harbor entrance and had reached the sea.

Masts creaked and sails billowed, and more ships cast off. As we neared the end of the quay I had a clear view of the harbor entrance. The breakwaters were as dark as the quay, horizontal smudges that seemed to rise barely above the waterline. A captain without keen night vision might easily run aground, trying to pass between them. I felt more out of my element than ever, plunged into a shadowy world ruled by the likes of Pompey and Caesar, where men manufac-tured avalanches, moved mountains of earth, built atop water, and made even darkness their weapon.

At the end of the quay, Pompey's ship waited. It was a smaller, sleeker, faster vessel than the big transport ships. A boarding plank was quickly laid in place. Pompey headed straight for it. I summoned my nerve and quickened my pace to catch up with him.

"Great One!"

He abruptly halted and turned about. Without torchlight, it was hard to read his expression. I saw only deep shadows where his eyes should be. The hard line of his mouth turned down sharply at the corners. "Hades take you, Finder! What do you want now?"

"Great One, my son-in-law—I want you to release him from your service. Leave him behind."

"Why?"

"It's the price for what I have to tell you. 'Not here, not now,' you said. On board your ship then, when time allows. I'll go with you. But you must leave Davus here."

Pompey was silent. He seemed to be staring at me, but I couldn't see his eyes. Finally he gestured for the rest of the party to commence boarding, then turned back to me. "Finder, why do I have the feeling that this is a trick of some sort—a ruse to trade places with your boneheaded son-in-law? I spared those street rats for trifling with me. I won't do the same for you."

"It's not a trick, Great One. I know who killed your kinsman, and why."

"Then tell me now."

I glanced at Davus, who stood awkwardly by while the others boarded. Tiro also hung back, waiting to see what would happen. "No. I'll tell you after we cast off."

"After Davus is out of my reach, you mean. Don't you trust me, Finder?"

"We must trust one another, Great One."

He cocked his head. "What a peculiar fellow you are, Finder, to dare to talk to me this way. Go on, then, board the ship." He turned about. "You too, Tiro. Stop gawking! As for you, Davus, I'm done with you. Off! Away! To Hades with you!"

Davus looked to me. I stepped forward, reached into my tunic, and pressed my moneybag into his hands. He looked down at the pouch and frowned. It was heavy with silver. Thanks to Tiro's largesse I had spent almost nothing during the journey. There was more than enough to see him safely home.

"But father-in-law," he whispered, "you can't give me all this! You'll need it."

"Just take it, Davus, and go!"

He looked into my eyes, then at his pouch in his hands, then into my eyes again. His shoulders rose and fell as he drew a deep breath. Finally he turned, but still hesitated.

"Go, Davus. Now!"

Without looking back he began walking down the quay, back toward the city.

Tiro boarded the ship. I waited for Pompey, but he gestured that I should go first. He followed after me. The boarding plank was withdrawn.

Orders were given in hushed voices. The sails snapped and billowed. The deck moved under me and the quay wheeled away.

I peered back the way we had come, and saw a figure I thought must be Davus, standing alone at the far end of the quay, framed by the gateway into the city. Then the ship turned and I lost sight of him.

XXII

I quickly lost sight of both Tiro and Pompey on the dark, crowded deck. No one questioned my presence. No one seemed to take any notice of me at all.

The soldiers were ordered into battle formation, but there was considerable confusion, with frantic movements back and forth and a great deal of arguing and cursing. After all Pompey's careful planning and what had appeared to be a perfect evacuation, I thought how ironic it would be if all his ships should escape except his own, for want of adequate naval drills among his hand-picked elite.

But the confusion was only temporary. Catapults and ballistic machines were rolled into position and clamped in place, then loaded and cocked by means of large wheels with ratchets. Infantrymen sheathed their swords, took up spears, and formed a tight cordon along the rail, their shields creating an unbroken barricade. At elevated positions behind them, archers took their places. Other soldiers attended the archers, standing by to shield them and supply them with arrows.

I found a place to stand atop an elevated platform amidship. All around us in the darkness loomed the big transport ships. Some were sailing for the harbor entrance while others hung back. Such a co-ordinated operation, without benefit of lights or other signals, meant they were following a precise order of evacuation determined before-hand.

The acoustics on the harbor were baffling. I heard indistinct shouts and the faraway clatter of battle, but couldn't tell which noises came from the city and which echoed across the water from the harbor entrance.

Ship after ship sailed past the breakwaters and into the open sea. I thought I could see exchanges of arrows and missiles between the ships and the men on the breakwaters, but the darkness and the dis-tance made it impossible to discern any details.

As Pompey's ship drew nearer to the harbor entrance, queuing up to run the gauntlet, the incendiary assault began. From both break-waters, catapults hurled flaming missiles toward the ship passing be-tween. By their illumination, I saw a bizarre sight: Caesar's men were frantically dismantling their own defenses on the breakwaters, tear-ing down the towers and mantlets and casting the debris into the water.

The missiles fell short. More incendiary missiles were fired. These, too, fell short, but the terrific splashes created great explo-sions of steam. At the same time, some of the debris cast into the waves caught fire, dotting the harbor entrance with points of flame.

The wrack of smoke and steam posed a hazard to the ship ahead of us, obscuring the captain's sightlines. He sailed off course, veering sharply toward the northern breakwater. I heard a loud curse behind me and looked over my shoulder. Pompey was only a few paces away. He seemed not to notice me. All his attention was on the battle.

The ship ahead of us veered farther off course, bedeviled now by a sudden change in the wind. It sailed directly toward the tip of the northern breakwater until, from our perspective, a collision appeared imminent. I heard Pompey suck in a breath.

But there was no collision. The ship skimmed past. For a mo-ment, because of the confusion of the smoke, the ship appeared to have sailed safely outside the breakwater, on the seaward side. Then

I heard a groan from Pompey, and realized the truth. The ship was still inside the harbor, sailing close alongside the breakwater, barely managing to avoid a scraping collision and apparently unable to pull back into the open harbor. It came to a standstill, held in place by the change in the wind, trapped against the breakwater, easily within range of arrows and missiles from Caesar's men, who let out a cheer that echoed across the water.

The vulnerable ship easily might have been deluged with incendiary missiles, but the enemy apparently preferred to take it intact. As we discovered in the next moment, they had the means to do so.

The officer Scribonius came running to Pompey. "Imperator, look behind us, back toward the city!"

The last of the transport ships had set sail, which meant that the last of Pompey's covering guard had safely withdrawn from the city walls and taken flight. But that also meant that the city was now completely open to Caesar's men. Given the barricades and traps in the streets, it was reasonable to assume that they should still be making their way through the city, yet the quays behind us glittered with torchlight. Not only had Caesar's men already taken the port, but some had manned fishing vessels and were boldly sailing toward the breakwater, evidently planning to board the trapped transport ship.

Scribonius gripped Pompey's arm. "Imperator, shall we turn about and engage them? We might fend them off and buy more time for the ship trapped against the breakwater."

"No! We can't risk running afoul of the breakwater ourselves. That ship is lost to us now. There's no saving it. If I could, I'd set fire to it myself, to keep Caesar from having it. Sail straight on!"

Scribonius withdrew.

"How can he do it?" Pompey pounded his fist against the mast. "How can he move so fast? What sort of pact has Caesar made with the gods? It isn't humanly possible! Even if the damned townspeople showed his soldiers safely past every barricade and trap, how can so many of them already be at the port? And what madness impels them to set out after us in those small ships? Caesar himself must be there, urging them on."

I gazed back at the port and imagined Caesar standing at the end of the quay, in the very spot where Pompey had stood only moments before, his red cape fluttering in the breeze, gazing out at Pompey's ship as we vanished into the clouds of smoke and vapor at the harbor entrance. I shut my eyes and prayed that Meto was there with Caesar, safe and whole, and that Davus was there as well, regretting not too bitterly that he had done as I told him. I imagined my son and my son-in-law together and safe on the quay, and clung to that image.

"Damn you, Finder!"

I opened my eyes to see Pompey glaring at me. Flames from burning flotsam in the water all around us pierced the smoke and lit up his eyes.

"You're Caesar's man, aren't you?"

I shook my head, not understanding.

Pompey scowled. "That slave you adopted, your precious son, Meto—he's been Caesar's cozy tentmate for years. And you're one of Caesar's spies. He's always had your loyalty. Admit it! Not even Caesar could have gotten so many men through the city so quickly, without spies to help him. How long have you been in contact with the townspeople? How well did you know those street rats who almost killed me? Was it you who put them up to it? No wonder you begged for their lives!"

"Great One, you're mistaken. What you're suggesting is impossible. Ask Tiro. He came with me all the way from Rome—"

"Yes, you managed to leech onto Tiro, and fool even him. Davus! He must have been your inside man, spying on me all this time! And I thought he was an idiot."

"Great One, this is madness."

Firelight danced across Pompey's face. I would not have recognized him. He seemed to be possessed by something not human—a god or a demon, I couldn't tell which. Hackles rose on the back of my neck.

Ahead of us loomed more smoke and flames. I heard shouting from either side, taunts and curses from the men on the breakwaters. I heard the creak and snap of catapults and ballistic engines. Fireballs hurtled toward us, shrieking like harpies. Scribonius screamed orders: "Catapults, return fire! Archers, return fire!"

Pompey stared at me, oblivious to the battle commencing around us.

"Great One, I haven't deceived you. There's no plot. I'm not Caesar's man."

He clutched my throat. In his grip I felt all the fury that must have been growing in him day by day ever since he fled Rome. My vision dimmed. His face swam before my eyes. Above the pounding blood in my ears the screams and shouts around us seemed hardly more than whispers.

A fireball landed so close that we were doused with cold water, followed by steaming mist. Soldiers cried out, broke ranks, and hastily reformed. Pompey's grip never loosened. I struggled to pry his fingers from my throat.

"If you're not Caesar's spy, then tell me what you came to tell me! Who murdered Numerius?"

All along, I had known it would come to this.

In my mind, especially on sleepless nights, I had rehearsed this moment many times. I had come almost to look forward to it. The secret was heavy. I wanted to lay it down. The shame was bitter, like wormwood on the tongue. I wanted to be cleansed of it. But in my imagination the time and place of my confession had always been quiet and dignified, in some private council chamber with all ears pricked to hear me out, like Oedipus on the stage—never like this, in the heat of battle with death and darkness all around, and Pompey already furious and ready to strangle me.

I was barely able to force the words past the hands around my throat. "I . . . killed . . . him."

What happened was the opposite of what I expected. Pompey abruptly released his grip and drew back.

"Why do you say such a thing, Finder? Why do you lie? Do you know who killed Numerius or not?"

"I killed him," I whispered.

I swallowed hard and rubbed the bruises on my throat. How peculiar, I thought: why bother to soothe the little irritations of a body that has no future beyond the next few moments?

I had known when I stepped aboard Pompey's ship that I would die there, though I hadn't expected the end to come so quickly. I had known when I set out from Rome that I would never come back. From the start I had hoped somehow to trade myself for Davus, and so gain some value from my death beyond an end to my own shame.

Scribonius ran the length of the ship, waving a sword over his head. "Starboard catapults, fire at will! All archers, fire to starboard!" We had sailed perilously close to the southern breakwater—so close that a fireball overshot and flew screaming over our heads, trailing streamers of smoke and a shower of sparks.

"Why?" said Pompey, his madness turning to confusion. "If you did such a thing, why confess?"

In the veils of smoke around us, I saw Numerius's bulging eyes and bloated, lifeless face. Above the roar of the battle, I heard his mother's tremulous voice and the sobs of Aemilia weeping for a child never to be born. "To be rid of the regret," I said. "The remorse. The guilt."

Pompey shook his head skeptically, as if he had heard of such emotions but had no firsthand knowledge of them. "But why would *you* kill Numerius?" The question contained another, unspoken: had he overlooked something obvious, been made a fool of?

"Numerius came to my house that morning to blackmail me."

"Never! Numerius was mine. He worked only for me."

"Numerius worked for himself! He was a schemer, a blackmailer. He had a document—evidence of a plot to kill Caesar, a pact signed by the conspirators. My son's was the first signature. The document was written in Meto's own hand. Even the grammar was his." I lowered my eyes.

"Your son? Caesar's favorite?"

"When and why Meto turned against Caesar, I don't know. Numerius said he had other incriminating documents, hidden somewhere. He demanded money, far more than I could pay. He refused to lower his price. He said he was about to leave Rome. Unless I paid, he would send the documents at once to Caesar. Caesar knows Meto's handwriting as well as I do! It would have been the end of him. I had only a moment to decide."

Pompey curled his upper lip. "The garrote around his neck . . ."

"A souvenir from a past investigation. Numerius waited in the garden. I went to fetch money from my study. But I brought back the garrote instead. He was standing at the foot of Minerva with his back to me, whistling at the sky. So arrogant! He was young, strong. I doubted my strength—but it wasn't as hard as I thought it would be."

Another fireball shrieked above our heads, so close I flinched. By its lurid glare I saw the growing rage on Pompey's face. "What happened to the document he showed you?"

"I took it to my study. I burned it in the brazier. That was when Davus came into the garden and found the body."

"Then Davus knew the truth? All along?"

"No! I told him nothing of the blackmail, or the murder. I told no one, not even my wife or daughter. To protect them. If they'd known, and you suspected . . . but that wasn't the real reason. It was shame . . . guilt . . ."

I had come full circle. How could I expect a man like Pompey to understand? To slaughter hundreds or thousands in battle was a glorious thing, pleasing to the gods. To kill a single man was murder, a crime against heaven.

I had killed men before, but only in desperate self-defense, when the choice was no choice at all, my life or another's. Never from behind. Never in cold blood. When I killed Numerius, something in me died.

I had always secretly imagined myself to be better than other men. Men like Pompey or Caesar or Cicero would doubtless look down at me and laugh at such a conceit, but I had always taken pride and comfort from knowing that while others might be richer or stronger or higher-born, still I was *better.* Gordianus freed slaves and adopted them. Gordianus stood aloof to the greed and grubby passions that drove "respectable" Romans into the law courts, where they tore at one another like vicious beasts. Gordianus did not cheat or steal, and seldom lied. Gordianus knew right from wrong by some infallible internal moral sense, yet had compassion for those who struggled with shades of gray. Gordianus would never murder. As Pompey had said, killing people was not his style.

Yet Gordianus had done just that, strangling the life out of another man in his own garden.

In doing so, I had forfeited the thing which set me apart from other men. I had lost the favor of the gods. I felt it the instant Numerius Pompeius crumpled lifeless at my feet. The sun withdrew behind a cloud. The world became colder and darker.

That moment had brought me directly, inevitably, to this moment. I was prepared for whatever happened next. I resigned myself to the Fates.

Davus was rescued. I had seen Meto alive and well. Bethesda and Diana and Eco and their children were all safe, or as safe as anyone could be in a broken world. If it was true that Numerius had other documents that compromised Meto hidden away somewhere, my only regret was that I had not been able to find them and destroy them, for Meto's sake.

In my mind, along with my confession, I had also pictured what would follow. I had imagined Pompey summoning henchmen to dispose of me, out of his sight. I had never imagined him leaping on me like a wild beast, his hands tearing at my face. I covered my eyes. He seized me by the hair and knocked my head against the mast. My ears rang. I tasted blood in my mouth. He threw me to the deck. He screamed and kicked me wildly.

I somehow scrambled to my feet. I ran blindly, stumbling and tripping over coils of rope, colliding with cold armor, cutting my cheeks and arms and shoulders on arrows and spears. Amid the smoke and sea spray, faces looked back at me aghast. They were frightened, not of me but of the madman behind me. Every man on the ship teetered on the sword's edge of Mars, poised between life and death. The sight of their commander reduced to an insane rage unnerved them.

A fireball flew over the ship. It grazed the mainsail, tracing a fringe of flame along the top edge. Soldiers panicked. Scribonius cried out, "Cut it loose! Cut it loose!" Men scurried up the mast, daggers flashing between their teeth.

Hands clutched my shoulders. I gave a start, then saw it was Tiro. "Gordianus, what have you done? What did you say to him?"

By the light of the leaping flames above our heads, I saw Pompey no more than five paces distant. The look on his face turned my blood to water. In another instant he would be close enough for me to see my reflection in his eyes; it was a dead man I would see there.

I broke from Tiro, turned and ran. Somehow I sprouted wings. How else can I explain the leap that took me over the heads of the men who stood in close formation along the ship's rail? For a moment I thought I would fall short and be impaled on their spears. A spearpoint did pierce my shin and rip through the flesh, scraping the bone. I screamed at the pain. An instant later I plunged face-first into water so cold it stopped my heart and froze the scream between my lips.

A powerful current sucked me deep beneath the surface. This was the end. Neptune, not Mars, would claim me. My crime would be purified by water, not fire.

The cold was excruciating. The darkness was infinite. The current twisted me this way and that. It spun me about almost playfully, as if to prove I was powerless to resist. I lost all sense of direction. Suddenly I was startled to see brightly flickering spots ahead of me, like sheets of yellow flame. Had the current sucked me all the way down to the seabed, to a fissure that opened into Hades? That seemed impossible, for my senses told me that I was traveling upward, not down. The frigid current drew me closer and closer to the flames, until I felt the heat of the burning flotsam on my face.

Done with me, the hand of Neptune expelled me from the water. I emerged into a scorching, airless void of flame. I sucked in a desperate, burning breath.

I was to be purified by water and fire alike.

PART THREE

DIONYSUS

XXIII

Hunched forward in a chair pulled close to my bedside, Davus propped his chin on his hands and stared at me. I wondered what profound thought was crossing his mind.

"Speak," I said.

The single word exacted an excruciating price. Bubbles of molten lead seemed to burst in my throat. I felt an urge to cough and struggled against it. Coughing caused unspeakable agony. I swallowed instead. Swallowing was a torment, but bearable.

Davus tilted his head and frowned. "I was only thinking, father-in-law, how much better you looked when you had eyebrows."

During endless hours of drifting in and out of consciousness, I had noticed a little mirror of polished silver hung on one of the walls, the room's only ornament. I had not yet asked Davus to take it down so that I could have a look at myself. Perhaps it was just as well.

I closed my eyes and drifted back into oblivion.

⌒

When I opened my eyes, Davus was just as he had been before.

I breathed in through my nose. My sinuses seemed to be lined with suppurating blisters. Still, it was less painful than breathing through my mouth. "How long—?"

Davus cocked his head attentively.

". . . since I was last awake?" I managed to say. The pain of speaking brought tears to my eyes. Nonetheless, it seemed slightly less painful than before.

"Yesterday," Davus said. "Yesterday, you woke up for a while. You said, 'Speak.' That's the most you've said since they pulled you out of the harbor."

"When was that?"

Davus counted on his fingers. "One . . . two . . . three days ago."

Three days had passed, and I remembered nothing, not even dreams. Nothing! Except—

Endless water, black and cold. Flames. Smoke. A floating plank. Fireballs careening overhead. The stench of singed hair and burning flesh. Men screaming. A sudden jolt. Jagged rocks beneath the water. Coming to rest, half in the water, half out. The sky above cold and black and endless, but mantled with stars, growing lighter each time I woke from fitful dozing—iron gray, then palest blue, then oyster pink. Voices. Arms lifting me aloft.

Useless, someone said. *Why bother? He's not one of ours.*

That big fellow knows him. And the big fellow's got silver in his pouch.

Wrapped in linen. Laid in a wagon. Other bodies in the wagon—alive or dead? Davus leaning over me, looking down, his face almost unrecognizable; I had never seen him weep before. An endless journey of bumps and jolts, then finally coming to rest upon a bed unimaginably soft, in a cool, dim, quiet room. A woman's voice: *If you need anything else*—Another voice: *I could use something to eat.* That was Davus. I felt hungry, too, but was too weak to speak, and when the food came, the smell of charred flesh sickened me.

What else could I remember? Pompey's face, contorted with rage. Tiro's face, alarmed and confused. I tried to push those images aside and see other faces. Bethesda . . . Diana . . .

"Meto," I said.

"No, it's me." Davus, misunderstanding, leaned over me and smiled.

I shook my head. "But where—?"

"Ah!" Davus understood. "He's with Caesar. On their way back to Rome."

"When?"

"They left the day after Pompey fled. Caesar made a speech in the town forum, thanked the citizens for their help, left a garrison in charge, and then headed north on the Appian Way. Meto went with him. That was three days ago."

"You saw Meto?"

"Oh, yes. Should I tell you about it? Are you up for listening?"

I nodded.

"Well, then. After I left you, not half an hour passed before I found Meto. Easy enough, since he was with Caesar. Hard to miss that red cape! I met them coming from the forum, on the same street we took with Pompey. Caesar's bodyguards might have killed me, but I did as you said and threw down my sword. Meto was glad to see me. I told him what you'd done, leaving with Pompey. Caesar was in a hurry to get to the port. I showed them how to avoid the traps. We got to the quay just as the last of Pompey's men were casting off.

"From the end of the quay, I recognized Pompey's ship, just starting to sail out the harbor entrance. I pointed it out to Meto. He pointed it out to Caesar. We watched the ship run the gauntlet. For a while it looked like Pompey was in big trouble, veering toward the southern breakwater. I said a prayer to Neptune for you. It was hard to see much on account of the darkness and the smoke—but I could swear I saw someone jump overboard! Meto didn't see it. Neither did anybody else. They told me I imagined it, that no one could have seen such a thing at that distance. But I was sure. Would you like some water?"

I nodded. Davus fetched a pitcher and poured water into a clay cup. I took it from him. There were cuts and burns on my hands, but nothing crippling. Swallowing was not as painful as I expected. My stomach growled.

"Hungry," I said.

Davus nodded. "I'll get the cook to make you something easy to eat, maybe some cold gruel. The food here is pretty good. Should be, for what we're paying. People say this is the best inn in Brundisium. Too much seafood for my taste."

I gestured for him to get on with the story.

"Where was I? Oh, yes: Pompey's ship. It got through all right, but just barely. You should have seen the look on Caesar's face, thinking he might have caught the Great One after all—like a cat staring at a bird. But in the end Pompey's ship squeezed out of the harbor, smooth as a dropping from a sheep's bottom. So did the rest, except for a couple of ships that ran afoul of the breakwater. Caesar sent little boats to board them and take the men prisoner. What a night that was—everything a mad scramble, and Meto always in the middle of things." Davus frowned. "He wasn't as upset as I thought he would be—about you sailing off with Pompey. He got that look on his face—you know, where you can't imagine what he's thinking, or at least I can't—and he said maybe it was all for the best, you running off with Pompey and Tiro.

"He asked me if I intended to go back to Rome with him, because if I did, I'd have to keep my mouth shut. He didn't want Caesar or Antony to know that you'd gone with Pompey, not yet. I suppose he thought it would make him look bad, having his father sail off with the enemy. I showed him the money you gave me and told him I didn't need his help getting home. I think he was glad to be rid of me. That was that. The next day, after his speech in the forum, Caesar was off. Just as well. I wanted to stay around here for a while longer anyway."

I took another sip of water. "Why?"

"Because I was *sure* I saw somebody jump off Pompey's ship—or get pushed off."

"And you thought it was me. Why?"

"I just had a feeling. I can't explain it. I knew something wasn't right. The way you gave me all that money. The way you talked, as if you didn't expect to ever come back." He shook his head. "I had to make sure. The afternoon after Caesar and Meto left, I decided to walk all the way around the harbor, starting at the southern break-water, since that was the end Pompey's ship sailed nearest to. Some of Caesar's men from the garrison were posted to watch for bodies washing up on shore, so there'd be no looting. Most of the men they found were dead. Some had arrows in them. Some were horribly burned. To tell you the truth . . . I never expected to find you alive. When I saw your face, and you opened your eyes—" His voice became husky. He lowered his eyes.

I nodded. "Then Meto doesn't know."

"No. He thinks you're with Pompey. Won't it be a surprise when we get back to Rome and he lays eyes on you! Maybe by then, your eyebrows will have grown back."

~

The cold gruel from the kitchen was actually rather soothing to swallow. I was famished, but Davus was careful to keep me from eating too much, too quickly.

Eventually I had the courage to ask him for the mirror.

I was not horribly disfigured after all. My eyebrows had been singed off, and the effect was not flattering, but there were no serious scars or burns on my face. I had inhaled more seawater and smoke and fiery vapors than was good for a man, I was covered with nicks, burns, blisters, and bruises (especially around my neck, where Pompey had choked me), and there was a nasty, pus-filled wound at my shin, inflicted by the spearpoint I scraped against when I leaped off Pompey's boat. I had been feverish and delirious when Davus found me, but once the fever broke I recuperated swiftly.

Some men in my position might have imagined that they had

been saved by divine intervention, spared from oblivion for the sake of a special destiny. I saw myself instead as a minnow too small to be caught in Neptune's net, or a sodden twig thrown onto Hades's brazier that had sputtered but failed to catch fire.

I was anxious to get back to Rome. I was even more anxious to see Meto again. In Caesar's camp, it had been impossible to speak to him candidly. There was much I wanted to tell him and to ask him.

We eschewed Tiro's "shortcut" through the mountains and set out on the Appian Way, following in Caesar's wake. He traveled at a pace that seemed almost impossible, considering the size of his army. Press as I might, I soon realized that we couldn't possibly match his speed, much less catch up with him. I would have to wait until we reached Rome to see Meto again.

At every town along the Appian Way, arriving a few days after Caesar, we found the people in the taverns and markets and stables talking of nothing else. Wherever he appeared, Caesar had been greeted with thanksgiving. Local magistrates pledged loyalty to his cause. If there were those who would have preferred to see Pompey triumphant, they kept their mouths shut.

The weather was mild. At Beneventum my fever recurred and we lost a day of travel, but otherwise we made good time. We returned to Rome through the Capena Gate as the sun set on the Nones, the fifth day of Aprilis.

Diana wept at the sight of Davus. Bethesda wept at the sight of me. Mopsus and Androcles did not weep, but laughed with joy. Meto had been to see the family only once, the day after he arrived in Rome. He had told them that Davus was on his way, but that I had gone off to Dyrrhachium with Pompey. My homecoming was unexpected by all concerned, not least myself, and all the sweeter for that.

One face was gone from the household, but missed by no one except perhaps Androcles and Mopsus. The bodyguard Cicatrix, posted by Pompey to watch my household, had been ordered by Meto to leave and never return. With his master across the sea and Caesar in charge of Rome, the slave had meekly obeyed, glad to keep his head. No one knew where he had gone.

Eco and his family came to the house that night. After a boisterous dinner, the two of us withdrew to my study and drank watered wine long into the night. I feared he would press me to explain how I had arranged for Davus's release and managed to escape from Pompey myself, but like the rest of the family he seemed to assume I had resorted to simple trickery. For the time being, I continued to keep secret the truth about Numerius's murder, and Meto's treachery.

Eco apprised me of the latest gossip from the Forum. News of Pompey's flight, followed almost at once by Caesar's arrival, had sent alternating tremors of dread and jubilation through the city. The Senate, or what remained of it, had been summoned by Caesar to meet on the Kalends of Aprilis. Exactly what Caesar had demanded and how the senators had responded was the subject of much speculation, but it was obvious that no senator with the stature or the will to stand up to Caesar remained in Rome.

There were persistent rumors that Caesar would appear in the Forum to speak to the citizenry, but so far that had not happened. It might be that he feared a hostile reception, even a riot. Rumblings of discontent had begun when Caesar broke into the sacred treasury in the Temple of Saturn, which was the people's security against foreign invasion. The huge stores of gold and silver ingots had been set aside for use only in case of barbarian invasion, and had remained intact for as long as anyone could remember. The fleeing consuls had debated whether to open it, and had decided to leave it untouched. Caesar had pilfered it like a common thief. His excuse: "The sacred treasury was originally established by our ancestors to be used in case of attack by the Gauls. Having personally eliminated any such threat by conquering Gaul, I now remove the gold." The tribune Metellus attempted to stop the illegal plunder. He barred the sealed doorway with his own body. Caesar told him, "If I must, Metellus, I shall have

you killed. Believe me, to threaten such a thing pains me considerably more than would the actual doing of it." Metellus withdrew.

Caesar had stolen the sacred treasury. He had threatened the life
of a tribune in the performance of his duties. For all his continuing
rhetoric about negotiating with Pompey and restoring the constitution, the message was clear. Caesar was prepared to break any law
that restrained him and to kill any man who opposed him.

What of Cicero? On his way to Rome, Caesar had visited him at
Formiae. He asked Cicero to return to the city and attend the Senate.
Cicero delicately refused, and made a point of going to his hometown of Arpinum instead, to celebrate his son's belated toga day.
Caesar was tolerating Cicero's neutrality, for now. Would Pompey be
as understanding if he came sweeping back through Italy with fire
and sword? Poor Cicero, trapped like Aesop's rabbit between the lion
and the fox.

"What of your brother Meto?" I asked. "I understand he paid the
family a visit the day after Caesar arrived."

"And that's the only time any of us have seen him," said Eco. "Too
busy to leave Caesar's side, I suppose. They'll be off again any day
now, if rumors are true. Caesar is leaving Antony in military command of Italy and hurrying off to Spain, to fend with Pompey's legions there."

I shook my head. "I must see Meto before he leaves."

"Of course, Papa. Caesar and his staff are housed in the Regia, in
the middle of the Forum. As Pontifex Maximus, that's his official
residence. You and I will stroll down there tomorrow. I want to be
there to see Meto's face—he'll be as surprised to see you as the rest of
us were!"

"No. I want to see Meto alone, in a place where the two of us can
speak privately." I pondered the problem, and had an idea. "I'll send
him a message tonight. I'll ask him to meet me tomorrow."

"Certainly." Eco reached for a stylus and wax tablet. "Dictate and
I'll write it for you."

"No, I'll write it myself."

Eco looked at me curiously, but handed me the stylus and tablet.
I wrote:

DIONYSUS

To Gordianus Meto, from his father:

Beloved son,

I am back in Rome. I am well. No doubt you are curious about my peregrinations, as I am curious about yours. Meet me tomorrow at midday at the Salacious Tavern.

I closed the wooden cover of the tablet, tied the ribbon, and sealed the ribbon with wax. I handed it to Eco.

"Would you see that one of the slaves delivers it? I'm too exhausted to keep my eyes open for another minute."

"Of course, Papa." Eco looked at the sealed letter and frowned, but made no comment.

XXIV

In contrast to the brilliant sunshine outside, the gloom of the Salacious Tavern was nearly impenetrable. The unnatural darkness, lit here and there by the lurid glow of lamps, filled me with a vague unease that mounted quickly and explicably into a kind of panic. I almost fled back to the street, until I realized what I was reminded of: the cold, murky waters beneath the flaming flotsam at Brundisium. I took a deep breath, managed to return the smile of the fawning proprietor, and walked across the room, bumping my knees against hard wooden benches. The place was empty except for a few silent patrons who sat hunched over their cups, drinking alone.

I found my way to the bench built into the corner at the far side of the room. It was where I had sat when I last visited the tavern, to meet with Tiro. According to both the tavernkeeper and Tiro, it was also where Numerius Pompeius liked to sit when negotiating his shady transactions. "*His* corner, he called it," Tiro had told me.

Did the lemur of Numerius lurk in the shadows of the Salacious Tavern? On my last visit, I had felt a twinge of uneasiness at occupying the place where Numerius had sat and schemed. Now I felt nothing. I suddenly realized that I had not seen his face in my dreams, nor thought much about him at all since the night I confessed to Pompey and leaped from his ship, expecting to die. With the murder of Numerius, my pretensions to moral superiority had died. At Brundisium, my feelings of guilt had likewise died. I was not proud of the fact. Nor did I question it. I was stripped of both self-righteousness and self-recrimination. I was like a man without gods, no longer sure what I felt, or thought, or believed, or where I belonged in the scheme of things.

According to a public sundial not far from the tavern entrance, I had arrived a little early. With the punctuality born of his military training, Meto arrived exactly on time. His eyes were younger than mine and adapted more quickly. He peered into the darkness for only a brief moment before spotting me and crossing the room with a firm stride, not bumping into a single bench.

It was hard to read his face in the dimness, but there was something stiff and uneasy in his manner. Before either of us could speak, our host descended on us. I asked for two cups of his best. Meto protested that he never drank wine so early in the day. I called after the tavernkeeper to bring water as well.

Meto smiled. "This is becoming a habit, Papa—turning up where you're least expected. The last I heard—"

"I was sailing to Dyrrhachium with Pompey himself. Davus says you weren't entirely displeased at the news."

Meto grunted. "Hardly a fair trade if you ask me—you taking the place of Davus. I didn't quite understand the point. Pompey had a kinsman murdered, and forced you under protest to look for the killer, and Davus was taken as a sort of surety?" He shook his head. "Awfully petty behavior for the Great One. Truly, he's lost his wits."

"It was rather more complicated than that, Meto. Did Davus not tell you the name of Pompey's murdered kinsman?"

"No."

"It was a young man named Numerius Pompeius." Even in the dim light, I saw the tension that creased Meto's face. "Does that name mean something to you?"

"Perhaps."

The tavernkeeper brought two cups of wine and a pitcher of water.

"Meto, on the day before Pompey fled Rome, Numerius came to my house. He showed me a document, a kind of pact, written in your hand—in your style, for that matter—signed by yourself and a few others. You must know what I'm talking about."

Meto ran a fingertip around the rim of his cup. "Numerius had this document?"

"Yes."

"What became of it?"

"I burned it."

"But how——?"

"I took it from him. He tried to blackmail me, Meto. He threatened to send the document to Caesar. To expose your part in plotting Caesar's assassination."

Meto turned his face so that a shadow fell across his eyes, but I could see the hard line of his mouth, and the scar he had received at Pistoria. "And Numerius was murdered?"

"He never left my house alive."

"You——"

"I did it for you, Meto."

His shoulders slumped. He shifted uneasily. He picked up his cup and drained it. He shook his head. "Papa, I never imagined——"

"Numerius told me he had other documents, equally compromising, also in your handwriting. Could that be true? Were there other such documents?"

"Papa——"

"Answer me."

He wiped his mouth. "Yes."

"Meto, Meto! How in Hades could you have been so careless, to let such documents fall into the hands of such a man? Numerius told me he hid them somewhere. I searched—I wanted to destroy them—but I never found them." I sighed. "What became of the plot, Meto? Did the others lose their nerve? I know you didn't;

you're anything but a coward. Did it become impossible to carry out? Are you still planning to do it? Or have you had a change of heart?"

He didn't answer.

"Why did you turn against him after all these years, Meto? Did you finally see him for what he is? Men like Caesar and Pompey—they're not heroes, Meto. They're monsters. They call their greed and ambition 'honor,' and to satisfy their so-called honor they'll tear the world apart." I grunted. "But who am I to judge them? Every man does what he must, to protect his share of the world. What's the difference between killing whole villages and armies, and killing a single man? Caesar's reasons and mine are different only in degree. The consequences and the suffering still spread to the innocent."

"Papa . . ."

"Perhaps you became too close to him, Meto. Intimacy can turn to bitterness. People say that you and he . . . Did he slight you in some way? Was that the break between you—a falling-out between lovers?"

"Papa, it isn't what you think."

"Then tell me."

He shook his head. "I can't explain."

"It doesn't matter. What matters is this: as long as Caesar remains alive, and those documents still exist somewhere, you're in terrible danger. Should they ever be discovered and brought to his attention—"

"Papa, what happened on Pompey's ship, in the harbor at Brundisium?"

"It was as Davus told you. I took his place by telling Pompey that I knew who killed Numerius. As we were about to run the gauntlet, Pompey demanded that I tell him then and there. So I did. I told him everything. He was like a raging animal. I went aboard his ship never expecting to leave alive, Meto. But I leaped overboard and somehow survived, and Davus found me the next day."

"Thank the gods for that, Papa!" He took a long breath. "You say that you told Pompey everything. Did you tell him about the plot to kill Caesar?"

"Yes."

"And about my part in it?"

"Yes."

"Did he believe you?"

"Not at first. But in the end, yes."

Meto fell silent for a long moment. "You must believe, Papa, that I never intended for you to be drawn into this." He turned toward me. Lamplight illuminated his eyes. The look on his face was so miserable that I reached for his hand and covered it with mine.

He allowed the touch for a moment, then abruptly stood up. "Papa, I have to go."

"Now? But Meto—"

His eyes glimmered brightly. "Papa, whatever happens, don't be ashamed of me. Forgive me."

"Meto!"

He turned and left, bumping blindly against the maze of benches. His silhouette reached the foyer and vanished.

What had I expected from our meeting? More than this. Meto had told me nothing. He was trying to protect me, of course, as I had tried to protect him. I was left with the same unanswered questions and blind conjectures that had been spinning in my head for months.

I had not yet touched my wine. I reached for the cup and drank slowly, gazing into the dark corners of the room. The murkiness that had unnerved me when I entered the tavern I now found comforting.

The tavernkeeper ambled over with a pitcher. "More wine?"

"Why not?"

He refilled the cup and ambled off. I sat and drank and thought. What would become of Meto? What would become of Caesar? And Pompey, and Cicero, and Tiro? And Maecia, and Aemilia . . . ?

The warmth of the wine spread through me. I found myself staring at one of the uncertain silhouettes across the room and imagining that it was the lemur of Numerius Pompeius. The fantasy became so powerful that I could almost feel him staring back at me. I felt no fear. Instead, I thought what a fine thing it would be if I could wave him over and invite him to share a cup, if lemures drink. What would I ask him? That was obvious. Had he lived, would he have married Aemilia after all, despite the fact that Pompey had plans for him to marry someone else? Or would he have spurned her, dooming the unborn child as surely as his death had doomed it?

And of course, I would ask him where in Hades he had hidden the other documents.

Where in Hades—indeed! I laughed a bit tipsily at the notion. I had eaten no breakfast that morning, and like Meto, I wasn't used to drinking in the middle of the day.

My thoughts wandered aimlessly, thanks to the wine. Thanks, I thought, to Dionysus, the god of wine, looser of loins, emancipator of minds, liberator of tongues. Even slaves could speak freely on the Liberalia, the day of Dionysus, because the sacred power of wine transcended all earthly shackles. Through wine, Dionysus illuminated the minds of men as could no other god, not even Minerva. So it was, there in the Salacious Tavern, that Dionysus gave me wisdom. How else to explain the chain of thoughts that led me to the thing I sought?

Something Tiro had said about Numerius popped into my head. In the very spot where I sat, Numerius had boasted to Tiro of certain documents he had come by, the evidence of the plot to assassinate Caesar. The sheer danger of possessing them and the lucrative possibilities for blackmail had exhilarated him. He had told Tiro, "I'm sitting on something enormous."

Where were those documents?

Numerius's mother had searched the family house. I had searched his secret love nest. Numerius must have had some other hiding place for the documents.

"I'm sitting on something enormous." Numerius had been drunk when he made that boast to Tiro. Perhaps only a man equally drunk could see that he meant exactly what he said.

With my fingers, I examined the bench beneath me. The seat was worn smooth from long use, the boards seamlessly joined. I leaned forward, reached between my legs and rapped my knuckles against the boards which formed the upright. The bench sounded hollow.

I remained bent over and blindly ran my fingertips over the flat surface behind my calves. The wood there was not as smooth and polished as the seat. There were little splinters and rough spots made by kicking heels, but no loose boards—except for one spot near the corner where a board was split. My finger discovered an empty nail hole.

"You're not throwing up on the floor, are you?" The tavernkeeper, alarmed at my posture, suddenly stood over me. "Gods, man, if you need a pot, ask for one!"

I ignored him and pushed at the loose bit of board, to no effect. I wriggled my little finger into the empty nail hole and pulled instead. Slowly but surely, a part of the split board yielded, just enough to allow me to slip my forefinger, then my middle finger, behind it. The hidden recess was small and narrow, but with two fingertips I was able to pinch the tip of something wedged within. I pulled too quickly and lost my purchase. I tried again, making grunts that further alarmed the tavernkeeper. Slowly, painstakingly, I extracted several pieces of parchment very tightly rolled into a cylinder the circumference of my little finger.

I sat upright and sucked in a deep breath, gripping the parchments in my fist. The tavernkeeper loomed over me, a lumpy silhouette with hands on hips.

"I think perhaps you should go now," he said.

"Yes," I said. "I think perhaps I should."

I longed to find Meto at once. The Regia was not far away, just across from the House of the Vestals. Then I realized, even as inebriated as I was, how foolish I would be to carry incriminating material into Caesar's residence. I had to destroy the documents first. But before I did that, I wanted to take a look at them. The only safe place to do so was in my own home. I made my way through a maze of alleys to the Ramp and trudged up the Palatine Hill, imagining I might be stopped at any moment by Caesar's spies.

Davus met me at the door. I told him to bar it behind me and rushed to my study. I unrolled the parchments and scanned them quickly, curious to see if they were as incriminating as Numerius had suggested. They were. The handwriting was indisputably Meto's. To judge by the dates, the plot to kill Caesar had been devised even before he crossed the Rubicon. One sheet was a manifesto of sorts, enumerating reasons why Caesar must be put to death. Chief among them was the absolute necessity to avoid a civil war that could end only in the destruction of the Republic. The men named in the documents were the same staff officers who had signed the pact Numerius had shown me on the day of his death, which I had taken from his dead body and burned.

I laid the documents in the brazier and set them aflame. I watched them burn and held my breath until the last bit of parchment withered to ashes. The fear that had gripped me ever since my visit from Numerius came to an end in the place where it began.

Now I needed to tell Meto.

I called for Davus. Together we made our way down to the Forum. Outside the Regia, the line of citizens waiting to be seen by Caesar stretched almost to the Capitoline Hill. Among them I recognized senators, bankers, and foreign diplomats. Some wore wide-brimmed hats. Others were attended by slaves who held parasols aloft to protect their masters from the glare of the sun, and from the gaze of gods who would be ashamed to look down and see what could only be described as supplicants awaiting audience with a king.

I went to the head of the line. I told a guard that I was the father of Gordianus Meto. "I've come to see my son," I said.

"Not here. Went out on some errand, a little before midday."

"Yes, he came to see me. I need to see him again."

"Hasn't come back yet."

"No? Do you know where he might be?"

"Should be here, but he's not. Nobody's seen him. I know, because the imperator was just asking for him."

"I see. When he comes back, will you give him a message?"

"Certainly."

"Tell him it's urgent that I talk to him, as soon as possible. I shall be at home, waiting to hear from him."

~

No reply from Meto came that day.

The next morning I went down to the Regia again. I found the same guard. I asked to see Meto.

"Not here." The man stared straight ahead with a stony countenance.

"Where is he?"

"Couldn't say."

"Did you give him my message yesterday?"

The guard hesitated. "Couldn't say."

"What do you mean, you couldn't—"

"I mean that I shouldn't be talking to you at all. I suggest you go home now."

I felt a cold weight on my chest. Something was wrong. "I want to find my son. If I have to, I'll stand in this line and wait my turn to see Caesar himself."

"I wouldn't suggest it. You won't get in to see him."

"Why not?"

The guard finally looked me in the eye. "Go home. Lock your door. Talk to no one. If the imperator wants to see you, he'll send for you soon enough. I hope for your sake he doesn't."

"What do you mean?" The guard refused to answer and stared stonily ahead. I lowered my voice. "Do you know my son?"

"I thought I did."

"What's become of him? Please tell me."

The guard worked his jaw back and forth. "Gone," he finally said.

"Gone? Where?"

He looked at me. His eyes were almost sympathetic. "Word is, he's run off to Massilia. To join up with Lucius Domitius. You didn't know?"

I lowered my eyes. My face flushed hotly.

"Meto, a traitor. Who'd have thought it?" The guard spoke without rancor. He felt sorry for me.

I did as the guard advised. I went home. I barred the door. I spoke to no one.

Was Meto's flight to Massilia the result of long deliberation, or was it the act of a desperate man, a would-be assassin who feared he might be discovered at any moment? If I had found Numerius's hiding place only moments earlier, while Meto was still with me, would he still have fled to Massilia?

I stirred the ashes in the brazier in my study, and wondered at the joke the gods had played on me.

XXV

A few days later, Caesar left Rome, headed for Spain.

His route would take him along the Mediterranean coast of Gaul and past the city-state of Massilia, which was now defended by Lucius Domitius with his six million sesterces and some semblance of an army. Domitius had lost Corfinium to Caesar without a struggle. Would he do better at Massilia? If Caesar took the city, would he pardon Domitius a second time? What sort of mercy would he mete out to the Massilians? What mercy would he show to a defector who had plotted to kill him?

To save Meto, I had done something unspeakable. Now he would have to save himself. I felt like an actor who leaves the stage before the final scene, with no more lines to speak, while the drama goes on. Was this how lemures felt, observing the living?

I felt abandoned by the Fates. The snarled thread of my life had come unraveled from their tapestry and dangled in the void. I felt mocked by the gods—who were not yet done with me.

One morning, about the middle of Aprilis, a stranger came to the door. He told Davus that he had olive oil to sell. Davus told him that the mistress of the house was out, Bethesda having gone with Diana to the fish market. The man asked if he might leave a sample of his product. He handed Davus a small, round clay jar and departed.

The incident seemed innocuous enough, but I had told Davus to report all visitors to me without exception. He came at once to the garden, where I sat brooding beneath the statue of Minerva.

"What's that?" I said.

"A jar of olive oil. At least, that's what the man said."

"What man?"

Davus explained.

I took the jar and examined it. A piece of cloth had been pulled over the short, narrow spout at the top, tied with twine and sealed with wax. The jar itself appeared unremarkable. Near the base, two words were etched into the clay. On one side was the word OLIVUM; on the other, MASSILIA.

"Olive oil of Massilia," I said. "A fine product. But a curious co-incidence. I wonder . . . Davus, bring an empty jar."

While he was gone, I untied the string and broke the wax seal. The cloth covering the spout appeared to be nothing more than a swatch of white linen. I removed the cork. It, too, appeared unre-markable. Even so, I cut it open. It was solid all through.

When Davus returned, I slowly decanted the contents into the empty jar, scrutinizing the thin stream that glistened with golden highlights.

"Do you think it might be . . . poisoned?" asked Davus.

I touched my finger to the stream and sniffed it. "It pours, looks, and smells like olive oil to me."

I finished emptying the little jar, then held it so that sunlight shone into the spout. I peered inside, but saw only flashes of oily residue. I shook the jar and turned it upside down. Nothing came out but a few more drops of oil.

"Curious," I said. "But why shouldn't a merchant of fine imported olive oil leave us a free sample of his wares? Stranger things have happened."

"What about this, father-in-law?" Davus held up the other jar, now brimming with golden oil.

"We'll offer it to Minerva." It seemed a logical solution. If the oil was what it was purported to be, it was of the highest quality and fit for an offering to the goddess. If it was what Davus feared, it could do no harm to a goddess made of bronze. I took the jar from Davus and set it on the pedestal at her feet.

"Accept this offering and grant us wisdom," I whispered. It couldn't hurt.

The jar which had originally held the oil, now empty, I placed on the paving stone beside my chair. I sat and closed my eyes, letting the warm sunlight of Aprilis warm my face. My thoughts wandered. I dozed.

Suddenly I was wide awake.

I went to my study. Among the scrolls in my pigeonhole bookcase I located the memoirs of the dictator Sulla. I scrolled past political scandals, slaughters, looted cities, visits to oracles, homages to favorite actors, sexual braggadocio, and finally found the passage I was looking for:

A military commander and political leader must often resort to sending secret messages. I credit myself with having invented a few clever methods of my own.

Once, when I needed to send secret orders to a confederate, I took the urinary bladder of a pig, inflated it stoutly, and let it dry that way. While it was still inflated, I wrote upon it with encaustic ink. After the ink was dry, I deflated the bladder and inserted it into a jar, then filled the jar with oil, which reinflated the bladder within. I sealed the jar and sent it as if it were a culinary gift to the recipient, who knew beforehand to open and empty the jar in private, then break the jar to retrieve the bladder, upon which the message remained perfectly intact.

I dimly recollected having read the passage long ago. I had no recollection of ever having discussed it with Meto, but I presumed he had read every volume in my small library. Besides that, Sulla's autobiography was exactly the sort of thing that Caesar would have pored over while composing his own memoirs and dictating them to Meto. The fact that the jar was manufactured in Massilia could hardly be a coincidence.

I returned to the garden. Minerva seemed to smile down sardonically as I struck the jar against the paving stones. It broke neatly in two and fell apart. The bladder within held the shape of the jar. I carefully unwrinkled the creases, then fully inflated it with my breath. The glistening coating of oil made the tiny wax letters appear still warm and pliant, as if Meto had just painted them. The message began at the top of the bladder and wound around it in a spiral. I turned it slowly as I read:

Papa, after you read this message, destroy it at once. I should not be writing to you at all, but I cannot let you go on believing a lie; the truth has always mattered so much to you. I have always been loyal to C. I still am, no matter what you may hear. The plot against C's life was a fiction. The documents which N obtained were false, contrived with C's knowledge and at his behest. They were deliberately passed to N through an intermediary whom N trusted. The intent was for N to pass them on to P, believing them to be genuine, so as to convince P that I and some others were hostile to C and could be suborned by the opposition. Thus we could infiltrate the enemy's higher circles. But instead of passing them on to P, N decided to use them for his own purpose. I never foresaw that he would blackmail you and draw you into the deceit. When I think of what you did, meaning to protect me, I feel hot with shame. I know how deeply that act went against your nature. Yet your confession to

P of my part in the fictitious plot may have done more to convince him of my disloyalty to C than my original scheme would have done. Thanks to you, my mission is at last feasible. Excuse these crude sentences. I write in haste. For my sake, destroy this message at once.

There was a crowded postscript added in a corner, in letters so small it made my eyes ache to read them:

The night before C crossed the Rubicon, he dreamed that he committed incest with his mother. I think the dream was a message from the gods: to pursue his destiny, he would be compelled to commit terrible acts of impiety. He chose destiny over conscience. So it is with me, Papa. To follow my duty, I dishonored the man who freed me from slavery and made me his son. I kept secrets from you. I let you believe a lie. I am an impious son. But I made a choice, as C did, and once the Rubicon is crossed, there can be no turning back. Forgive me, Papa.

I read the entire message again, slowly, to be sure I understood it. Then I took it to the brazier in my study. The burning oil and pig's flesh gave off a smell that reminded me of Brundisium.

The crime I committed, thinking to save my son, had actually served to thwart his secret plans.

The confession I made to Pompey, thinking to cleanse my own conscience, had actually served to let Meto proceed with his scheme.

The world believed my son had fled to Massilia as a traitor to Caesar. In fact, he was Caesar's spy, now deep in the enemy's camp. Was his peril less than I had thought, or greater?

I returned to the garden. I sat and gazed at Minerva. I had prayed for wisdom and received it. But instead of making things simpler, each new piece of knowledge only made the world more mystifying.

From the front of the house, I heard the sounds of Bethesda and Diana returning from the fish market. I called their names. A moment later they appeared in the garden.

"Daughter, bring Davus. Wife, send for Eco. It's time for this family to have a meeting. It's time for me to tell my family . . . the truth."

~

Aprilis passed. The month of Maius brought clear skies and mild sunshine. Trees came into leaf. Weeds sprang up and wildflowers bloomed amid gaps in the paving stones. The coming of spring brought a sense of relief, however illusory, from the dreadful uncertainties of war.

From Gaul came word that Massilia had closed her gates to Caesar, who left behind officers to mount a siege while he pressed on to Spain. Old soldiers in the Forum argued over how long the siege would last. The Massilians were stubborn, fiercely proud people. Some thought they could easily fend off any army for however long it took for reinforcements to arrive from Pompey. Others argued that Fortune was with Caesar, and the siege would be over in a matter of days rather than months. Could the Massilians expect the same clemency Caesar had shown in Italy, or would the city be leveled, its defenders slaughtered, and its people sold into slavery? I tried not to imagine what might happen to a spy discovered in such desperate circumstances, or mistaken for the enemy by his own side.

One morning as I headed down the Ramp with Mopsus and Androcles, the sheer perfection of the spring day banished all gloomy thoughts. My spirits rose on a zephyr of warm, sun-drenched air. On a sudden whim, I decided to tend to a task I had been putting off ever since my return.

We walked straight through the Forum without pausing. I wanted no rumors of catastrophe to spoil my mood. The daily dose of fear and mayhem could wait for another hour.

The boys didn't ask where we were going. They didn't care. To be out and about in the city on such a glorious morning was its own reward. Vendors hawked their wares. Slaves carried baskets to market.

Matrons flung open their shutters to let in the mild, sweet air of spring.

We came to the Carinae district on the lower slopes of the Esquiline Hill, and walked down the quiet street to the blue and yellow house where Maecia lived. The black wreath of mourning still hung on the door. My buoyant mood faltered, but I took a deep breath and gave the door a few polite knocks with the side of my foot.

An eye peered at us through the peephole. Before I had time to state my name, the door swung open.

Mopsus and Androcles emitted squeals of delight. The noise startled me almost as much as the sight of Cicatrix abruptly towering over me.

My heart raced. I braced myself for one last joke from the gods. Had I unwittingly, on a perfect spring morning, delivered myself to Nemesis in the form of one of Pompey's trained killers? But the thought was irrational, a guilty reflex at the sight of the black wreath. Unless some secret network of messengers had relayed the news directly from Pompey, Cicatrix knew nothing about my crime. Nor did Maecia.

I cleared my throat. "So this is where you ended up." It made sense. All of Pompey's other relatives had left town.

Cicatrix raised an eyebrow, which further contorted the scars on his face. "Until the Great One comes home."

I grunted and made no comment.

Cicatrix glowered at me, then helplessly cracked a grin as he lowered his gaze to Mopsus and Androcles. "But I left these two spies behind to take my place." He crouched and playfully boxed at the two of them. The boys jabbed back at him and burst out laughing.

"Cicatrix, who's there?" The voice came from within.

He straightened immediately. "A visitor, Mistress. Gordianus." He stepped aside. Maecia appeared in the foyer.

The light from the atrium silhouetted her slender figure and haloed her sheer blue stola and the great shell-like fan of hair arranged atop her head. With her green eyes and creamy skin, without makeup or adornment, she had been beautiful when I last saw her. Now she took my breath away. More than anything else, it was her smile that transformed her. I had not seen her smile before.

"Gordianus! I understood from Cicatrix that you sailed to Dyrrhachium with Pompey."

I looked sidelong at Cicatrix. "An untrue rumor," I said. "There are so many circulating these days."

"Come in. As for your slave boys . . ."

"I think they'd like to visit with Cicatrix—if that won't compromise his duties."

"Of course not. They can help him guard the door."

We stepped into the atrium. Where previously the corpse of Numerius had been displayed upon its bier, there was only bright sunshine. Through a colonnade I could see into the garden at the heart of the house. I caught a glimpse of another woman, seated amid flowering shrubs.

"Do you have a visitor, Maecia? If I'm intruding . . ."

"No, I'm glad you've come. We'll sit and talk in the garden for a while—the day's too beautiful to do anything else. But I want to speak to you privately first." She led me to a little room off the atrium. She lowered her voice. "Before he was expelled from your house, Cicatrix overheard your son say that you'd gone with Pompey."

"A misunderstanding."

"But you did go to Brundisium?"

"Yes."

"You saw Pompey?"

"I did."

She hesitated. "Did you ever find out why my son was murdered?"

I drew a breath. Perhaps, eventually, Pompey would tell her—if Pompey ever came back to Rome alive—but there was no way I could tell Maecia the whole truth. I could, however, answer this question.

"Yes, I know *why* Numerius was killed. He was attempting to blackmail someone, using information that he should have passed directly to Pompey."

"And the gold I found?"

"He may have blackmailed others."

"I knew it was something like that. But it wasn't Pompey who—"

I shook my head. "No. Pompey was in no way responsible for Numerius's death."

She sighed. "Good. That was what I feared most, that Numerius betrayed Pompey, and Pompey found out. If my son had been a traitor, and Pompey put him to death for it—I could endure anything but the shame of that."

"Then you must never think of it again, Maecia. I can't tell you who killed Numerius . . . but I know beyond any doubt that it wasn't Pompey. Your son wasn't as loyal to the Great One as he might have been, but he never betrayed him."

"Thank you, Gordianus. You comfort me." She touched my hand. My face flushed hotly.

Maecia noticed. "You need a cool drink, Gordianus. Come into the garden. We're drinking honeyed wine."

She led me down a hallway and through a colonnade into bright sunlight. The woman in the garden sat with her back to me. She wore a matronly stola and her hair was styled much like Maecia's. She looked over her shoulder. For a moment I failed to recognize her smiling face. I sucked in a breath when I realized it was Aemilia.

Maecia sat beside her and the two linked hands. A slave brought another chair and poured me a cup of wine, for which I was grateful. My face was still flushed and my mouth was suddenly dry. I had come prepared to see Numerius's mother, but not his lover.

The two of them seemed to be in unaccountably high spirits, holding hands and practically beaming. Perhaps it was simply the weather, I thought. Perhaps it was the honeyed wine. But why was Aemilia dressed as a married woman? As I observed the loose folds of her stola, I noticed a telltale swelling at her belly.

Aemilia saw the expression on my face. She grinned.

"You kept the baby," I said, my voice hardly more than a whisper.

She patted her belly proudly. "Yes."

"But how? I thought . . ."

"My mother insisted that I get rid of it, at first. But Maecia wanted me to keep it. It's Numerius's child, after all. Maecia went to see my mother. It wasn't easy, but the three of us found a solution."

Maecia explained. "We devised a little fiction. Numerius and Aemilia were secretly married, you see, behind everyone's backs—why not? There's no one to say that they weren't. I even had the marriage recorded officially; the bribe was ridiculously cheap. As Numerius's widow, there's no reason Aemilia shouldn't have his child. That's why she's living with me now, as my daughter-in-law. And when Pompey, and Aemilia's father, and my brother and sons all come back . . ." Her eyes misted and there was a catch in her voice. "When they come back, they may not be happy with what happened behind their backs, but what can they do but accept it?" She sighed. "These things are so much easier to work out, with all the men out of the way."

I nodded dumbly. Another conspiracy! More deceits and secrets and schemes—but meant to save life, not destroy it. From the foyer, I heard Mopsus and Androcles burst into giggles, joined by Cicatrix's braying laughter. The noise was infectious. Maecia patted Aemilia's belly and the two of them laughed as well.

I sipped my honeyed wine, and heard the echo of gods laughing.

AUTHOR'S NOTE

The story of the first days and months of the Roman Civil War comes from many sources. Chief among them are two documents which could hardly be more dissimilar in tone: Caesar's own account, delivered in cool, self-serving retrospect, and Cicero's riveting series of letters written as the events occurred, which read like white-hot dispatches from the maelstrom. Where critics of Cicero see weakness and vacillation, sympathizers see Hamlet-like indecision.

We are fortunate to have some of the letters Cicero received during this period, including messages from Caesar and Pompey. We also have a handful of increasingly frustrated letters, preceding the loss of Corfinium, written by Pompey to Lucius Domitius and to the consuls.

Additional details are given by later historians including Appian and Dio Cassius, by Suetonius and Plutarch in their biographies of the principals, and by the poet Lucan in his epic poem of the war, *Pharsalia.* In the road trip of Gordianus and Tiro, readers may detect echoes of Horace's Satire I.5, with its itinerary of a journey from Rome to Brundisium (modern Brindisi).

The Vitruvius whom Gordianus meets outside Brundisium is of course Marcus Vitruvius Pollio. From certain passages in his famous treatise on architecture, Vitruvius appears to have served as a military engineer for Caesar in the African campaign. His earlier participation in the siege of Brundisium is a conjecture on my part.

Cicero's get-well messages addressed to Tiro at Patrae are among the most famous of his letters. The role played by those letters and by Tiro in these pages is another conjecture on my part.

Sulla's curious method of sending a secret message is known to us from a second-century author, Polyaenus, who compiled a digest of such stratagems for the edification of Marcus Aurelius. It is my conceit that Sulla himself might have bragged of the incident in his (regrettably, lost) memoirs.

I have not attempted in *Rubicon* to give a detailed explanation of the fiendishly complicated and much disputed causes of the Roman Civil War. For readers with Machiavellian appetites, two books delve exhaustively into the political minutiae of the Late Republic with strikingly different interpretations: Erich S. Gruen's *The Last Generation of the Roman Republic* (University of California Press, 1974) and Arthur D. Kahn's *The Education of Julius Caesar* (Schocken Books, 1986). A more succinct (if decidedly pro-Caesar) explanation of events leading up to the conflict can be found in the first nine pages of Jane F. Gardner's introduction to the Penguin edition of Caesar's *Civil War.*

My research for *Rubicon* was conducted chiefly at Doe Library at the University of California at Berkeley. To Penni Kimmel, for her close reading of the first-draft manuscript, and to Terri Odom, for reading the galleys, my heartfelt thanks. Thanks also, for their steadfast support and encouragement, to my agent, Alan Nevins, and my editor, Keith Kahla. Thanks always to Rick Solomon, with a renewal of the dedication I made at the decade's outset in *Roman Blood:*

AUSPICIUM MELIORIS ÆVI